POOR BARNUM'S JOURNAL

BY

LARRY HANKIN

ARPress
45 Dan Road Suite 15
Canton MA 02021

Hotline:	1(888) 821-0229
Fax:	1(508) 545-7580

Ordering Information:
Quantity sales. Special discounts are available on quantity purchases by corporations, associations, and others. For details, contact the publisher at the address above.

Printed in the United States of America.

ISBN-13:	Softcover	979-8-89676-439-7
	eBook	979-8-89676-440-3

Library of Congress Control Number: 2025915353

BARNUM'S JOURNAL

Table of Contents

*

*

FOREWARD

My name is Theodore Jinsky. Presently I'm an assistant Agent to Michael Berman of Berman & Nadler, one of the larger Literary Agencies in New York.

Back in February of 2018, when I was 20, I was about to start work for B&N as an assistant to Mr. Berman with the possibility of becoming an agent within a year-if I lasted that long. Before starting, I decided to take a few weeks sabbatical/vacation in Southern California and visit a few of my former filmmaker friends.

One evening, as I was having a cup of coffee in a late-night diner in Venice, California, my old stomping grounds, an elderly homeless gentleman approached asking for some spare change. He seemed friendly so I gave him 50 cents, and he gratefully struck up an innocuous conversation. He seemed harmless, calm, intelligent, didn't smell of liquor or appear to be high - an elder gentleman looking for a few moments of common human contact. I responded, he seemed interesting, and I invited him to sit down, and we chatted for about a half hour. He told me his name was Barnum Justice; he'd been homeless for more than 20 years and seemed to know a lot about the "living" part of street life.

We were from worlds that were as different as chicken soup and sow belly. he seemed to be between at least 40 or 50 years my senior; tall, long grey

hair, mustached and goateed, he maintained he
was a non-religious, independent, urban-survivalist,
entrepreneurial, panhandler-beggar-saint and self-
described doggerel poet, writer, storyteller and windowwasher from Belle Harbor, Long Island in New York by
way of Flat Rock, Texas and points east: A harmless,
older, homeless gentleman or a 75-year-old, quirky
,'Know-it-all' depending on what we were talking
about. In passing, I mentioned that I was jobless at-
the-moment but was about to start work for a literary
agency back in New York: B&N - only as an assistant,
but it was understood that I'd be working towards
being an agent there. This information was a mistake.
First, he was completely familiar with B&N as a big,
well known 'Lit Shop' – a highly successful Literary
Agency. He confessed he was in the middle of writing
his fifteenth book – a memoir, and all he wanted was to
be published: "Spread my Words", was how he put it.

Suddenly he was a righteous visionary – the worst
kind: retro, feisty, a street survivor; a temp-working
blood donor; an unhoused Neal Cassady fan who lived
in his old, '65 VW Bus-Van and talked to his hand-held
tape recorder-journal with an idea for his next chapter
and carried an old fashioned black and white crinkled-
design covered school notebook with him. I decided
this old guy was a definite, reader-interesting, central
character for a popular fiction novel release; a story I'd
been thinking of writing for two years. I stuck with his
conversation.

Barnum was Dickensian and Quixotic: Fagan and Don
Quixote, A main character in a book that could be a
best seller – a book about a sympathetic Homeless
Man: Gulley Jimson, Chaplin, Don Quixote, Zampano,
homeless wanderers looking for love and a reason.
Barnum was a perfect, modern, Don Quixote sans both
Rosinante & Sancho. Perfect for today's readers. The

ladies would understand him - have feelings about him; we all know of old guys like him.

When I asked him if it was okay for me to record him for a book I wanted to write, he immediately insisted he be the one to write it. He insisted he was a writer, a storyteller. His idea was to write a book full of his stories and pomes (his name for his doggerel poetry) or about his extremely interesting life and it being a best-seller that would make him a millionaire and he'd give it all to his own UCFHA - "Unhoused Charity Fund Hospital Association" (sic).

Barnum was either a very shrewd negotiator or else his failure to see the Big Picture (money) made him shrewder than Professor Conrad, my Contract Negotiations professor at UC. Barnum wanted control – "Fuck the money: Full Control of Everything". and he wouldn't budge. He was one of those: A Poet. Over the next few days and weeks we'd meet over coffee at the same "Benji's Burgers & Eggs" Diner - open all night. Barnum mentioned he kept a semi-hemi-demi-daily journal full of his stories, adventures and observations. He deigned to let me read two of his fiction stories and "pomes".

Amazingly, they were amazing: Two short stories, one about a politician and the other was a fable about a runaway kid plus, some of his 'pomes'. I was impressed. Barnum was a real writer - just a bit addled by age or from his choice of living accommodations, but he also seemed informed about the process of writing and some lit history. Like a savant.   Not a bad idea: How to make the book sell: Written by a savant. That would sell. "Barnum". Perfect: One name: A homeless, old, one-named savant who writes about how he sees the world. I can smell a best seller a mile away. The ladies'll lap him up. The kids will love his crazy, quirky takes on things you and I take for granted or totally disagree with. Off-Center is On-Target right now. His stories: Two different styles; different constructions. Doggerel poems, rants, his friends, adventures, love stories - a genuine, F-ing *savant*. I found a savant. I started listening to him differently.

The irony (he loved irony) of being a poet-window-washer will be lost on no one. I told him, if he could get me a manuscript of not less than 70,000 words and be sure to include some doggerels and the story about the runaway kid and the politician, I could get him a book deal easy, if he'd agree to split the publishers signing fee with me. That's all. He said, "You get one 40%, I get 40%, and 20% goes my Homeless Hospital Fund Association. And he also keeps complete legal ownership of all Rights and Artistic and Financial control of everything else." "...Agreed."

I got a local lawyer to draw up a two-pager-or-less on those terms, made 2 xeroxed copies, bought Barnum breakfast at Benji's Burgers, handed him his copy, he read it, agreed, we shook on it, and we both signed. When he put down the pen and said: "Now what?" I reached over, gathered the needed documents, touched his shoulder: "70,000 words. Tag, you're it." Barnum gave me a thumbs-up, "I'm on it," and just shoved another forkful of eggs and sausage into his mouth.

That breakfast was the last I heard or saw of him. Or anyone did. I had to go back to New York and B&N. No Barnum. I left. As soon as I hit the East Coast, I called West Coast friends: No one saw or heard of or from him in two months. He'll turn up. Six months. He was old. He probably died. I finally let it go.

5 years later, I had become an Official Assistant Agent to the head of the agency at B&N. This morning a cardboard box was delivered to my desk from Katherine

Lamarr Jefferson – in San Diego, California. Who I knew as Kaye Lamarr, a barmaid, 3 nights a week at Duke's Bar & Grill in Venice, California in the beginning of 2018 - a bar Barnum would frequent the same 3 nights. I assumed Kaye was Barnum's next conquest. Back then, I'd guess she was in her 50's. Smart, cool, independent. Good bartender. Been around. Played a mean game of Bar-Dice. I didn't know her that well.

Back to her delivered box. I opened it. Some stuff was wrapped in protective bubble wrap with a note addressed to me taped to it.

"Dear Theo,

it's taken me a year to track you down. You were Barnum's friend. Barnum left everything to me but hs instructions were that I should pass these on to you. Barnum drove Babe to Saskatoon, Canada to visit his two cousins and their wives in the middle of winter, caught pneumonia, was hospitalized and complications ensued. He passed in December of 2023 in a hospital in Saskatoon at the official age of 83. Before he died, his relatives said B&N's business address is the last address anyone they could get in touch with has for you. I hope this box finds you! Stay well and be happy.
Kaye Jefferson."

I ripped off the bubble-wrap and there it was: The manuscript.

Barnum's Journal

By Barnum Justice

There was a small envelope stuck between the first and second pages with a note enclosed. All the note said was:

Tag. You're it.

xxx

*

The following is Barnum Justice's Book as he wrote it: A treasure-trove of cool bios, stories, doggerel poetry(("pomes"), fables, rants, seminars, and street life in Barnum's own words and writings, all laid out in the real-time order in which Barnum wrote and recorded them. Sorry it took so long.

T.J.,
 N.Y.C., N.Y.
09/23/2025

HOW TO BE HOMELESS

"You gotta get serious. Get calm. See patterns. Figure it out. Use it. Mean it. Either get out fast or, by default, you're committing. The street resurrects, the street teaches, the street deteriorates to the bone; rots your teeth and reason. Or sharpens them. Eye of the Tiger."

-- B.J.

My name's Barnum Justice, formerly Bernard David Lumpitt. Not "Barney". Ever. My hair's all grey now. I changed my own last name to 'Justice' because I wanted to and could and because Mr. Hoover Clement Justice and his wife Mrs. June-Anne Marlene Justice took me in when I finally succeeded in running away for the last time.

I'm what they call an elder street poet: a renaissance re-assembler of realities for re-imbursements; a player of paradigms for pay; a maker of magic metaphors; a collagist of clarity for cash: Basically, I fuck with the truth for money as opposed to lawyers who fuck with the facts for financial benefit. I'm also a Squeegee Enthusiast: A Washer of Windows, a Poet: Storefronts to Monocles. I love irony.

My problem is, I ain't real. I'm a symbol. Friggin' artists. But see, I smell bad, I shit in dumpsters, I got an attitude, I scare away business, I block the sidewalks, I go through your garbage. Raccoons and useless people keep you awake at night, right? So, then you know what my problem is? I'm too real: Friggin' reality: That's the problem. I'm too real, I'm not real, I'm too real, I'm not real, I'm…

I can't find that fine line. Humble!? No such animal. Ever. Why? Because *Bigger Picture*, the unsheltered, hungry, & homeless don't have any heroes; no Role Models; no contemporary nor mythical mentors. No one to look up to – to emulate besides The Humble Beggar of Biblical, Horse-Pucky Fame or Chaplin's cute, angry little tramp or Emmett Kelly's passive, stone-faced stunt-clown. All homeless. Real Clowns ain't cute or clever. They're clowns and they're pissed off. They use a banana peel like Zorro uses a sword or Thor his hammer or a Bully, his bludgeon.

*

The Goddam Duke of Kent

Now I never had dinner with a bank president
And I never was a split-level house resident
And I never sold nuthin' to the Russian
Government
And I fell on my head, and it didn't make a dent
Cuz, God covered it with hair and filled it with
cement

I'm a drinker, I'm a thinker, I'm the God-Damned
Duke of Kent
And I'll never really know what my momma
musta' meant
When she said the Holy Ghost gonna rest my
bones content
'Cause dyin' cost a dollar and I ain't got a cent

When I used to sin, I'd get Holy Rolled
But I took it on the chin and I think I'm gonna fold
I tried to win it all, I tried to keep the gold
I tried coke and gin 'til my coat got sold

An' I lied for my love and I stole for my rent
Made love on a ship, made love in a tent
Made love to the wife of a very rich gent
And I'm glad a' what I did and I never will repent

But my bottles got blurry and my soul got bent
And my eyes got old and my money got spent
And I followed down the drainpipes to see just
where it went
Till I had to look up to see Dante's descent

Yeah, my head got in a spin and my center wouldn't hold
Now my teeth are mostly tin, and my feet are feelin' cold
An' my hair is gettin' thin, an' I think I'm gettin' old
An' when it's time to turn it in you don't have to be told.

I'm a drinker, I'm a thinker, I'm the goddamn Duke of Kent
And I'll never really know what my momma musta' meant
When she said, "The Holy Ghost gonna rest my bones content" 'Cause dyin' costs a dollar an' I ain't got a cent

*

Will Rogers State Park Rant

How would you like your son or daughter to walk into breakfast one morning and hit you with: "Mom, Dad, when I grow up, I want to be a Humble Beggar!" Pop Quiz! Name some F.U.P.H.H.H.'s – *Famous Unhoused Poor Hungry Heroes of History*. Hint: St. Francis of Assisi, St. Augustine, Jesus, Heyoka (Dakota Indian Sacred Homeless, Trickster Clown), Loki (American Indian Trickster Clown), Charlie-the- little-tramp-friggin' Chaplin (American Cute, Angry, Trickster Clown), Emmett Kelly (American Sad Homeless Clever Hobo Clown; Nasrudin: East Indian Sufi Priest Clown; Ratso Rizzo: American Tragic Clown; Fagin: English Evil Clown; etc. (What do they all have in common except the urge to make you laff (sic)? All are homeless. Ever wonder why so many are _homeless_? They could be funny and dress like any Social Class of clown they want: But could they be _as_ funny - or funnier?). But I digress:

So, my choices of classic, homeless role-models are: Broke Fanatics or Loser Clowns. But they were _characters - not real_. These were some story-teller's inventions to highlight an unacceptable situation, and the intent of The Humble beggar _"character"_ was to highlight - through suffering, humor, and possibly combat - the evils of Greed & Power. Not-Solve-Poverty. The Humble Beggar of Biblical Fame-and-no- Fortune Doesn't Exist in reality. Never did. It was a character to contrast with Greed and Lack of Compassion. The beggar had to be _"humble"_ to give The Greedy no excuse for being greedy. "Humble Beggars" were those storytellers' inventions to show how greedy people behaved in the face of dire helplessness, extremis, painful lack, and/or danger.

But it put a curse on Beggars to be known as Humble from The Bible on down. "Beggars" and "The Poor" are still interchangeable. And if you were either, you were humble. And if you weren't Humble this is obviously your God-Given punishment for being wrong and bad, so please take it somewhere else.

Humble, back-in-the-day, was a good symbol, it worked-kind-of, for small change, but how about Destitute Beggar or Dying of Hunger, Scabies, and Alcohol Poisoning Beggar; Beaten-Down, Starving Homo sapiens; Displaced, Unsheltered, Homeless Human Being; Orphan of The Storm, Invisible, Forgotten, Demeaned - anything but Humble: Angry, Subservient, Numb, Mentally Unstable, Broken, yet all: Homo sapiens. It's like the gangster bullshit they used to say about women in old, b&w "Noir" movies: "All women are whores except my mother and she's a saint." Same

Phonus-Balonus. "*PTSD* Beggar"; "*Battered House-Wife Syndrome* Beggar"; "*PTSD* wife"; "*Humble* War Vet". They're all shell-shocked: all PTSD-Triggered: under prolonged, *sensually overloaded*, extreme, continuous, and confined circumstances. Dogs cower and shake, Elephants break their chains.

When you're unhoused and hungry, there's a *way* -- a certain "Tao", a "Vibe", an "Energy Knowledge of Place" available for use: For good or evil. The unwritten foundation law of this place. The sum calculus of a specific street's energy for use as references to help you navigate the reefs and sea-lanes, the dos and don'ts of living in the specific locale. Food, shoes, access to bathrooms, showers, toilet paper, clean water, blankets, a safe place to sleep, medicines, drugs, who's who, prices, the goods, the bads, the "Tells". There's a little light inside of you. Burn it out.

If you want to know what life was like 250-350,000 years ago for our foremothers and fathers: It was pretty much no baths for days or weeks, sometimes on purpose because a thick layer of dried mud or dirt could protect you from bugs and the sun. Living in the same animal skins for long periods, living off what you could find on the landscape, permanent bruises and infections, exposed to the elements, nomadic, or at least having several places to sleep depending on the weather or where you were safest when it got dark, information was passed on mostly orally and manually one to another or through experience, trial and error, and you generally took your important belongings with you. It was what it was, and our species adapted, depending on the weather, catastrophic events, accidental or intentional.

If you want to know what life was like 250-300,000 years ago, talk to the Unhoused. The only difference is, back then they weren't made to feel guilty and humiliated about it.

*

When you become unhoused, you're gonna miss certain things. Doorknobs. No doorknobs. A wall. No wall. No wall, no doorknob, no table, no bathroom. If you're missing these four key items and you think you're not unhoused, I suggest you think again. You're unhoused - Unsheltered – Homeless - A Loser Blindsided by Life or Just Another Tricky Day in Peopleland. To partially quote someone famous, "When you got nothing, you got nothing. Period." When you run out of gas on a lonely highway, nothing to lose gets you nowhere fast without a little moxie and a Plan B, C, & D. Here's the rule: Being Unhoused is not, "A State of Mind"; Being Unsheltered is not, "A Situation" or "Unlucky", or "a Vacay on the Dole". Being Homeless is _A Job_.   Like any other Job. It's _not fun_. That's why it's called a Job and not Jazz. So, what _IS_ the Job of The Unhoused?

1: Get housed.

That's it. A no-brainer. Failing that proceed to:

2: Get thru today and find _a safe place to Sleep and Poop_ (not the same place). Sounds easy. Try it. Every day for the rest of your foreseeable-life-expectancy odds.

Here are The _Specs_ of The Job: Three consecutive 8-hour shifts, no pay, no time off, no day off, no one's in charge, there are no rules, but if there are they change every forty feet. People with homes don't like you, there's no bathroom, and there's no place else to go - literally and figuratively - but all you have to do is get through today and find a safe place to sleep tonight - and you're home free. Completely: Home - Free. Knowledge is power.

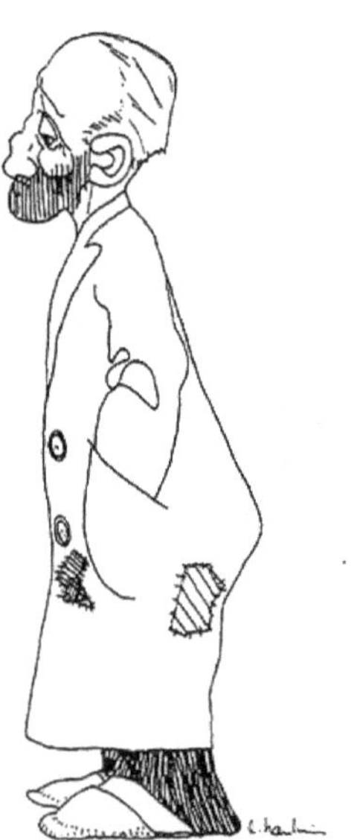

MANIFESTO

Since the United States is on the brink of having a permanent, unhoused pauper class and, since it's been proven beyond a shadow of a doubt that it's impossible to get rid of paupers, beggars, and the unhoused throughout all cultures, ages & civilizations, if we can't have less: we will have the _best_ paupers and unsheltered, homeless, unhoused, and independent entrepreneurial beggar-panhandler-saints.

GEAR

What you'll need is a box, backpack, or something to put your stuff in like a shopping cart (Two or three shopping carts may seem like a good idea at the time, but the opposite proves truer), a sleeping bag or your definition or facsimile thereof, most of your arrest-provoking body-parts suitably covered - I'll talk about that in a minute - _two_ serviceable shoes, a minimum of two rolls of toilet paper, and an attitude of Heroic Buddhism.

"Hell is other people."
                                    --Jean Paul Sartre
"Jean never outgrew his Terrible Twos."
                                    --My Mom

*

I didn't know my mom very well. She was a good Mom and always on my side. She was cool. If I could have worshipped her then, when she was simply my Mom, like I worship her now, I'd be further along. But, back then, home or at school, I was, 'Quirky'. 'Clueless'.

Dyslexia was unknown at the time. Mom was just Mom back then. Not quite "Ozzie and Harriet". But my mom was real. She still had dreams. We spent time together, but my father always loomed large in my thoughts and reality, his dreams were buried far deeper if not tossed in a nearby dumpster as a firstborn American. No vibes. Nada that I could invite friends over to dig. It shut out any idea that I could dare relate to any of my Family for Sanctuary. My Dad was really the weird one of the household. Not even my awesome younger sister Carmella, 5 years younger, was safe from my fear of attachment. For me, life up to age 11 was a psychic tightrope walk. Little did I know it would develop into a deep, driving, subconscious and rigid series of belief systems I'm still working on.

Venice Beach Pier Rant

I don't dream about money, mansions, power, sex, flying, or running. I dream about indoor bathrooms. Here's something nobody mentions: *Self-Esteem & Dignity* are based on free and able access to proper waste management facilities. That's something you won't learn from your parents or in Soc.-101: When unhoused for a protracted period, your self-esteem will be based on a direct correlation between you and your access to bathroom facilities. The organism with the least access to a bathroom is the most disadvantaged, a priori.

"Disadvantaged" is the name of the game.

Where do I do go to the John? How far is it from where I am right now? Diapers, Plastic Garbage Bags, Depenz, etc. (Until Civic Leaders Legislate Civilly, use your noodle. Behind Something and/or In Something are to be considered priorities).

It's always on my mind. In the back. Where's the nearest public facility? Different places, different customs. In Calcutta, it's pretty much anywhere.

However, all countries' street rules are subject to time, place, and proximity to authority figures. Access and distance from or to the nearest public restroom and/or appropriate facility, made-made or natural: This will be the North Star of your life while you're living on the street.

Find your spots; know your distances and personal timing and where the public bathrooms and showers at most public beaches are. Same with libraries. Unhoused people hang near convenient accesses to public bathrooms and showers, spare change spots, food, and places to sit. Homeless sapiens are unhoused, unsheltered, unbathroomed and undernourished - not stupid, unclean, or lazy. It's just a lot freaking harder and takes a lot more planning than I imagined if I thought about it at all.

A). Am I on a cross-town bus? In a doorway? on a street, a woodsy path, in a department store, tent, beach. How much do I smell? Can anyone smell me? Do I really care at this point? You don't care, Okay, neither do I, etc.

B). Where do I or don't I sleep? When? & For How Long? Play it by ear, improvise: Diapers, Plastic Garbage Bags, Depenz, etc. (Until Civic Leaders Legislate Civilly, use your noodle Behind Something and/or In Something are to be considered priorities).

C). We're the only species that excretes, eats, drinks, sleeps, creates, pro-creates, and grows up, all over, under, around, in, on and throughout this planet - our "territory". We've staked it out. This is *our* planet: The species Homo sapiens owns Earth. We'll defend it against aliens. What other species will – or could? What other Species or Entity has the sheer fire power of Homo sapiens?

D). The problem now is we (Homo sapiens) have altered and armed our entire planet against *ourselves* as well as most other living organisms including our pets.

E). Homo sapiens have yet to prove they're *a sustainable, viable species for the long haul.* Forget 'In the Universe'. I'm talking about on this Planet for at least the next couple of years. To quote Pogo Possum: "We have met The Enemy and They are Us."

*

Trinity Church Panel Discussion:
Flat Earth or Round Planet?
God & Jesus: What did they know & When

On the one hand, thankfully, we don't have to worry about dinosaurs anymore. On the other hand, the way we treat this flat or round Orb thing, someday there'll be a species that won't have to worry about Homo sapiens anymore. And if it isn't round, what's all this bullshit about it being round? Is our God a prankster God? When was he going to tell us -- Never mind. On the other hand, flat or round, we clog it, dam it, trash it, chop it, farm it, weed it, mow it, till it, drill it, mill it, mine it, harness it, deplete it - and now we're going to have to FIX IT? Where's that in the Planet Lease? AND THE SKY? YES: The Sky: The Air We Breathe. That's The Sky. Remember? <u>We</u> broke it, <u>we</u> bought it: <u>We</u> own it, <u>we</u> fix it. And the cost ain't cheap. The Good News: The Sky is not falling and never will. If anything, it'll float up, up and away.

But it's changing. <u>Not</u> *much,* but just enough so we won't be able to use it to breathe anymore.

The upside is: Rich, warm, green Island Get-Aways don't really matter to gentle ocean breezes of Non-Breathable Air. And the icebergs and trees and lions and tigers and Monarch Butterflies and Honeybees and Elephants ain't gonna pay for it or fix it or even come back at all. *Ever!* They just know, right now, something's going down. Even the pigeons know something's up.

(Stock Market Tip: Individual Home Oxygen Tanks)

*

SHRINK & THE GREAT ASSUMPTION

I taped this conversation I was having with Shrink about reading books and finally we tried to decide if the bible was a good book or not. Shrink is an amazing dude. He was going on about how every squirrel, ant, child, and one sorry-assed grasshopper knows about winter.

"Right? Prep now for the Big Move – whatever that is. For the long haul. Like, if we won't-don't stop screwing around with our very own planet-and-home-sweet-home's ecosystem, Mother Nature or physics will stop us, once and for all. God has nothing to do with nothin' but God Stuff. Magic stuff.

"Miracles."

"Miracles. Yeah. Magic Stuff. Visions. Every species that's survived learned the first lesson of existence: Don't mess with Mother Nature, The Universe or Each Other.

"A Well-Known Southern Politician said, "The quickest and longest-lasting education is the second kick of a mule."

"Darwin said: "'Adapt or die'."

"Okay. What's that got to--!?"

"Every species that became extinct never survived the second mule kick. Happens all the time. It's only in the last few centuries that we've found out that all those thousands of years of accumulated knowledge was Just Not So. Our World is Not Flat."

"The world's known that for--!?"

"You know how long it took for homo sapiens to realize and prove the world is _not_ flat?

"What's it got to do with--!?"

"Did Jesus know the earth was round?"

"What's that--!?

"Our supply of drinkable water is not quite as infinite as Gods' Grace might lead you to believe. Our world happens to be round and extremely finite and depletable while it's _The Universe that's_ not _(so far)_.

"So?"

"So, our subconscious and DNA have yet to get with the program. Species-wise, Leary and the Buddhists are phony-baloneys now. "Living in the now", _right now_, is not only bullshit – it's also not sustainably successful or proactive, species-wise. It doesn't move the ball down the field. Living in the Now is not Now anyway for very long. Not even a part of a nanosecond. It almost instantaneously becomes: "Just then". Now is near useless. It's hardly now at all. Ever. The future is the savior. Thinking and living for the future about the future in the now is the real reality now. Now, the future is realer than now is. Now is all Kabuki Theater. We're goners unless, as a species, we really get our shit together."

*

Species Refusal-To-Learn-Evolve-Goddammit Syndrome

Mother nature only cares as much as you do and if you don't that's okay and goodbye. The point is learning to Care: An emotion that hardens with time. As a member of our species, I'm speaking up and saying, Get Real! (as someone once wrote or sang about) The New Reality is: The realer things get the less of it there is.

Where is evolution going with this compulsive "Reality Best Quest" of Homo sapiens? The Realer things get the less of It there is. Basically, Reality is just Sparks in the Darkness. How long do we keep morphing till it feels right?

With the present tenner of global events as-they-are, I feel going The Homeless Sapiens Way, as an Independent Entrepreneurial Beggar Panhandler Saint, is the correct, pro-active, pre-emptive, offensive direction for me to take, personally, politically, financially, presently, and mentally speaking. However, I'd like to know Who's Guardin' the Garden of Eden? And where's *That* song? Specieswise. I'm just sayin'."

*

WEEMS "SHRINK" DUNBAR

Is originally from Ohio. The Midwest (in his mid-40's). That's his disguise and thus, how he gets by delivering small items that can be concealed without using his hands. I deliver legal things only; I can't speak for anyone else. Shrink also gets by panhandling, Temp jobs, donating blood - the usual. He's trying to "Get Out": Get Straight". Same-old-same-old for the whole time I've known him. It's tough. But so is he. Shrink likes Venice Beach and Southern California and talks a-mile-a-minute. "Shrink", because he always thinks he's got you figured out, but it's mostly him assuming and concluding. He's been tripping on bennies trying to raise money to get resumes printed up for his one job interview coming up - a part-time teller's job in a bank. "Where can I get clean clothes and a shower and shave for my interview in three days?" On and on. He's not going to get the job.

Shrink doesn't have a clue. He's a buddy of Fried Sal. His thing is liquor. He's some-kind-of-genius, but I can't figure about what. "Surviving" is a guess. It's almost a conditioned reflex for me to start taping when he starts spouting. But this time I didn't have any replacement batteries, so I waited till he got good and wound up. Finally, this is what I got. It's verbatim. He was loudly talking to a passing couple - in their 60's - looked like Asian tourists to me - about what he believed they had concluded about him because he was living on the sidewalk in one of those small, fold-up tents. A bit drunk; not much, it was early.

SHRINK: "No, see, don't *assume.* Bullshit. Back-in-the-day, yeah, see everything was fine and nice: I had a nice girlfriend and a nice apartment and a nice job and then I got laid off, and then I missed a rent payment or two and then my unemployment benefits ran out and I couldn't find enough temp jobs to keep up my rent so I was evicted and lost my girlfriend and when I finally found a job available that I was qualified for they wouldn't hire me because of the way that I looked & I smelled because I was living in my car by then and nobody's gonna hire anybody who doesn't have a legal permanent mailing address or has job references that're a year old and wears these clothes which I'm still wearing now and even wore then which is all I have now because I have no money to buy better ones so I keep getting arrested all the time because I have no place to live because I have no job and no money so everyone *assumes* I'm a kleptomaniac and a pathological liar because nobody believes anything I do or say because of the way that I look and I smell because I have no access to clean clothes or a bath because I have no job so to get by and survive I had to become a kleptomaniac and a pathological liar which I did and still am now. I'm a pathological liar. I swear-to-God, that's the truth. Okay: I'm *not* a pathological liar. Believe me now? Doesn't matter."

He stopped, took out a half-smoked doobie, lit it, took a big toke, and passed it to me. I passed: "I'm good." He took a toke for me, then offered the transfixed Asian LOL who waved it away like I did, smiled courteously and said, "I good" (sic), The man just waved like she did, smiled kindly and shook his head "No", but both remained transfixed. Shrink shrugged, took a last, quick toke, dabbed the ash-end out on his tongue, put it in his shirt pocket, and continued:

> "So, yeah...I finally figured out what I should do about it. I figured out I should go crazy - allow myself to cop to it - really. Because under the circumstances it was the only option I had left because under the circumstances if I didn't go crazy, which is okay, no biggie, I get it, but if I didn't, I'd go totally insane which is not fine or nice at all. So, that's what I did. "What did you do?" (he suddenly asked himself like another person, then answered as himself) I went crazy. And then everything was fine; really nice, because now it all fit with the smell & the clothes & the no job & the no place to live; the rejection, the attitude, the anger: Whose? Mine? Theirs? None of the above? I fit the M.O. of someone who's crazy! Here's the proof: *I can't tell the difference between right and wrong anymore. I can't tell the difference!* Does that make sense to you? Because I can't tell the difference anymore. What I just told you: To me, is senseless. what I just told you makes no sense at all. But what do I know? I'm crazy."

The nice couple calmly nodded in agreement, smiled, and moved on.

*

THE EXTINCTION of HOMO SAPIENS

We Homo sapiens became extinct by a process called
SENPA
(Species Extinction by Not Paying Attention)
(*from* "Dodoism": A species inability to either evolve
faster than predators could eat them or change the way
they taste)

I'm talking about *Sustainability* (if you're Street:
"*Survival*"). How ignominious. Homo sapiens, The Dodo
Birds-of-Self-Awareness. We had a shot at going into
the Graphic History Books along with fish, tadpoles all
the way up the line through Monkeys and Apes, past
Homo Erectus, Cro-Magnon, Piltdown. We were about
to become the next, new Homographic on The Evolution
& Visual-Aide Chart in classrooms all over the world.
Sapiens. Us. We may still blow it. The direct branch line
from algae, thru tadpoles, past monkeys and apes to
Homo sapiens w/a Briefcase. Homo sapiens: The "Nice
Try" species. They almost made it. They had so much
going for them - and the worst curse of all - so much
Potential.

No Biggie. Bats learned that if there's too much
shit on the floor, grow wings, hang from the ceiling,
and learn to poop upside down. *They worked it out.*
Sapiens: not enough time to clean up the mess or find
and reach another planet and move all 4 to 7.5 billion of
us there including meals, air-conditioning, and 1st class
accommodations and in less than 30 years hurtling at
the speed of light past nothing at all out the window
but All Black All Over full of pinholes of light in every
direction several generations away.

We hurtle along - for all intents and purposes - just
like The Earth, but back then, we at least had The Sun
and Moon for companionship while hurtling aimlessly

into infinity or somewhere else.

*

THE ART OF HURTLING AIMLESSLY

To this huge, round rock of a singular planet spinning thru space - the only one within several hundred thousand light years – the only one with a finite and exceedingly thin layer of breathable oxygen and survivable temperature range, potable water, and enough arable land to support and sustain all now-known biological species to thrive - to *this* singular planet: the problems of Boundaries, National Borders, and Flags will be solved in the 3rd way and probably not by our species.

I see everybody's buried in their hand-held-Worry-Beads-Do-Me- Friend-Me Apps. I've got extremely serious doubts about the survivability of our species. Everybody's money was on oil and the combustion engine (lightning, to spark to brush-to-wood-to-Oil-to-Plastics & Digital-to...The Sun! The Ancient Egyptians almost got it right. They had a choice – Every Pharoah had a choice - Pyramid or Solar Panels. "Pyramid!" Every time. Size: Height, Weight. "A Solar Panel is light, thin, like papyrus. Bricks last much longer." Pretty soon The Wheel will become obsolete. Money's the next thing to go, then water. Then Air. Wake me when the world is flat again and God feeds me as he does the birds on high.

*

GEMSTONES & ROCKS

1. Sleeping on a steam grate ain't all it's cracked up to be and they're hard to find now-a-days, most gone to legend and myth.

2. You can't sleep next to a fire hydrant: Red Zone. Can't Park in a red zone, can't sleep in a red zone, can't have sex in a red zone, can't alleviate in a red zone; Homo sapiens can't do anything in a red zone (Dogs are considered Special Needs). Boundaries. Authority. Screw The Man.

3. Shoes: Very important. But how many? No Shoes? Better than no feet. One Shoe: Great. Two shoes: Perfect. Three shoes: Thinking ahead. Four shoes: No way Jose': you're on your way to becoming Imelda Marcos. When you're unhoused and hungry, "The fourth shoe defeats its own purpose". Three shoes plus two feet - in rotation – will last you a lifetime in unhoused years.

4. If you're gonna sleep in a doorway: Check the hours. You can't sleep in a working doorway. You gotta do the homework, folks. Use your noodle. Gettin' through one day-at-a-time & finding a safe place to sleep and do your business day after day after day after day, over and over and over-yeah: mind-boggling. Time. Eye of The Tiger.

5. In one hundred years from now we'll be the Dodos: Homo Sapiens. In one hundred years all the different A.I. systems sent into outer space by then will communicate with each other on their own Dark Matter Wavelength and come up with a Roach Killer spray but for Water-Based, Consciousness-Carrying Life Forms who might run rampant and infect the entire Universe with Consciousness and Free Will.

*

EVOLUTION

Way-Back-In-The-Day, bats looked like mice in all-black, long-sleeved t- shirts. They were cool back then, but two things were working against them: they didn't have wings, and they had short legs so they couldn't run fast. So, the birds flying above could easy spot them because of their color and would easily swoop down and catch them because these wingless bats were very slow runners.

Finally, Barry, a very smart Bat, figured out that the way to escape birds above from spotting them on the ground was to put a ceiling between the birds and them. Then the birds couldn't see them at all. Ever. It was a great idea but back then there were no buildings or rooms invented yet to put a ceiling on or over. Way back then, the only things that had ceilings were caves.

"Too dark to see! We'll go blind."
"So what? You have two eyes now and you can't see in the dark so obviously you don't need eyes in the dark, you need ears. Hearing is key: If you hear "Ouch" ahead, make a quick, sharp turn right or left. You'll get the hang of it."

So that's what Bats did, and it worked. They hid in caves, multiplied, and only went out at night when it was too dark for birds to fly. But the slow-running, wingless bats had another, bigger problem. They were slobs. They never cleaned up after themselves or threw their garbage in the proper receptacle plus they relieved themselves wherever they were and operated around it, left the area, or slipped and fell in it. Several bat deaths have been reported to have died this way. The carcasses are left where they died and eventually consumed by much smaller things that considered this mana from heaven. These no-winged, slow- running bats never picked up after themselves or anyone else. However, at the same time they were able to solve the number one cause of death of bats: Letting go during sex.

Garbage, bat poop, and dead bugs and bat bodies started to pile up so high on the floor they couldn't walk or run in or on it. That's when Smart Barry, The Wingless, Slow Running Bat came up with the species changing "Bat Hypothetical": "_If_ we could grow wings and learn to fly, eat, sleep, have sex, and poop upside down while hanging from the ceiling and survive as a species, _THEN_: We could be as sloppy as we want in here because everything falls to the ground and we don't have to wade through all our own poop and candy wrappers and piss and dumpster stuff and to Hell with the Smell. Easy-Peasy."

With Pluck, Determination, and a Mighty Vision of the Future Safety of Bats, it took 400,000 years for all bats to finally learn how to grow wings, fly, breed, give birth, sleep, and poop while hanging upside down. Soon, they forgot the floor ever existed except when one of them fell to the bottom of the cave.

If you fall, the smell stays with you for weeks. And Bats don't take bathes. Remember: We're not rats or mice-with-wings. We're Bats: Apples and Oranges."

*

Paying Attention and Common Sense

Are Key Items for Species Sustainability. Time and or Evolution finally work it out, but indoor plumbing evolved faster. A.I. is faster than indoor plumbing. Almost as fast as the 2nd kick of a mule.

What if someone turns the electricity off or pulls the plug? It took Homo sapiens a couple of thousand years to work out the kinks and finesse "Indoor Plumbing", but Problem Solved.   I understand: Different times, different strokes. I get it. However, I think This Planet got us this far, and she's finally fed up with us and the garbage we produce that doesn't disintegrate as fast as everything else on this planet and disrupts every other living thing's DNA-century-learned-food-chains!

Okay, WE WIN: Top Dog. Our species has eradicated more "Other" species than any other species. We kill too many other species. _Not too many Animals_: Too many _Other Species_ - including our own. We're starting to throw the balance of nature out of whack with our plundering of our planet's resources.   The nearest "other one like Earth but uninhabited", is more than one hundred thousand light years away. Our species is starting to be the punchline to old lemmings jokes.

*

FRIED SAL

The street just makes Fried Sal's PTSD worse because it's compounded by street paradigms of how to deal with street reality. PTSD works great on the street or in a war zone pretty good *for a while:* It can help keep you alive. But in non-threatening situations PTSD really gets in the way of a friendly conversation or business deal.

Have you any idea what it costs to replace primal fear and adrenalin with dignity and trust? It's expensive, time-consuming, labor-intensive plus, progress doesn't show fast enough.

Wars have huge financial problems directly after winning or losing hundreds of thousands of gallons of blood, tons of brains, and Billions of dollars for postponed bridesmaids' outfits and rental halls. Plus, it causes an amazing number of fatherless children in foreign countries.

It's not like the old days in the 50's when you had the old blind guy with the tin cup and German Shepherd selling pencils. What happened to them? Or the old guy selling apples? The Last of the Pre-War Humble Beggars went into the garage or the attic with the old Life magazines.

In the 60's a whole New Generation of Panhandlers started easing The Old-Schoolers and unhoused, unemployed workers out: 'The Professional Beggars' & Thieves' showed up: The white and colored middle-class, teenage-hippie-runaways and white high school dropouts showed up. Kids. The easily busted, no hassle criminals. They *wanted* to be out here. They were asking for it! They weren't forced to survive – they volunteered to survive. They were curious. Above average. Sue me: They were amateurs, but eager to learn. Flower Kids trying to run away from Norman Rockwellian magazine covers and mindless, middleclass backgrounds. They were simply curious, a way to meet a significant other and get a bit higher and a bit more real while wearing costumes. Something to get into for a year or two. Curious, hapless kids just finding out about bullshit and its consequences. The '60's. Nice Try. Really. It just wasn't fed, watered, and tended to while everybody got mortgagedup, had kids, and got insurance. I'm not complaining. I'm explaining. The street didn't say a word. It never does. Come one, come all. We know you. We have seen you before. Many times. Down the cobblestones and dirt alleys of Rome way back-in-the-day, and Far East. No difference to The Street. Crazies out of the County Mental Wards were just dumped into the mix now and then. The more the merrier into the late 60's and the LSD, amphetamine street junkies, Dobermans, and the new-age hookers and pimps and vets and second-recession jobless and the middle-class engineers, and then women, young child-mothers with babies in tie- dyed diapers – Christ, that was a whole new ballgame. Women's lib on the street. Ladies burning their underwear: arms akimbo, bras ablaze, and the daughters of the permanent homeless, the newly unhoused, the female addicts and the up-front female crazies, sales execs, computer programmers, aerospace engineers, all fallen through the cracks from before. The leftovers, the savings & loan managers and vice presidents and their families – The Newbies: Surviving. Middle-Class families, kids getting out, dealing, getting' busted, or being taken away. I mean it became the real deal Star Wars Bar while kids were stealing to feed their siblings and parents. What we have growing here now is a permanent unhoused class. And some of us just went professional. Simple as that. You keep doing something for so long, it either drives you bat-shit crazy, or you figure it out and correct it, or your autonomic nervous system figures it out and makes the adjustment for you without you having to lift a frigging finger. It's Sisyphus's own O.C.D. that wouldn't let him try another way or figure out The 3rd Way.

Survival is amoral and extremely prejudicial towards itself and its keep, so when the Second Cortex can't handle anymore: Ol' Lizard Brain's got your back n' sez: "Survive, find safe place to sleep; poop far away (if possible, bury)". But it ain't as easy as you think. It's Rocket Science plus Hunt and Peck: You do any way you can. However: There may be a way out. Our Urban Survivalist Science Staff are working on a way off this societal-suicidal treadmill - to the best of their knowledge, circumstance, lack of nutrients, equipment, sleep, and ability to think.

Running food, jumping food, flying food, dancing food, singing food, skiing food all along a wall of a Big Box store. Twenty or thirty 80- inch, color TV screens all at the same time. Looks great. I love taking short cut-tours through big box stores. I'm persona-non-grata in most of the big box stores in Hollywood and the West Side.

For food, mostly I go to the supermarket on Rose or behind health food markets, their dumpsters. That's generally where the tomatoes and past-dated foods are. Restaurant dumpsters are good, too. You go by smell, mostly. You can tell. Tomatoes: Vitamin C. Sometimes behind pizza joints they toss a screwed-up pizza in their dumpster. Timing is everything. Protein: Harder to come by. Protein you mostly have to pay for, catch, steal, or share.

*

The Importance of Batting Averages

Lately, a lot of people have been asking me about what the chances are of waking up on fire. Probably something on the news and they conclude I'm an expert on the hazards of the under- represented. Like I might conclude they're an expert on the downsides of liposuction.

"Waking aflame?" Statistically: Rara Avis. A lot less than being struck by lightning or shot in a schoolroom or randomly in public. Remember, half the job is to find a *safe* place to sleep tonight. There's a reason for that. Being homeless, unhoused, and/or unsheltered has a steep learning curve. The Four Mighty Pillars of Learning are Pain, Fear, Guilt, and Love. There are many baseball team owners and managers who maintain three-out-of-four is an impossibly great, championship batting average.

Many people are curious: How long have there been Poor People? Ironically: Exactly as long as there's been Rich People: *i.e.: "Homo sapiens that weaponize money and connections for their own monetary advantage over all others of lesser means by any means undiscoverable."*

Some rich people - a precious few - are okay. Sadly, it makes little difference. It's The Hoarding, not The Person. I look at it this way: I consider greedy people as One More God-Given Natural Resource. You got rain, sunshine, dandelion wine, green leafy vegetables, week-old tomatoes, and arrogant, angry, pompous, self-righteous people. So, like any God-Given Natural Resource, you don't waste it. You nurture it, you harvest it. But you don't over-harvest. Sustainability over the long haul is basic street cred for becoming a member of

The Successful Species Club. Also, some people want to be rich. Go for it. Me, personally, I haven't got the time.

*

Why do people with doorknobs - or, as I like to call them, the "Homelessless" – why don't The Homelessless not like me, The Homeless (Unsheltered; Unhoused?)"

Simple Logic: *Normal people have doorknobs. Ergo:* People without doorknobs are lying, cheating, pariahs. It's called Simple Logic. Don't take it personally. It's not you – it's them: The Homelessless. The nightmare of all Homelessless Homo-sapiens: Becoming Homeless,

To The Homelessless, we are their own, waking, walking nightmares. We freak them out a priori, just on visual sighting alone. However: To be fair-&-balanced, we've got to look at ourselves from the Homelessless Citizen's Point-of-View: Walk a mile in a doorknob owner's eyes and don't see what they don't see.

'Don't see' what gifts our genius has contributed to the world. Our gifts of Found Object Domicile Development from other Homo sapiens' corrugated scraps, waste, junk, detritus, flotsam, jetsam, cloth, bubble wrap and duct tape that have advanced The Art and Science of Instant Domicile Recycling Architecture by leaps and bounds.

That, alone, should have them bowing to our ranks but, no. What they see is us walking or sitting around or panhandling for spare change, or drinking a Café Latte:

"Look at the unhoused guy sitting drinking that Latte. I gave him a quarter last week and now he's blowing it on a Latte. These friggin' people are lazy pariahs".

The Challenge is: how do you get people to care for a dirty, focus-damaged stranger who's become hard-wired into short-term, survival behavior known as PTSD and has no access to a bathroom, income, or An Accessible Relative? A very tough sell.

Angry Apes and A.I. have come up with the same way to kill all the fire ants. Set fire to the planet. Poof. No more fire ants. But that's how A.I. and Angry Apes "think". Can A.I. come up with a plan "B"? An *Okay; But Besides That",* button.

The less you have, the more you get, e.g.: A person with two legs gets a quarter. A person with one leg gets a dollar. You gotta get serious. Get calm. See patterns. Figure it out. Use it. Mean it. Either get out fast or, by default, you're committing. The street resurrects, the street teaches, the street deteriorates to the bone; rots your teeth and reason. Eye of the Tiger.

*

Our Lord's Church of Sacred Angels

I was booked to lecture a class on what it's like to be homeless at The Congregation of Our Lord's Church of Sacred Angels in Harris County in Upper New York State. I was hired for one, one-hour talk on Homelessness for $100 cash, and I was guaranteed a packed house.

They also paid for my round-trip bus fare, and I was met at the bus station by Father Yaphet Sulumon in his full, priestly vestments and glory. He drove me back to the Church in an empty, yellow-orange school bus.

Over hamburgers-with-everything at Puffy-Marie's Diner, Father Sulumon and I discussed poverty. He was interested in changing things. Me too. Afterwards, we walked just down the block to the Sacred Angels

Church: My "stage". My show was standing room only. I spoke from the pulpit. It was empowering and weird, but I was determined to have this turn into a once-a-week series of Homeless Lectures at 200 dollars a pop. I was introduced to warm applause, turned on my little, handy-dandy tape recorder, and began:

> "The Unhoused have certain unalienable rights and privileges that the Doorknob Set are not privy to or even allowed to use or employ. Exempla gratia: Sleeping or Lying Unconscious on the sidewalk. An ordinary citizen wouldn't last two seconds. Here comes a policeman, a store owner, an ambulance, a fire truck, a Good Samaritan, whatever. They carefully pick you up and gently Deposit you in the back of a vehicle that takes you away.
>
> Where to: a hospital? A Jail? An Asylum?! A River?! All I'm saying is: I've never seen these people again."

Father Sulumon, rose from his front row seat in all his glory and vestments and disappeared stage left. I kept going:

> "What I'm saying is, if you're _Unhoused_ and you're lying on the sidewalk, people walk _around_ you. I personally take it as an act of respect".

After about 10 minutes Father Sulumon still hadn't returned, and I noticed people in the back pews starting randomly to head for the exit doors at the rear of the chapel.

I see people in the middle section of pews getting up and slowly heading towards the rear exits. I soldier on.

> "I use it as a chance to get a nap out in the open where nobody's going to beat me up and rob me. As much - _and,_ _i_f I die there: it's a statement. So, whichever, it's a win/win/win."

I cut it short.

"Thank you."

Scattered, polite applause from those few too close and timid to be seen leaving before it was over – no doubt polite church regulars. I had pretty much cleared the pews of both doubters and worshippers within 20 to 25 minutes. Okay...now what? Where's somebody with my —

"Mr. Justice?"

Father Sulumon, still in his priestly vestments, hands me 5 bills. I count it out in front of him.

"20, 40, 60, 80. 100. Thank—!?"

"This way."

He leads me out the back door of the church where his empty, yellow- orange school bus's motor is idling to an empty driver's seat. Father Sulumon gestures me in, follows me up, gets behind the wheel, lever- shuts the door, puts it in gear and pulls away. I chose to sit right across from him.

"You shoulda' stayed. I really got into it right after you--!"

"I watched your show on our tv in my office. The camera's behind the cross at the altar. That one monitors you from behind and into the audience."

"They didn't understand what I was trying to do. Not my crowd. Yet. A couple of shows – they'll come around. They always do.

I've been doing this a long time, Father. Win a few, lose a few. Wait; you'll see. I know what I'm doing. If we're gonna work together we've got to trust each other, Father."

Father Sulumon never said another word to me. When we got to the bus station he stopped, lever-opened the bus door, I said, "Goodbye; thanks", as I got off.

Silence. Father Sulumon lever-closed the door in his full priestly vestments and drove off in his empty, yellow-orange school bus.

I never heard from him, but I like those gigs because it's money. Can I get a "Heyman"?

*

UNHOUSED OWNERSHIP & ETC.

("Your Stuff", as defined herein)

<u>Unhoused Ownership</u> encompasses The Pros, Cons, & Differentiations between Your Most Prized versus your most Necessary Possessions; or as the late, great pataphysician, Professor George C., defined it: "Stuff" (Some of Professor C.'s 'Stuff' I would now-a-days categorize as 'Baggage', But that's just me. I travel light). Unhoused Definitions:

a. <u>Your Stuff</u>: That which you have and can carry with you, and which is necessary to getting through today and finding a safe place to sleep tonight (Professor C's definition of "Stuff" is far more extensive and all-encompassing).

b. <u>Legal Ownership</u>: To own, to consider "yours" or "mine"; that which one refers to as "having". Things that the law legally defines as belonging to a person or persons through manifest proof.

c. <u>Unhoused Ownership</u>: What you have with you now.

d. <u>Your Things &/or Acquisitions</u>: all other possessions of value to you that are not with you now. These are also defined on The Street as:

e. <u>Your Second Job:</u> "To care and protect things you value but are not with you"

f.   <u>Baggage:</u> Anchors; your things that slow you up, drag you down, and/or impede forward, pro-active, uplifting motion and emotion (see: d. *Your Things,* above).

When you're unhoused and hungry, having "things" isn't necessarily Ownership. On the street, having things is simply A Second Job.

Generally, in the Doorknob-Owner's World, Stuff & Things are vast and interchangeable. They mainly refer to either of four categories: Money, Bling, Real Estate, and People-Pets-&-Food.

In the "Stuff" Owner's World there are only two categories – "Stuff & Things":

1.   "I left my *Things* under the overpass.
2.   I took my *Stuff* with me."

Having Things as an Unhoused Person, an Urban Survivalist, or Independent, Entrepreneurial, Beggar, Panhandler-Saint is known as a Second Job.

"Talking About HavingThings" (In-General) While Unhoused is easily done. Let's talk about <u>*The Keeping of Acquisitions & Things While Unhoused.*</u> How many Things should or shouldn't an Unhoused Person have if an Unhoused Person could, would, or should have Things? How much Stuff is enough stuff and how much stuff is too much?

When does 'Stuff' become 'Baggage'? When you're unhoused and hungry and some of your Stuff's not with you.

Therefore: When you're unhoused: The less stuff, the better. So, where Professor C. asks: "Where can I put my stuff?" I ask: "How much stuff are we talking about?" Do I need another shopping cart or a storage facility? Yes, I need *some* stuff; but how much of which? A pair of slippers and a collapsible drinking cup? Fine.

$50? It's possible. A Grandfather Clock and a doorknob? I don't think so.

*

THE GIFTS OF DEMONIZATION

With the discovery of fire, religion cleverly figured out how to monetize Belief: Not the discovery of "How to Make Fire", but the discovery of "*Demonization <u>Over</u> Fire*": For letting this magical and rare "Fire" go out, causing <u>others</u> <u>to</u> <u>suffer</u>. *Now all shall be cold, freeze, and die because of me. Bad, careless, selfish, stupid ME!* Demonization: BAM: *GUILT!* You're Owned. Not Nature-Natural, but Homo-Natural! *Guilt: The Superpower!* The Church's Job is to instill guilt. My job is to leverage it.

*

Once you get the gift from the passing prospect, move on. It's not a relationship. You can't hang with them now. They got rid of some money or guilt or both, and you got some money. Done and done. Let 'em pass or they'll want their alms back.

Find a good spot, assume a proper attitude, place your look on the fulcrum of pity, and leveraged by guilt, you simply tell your story: "My dog needs an eye operation" – "My brother is trapped in a pay toilet"; whatever. Some good examples of Good Spots are at least thirty feet up-wind of an ATM; a 7-11 parking lot; supermarket exit; and – the sweet spot – in front of a Ben & Jerry's. Some good areas are parks, bus depots, busy intersections, freeway exits. Some bad spots are in front of a police station, inside a steam room, the suburbs of Boston.

The hardest part of the job is to get anything from the guy who sees me more than three days in a row. The first day I'm a sorrowful victim: That's worth 50 cents. The second day I'm a tenacious survivor: That's worth a quarter. The third day I'm a dysfunctional, lazy, social pariah that shouldn't be encouraged plus, charged with vagrancy, fined, and given jail time. A) Don't carry a grudge. B) Don't be Discouraged. C) Always be Couraged. D) Stay Accessible.

*

COMPASSION

I do not bear malice. I accept Lack of Compassion as part of the territory – the prevailing circumstances under which I ply my trade, stories, pomes; whatever. All The Urban Survivalists have got to do is to stay accessible. I call it: "Accessible Confrontation": Embarrassment, Pity, Worthiness, Worthlessness, Earnestness, Craziness, Disability, Humor, Bad Penmanship: All are useful; whatever it takes to get across and no hard feelings. You got a flaw? A scar? An amputation? Use it.

Bottom line: what we're fighting here is Compassion Burnout, also known as Sympathetic Dysfunctionality. Thus, Priest's Law: "Guilt Production must be a direct function of Compassion Burn-out: As Compassion wanes, Guilt must be increased." Which then gives rise to Potso's Constant: "Though Compassion-Burnout is quite common, there has never been one reported instance of Guilt Burnout."

We've only been here for around 300-350,000 years and already we've created more waste than our entire planet's filtering system can absorb or recycle.

Question: Should we move to Mars, yell for help, hold our breath, evolve faster, pretend it's not happening or do the worst thing possible given the circumstances?

Simply turning all the internal combustion engines off is not an option as it will destroy the planet's sources of mortgage payments, debt management, candy, toys, and clothing imports. And food. Back-in-the-day, The Ancient Egyptians had the right idea but not the right tools. How long before we start to fully embrace the worship of our sun again and global nature instead of our front lawns. If you're looking for a God, The Sun is still a solid candidate. The Ancient Egyptians where on to something. The Egyptians and plants.

You know what's the weirdest thing is, about being unhoused? The nut jobs you have to deal with. Like Fried Sal: He's fried. Really. He doesn't need food or shelter. He needs more love and help than is accessible at present.

We were walking down the street and Sal sees a lone man sitting at a bus stop, reading a newspaper while waiting, so he walks over. I hang back.

"S'cuse me, sir. Got any spare change? Haven't eatin' all day." The Guy goes:

"Or taken a bath in a year."

And goes back to his paper.

"You got me: I dress and smell and walk around all day like this and sleep in a bag in a fold-up tent on the sidewalk all night for a year just so I can scam you out of some spare change and you caught me and blew my cover. A true patriot. I'm a changed man."

"You didn't say, 'Please'."

"What for?"

"For respect."

"For what?"

"Respect for another fellow human being."

"*I'm* another fellow human being. Could *you* be more respectful? And more specific?"

"Respect for me! Is that specific enough? For yourself." Sal fishes in his pants-pocket, comes out with a crumpled dollar bill and offers it to The Guy.

"I'll give you a dollar if you skip the lecture and just gimme some spare change. Any amount."

"No."

"Why not?"

"Because you're rude. You're lazy, you're either on drugs or crazy, you smell, you're dirty. Filthy. You're probably carrying every disease and insect known to mankind."

"$1.50, same deal."

"No."

"Lemme take a bath at your house."

"No."

"Then gimme a dollar."

"No. Get a job."

"Would you hire me?"

"No."

"Please."

"Too late."

Sal turns to me, shrugs, and we keep walking. That's why I prefer beaches. The further inland you go, the weirder Homo sapiens get. Either side. Any continent.

*

$$E=mc^2$$

E=mc² is the universe's mathematical formula for recycling. The unhoused know how to recycle. Great vegetables in the dumpsters behind supermarkets; shelters made from refrigerator cartons; old, corrugated tin sheets; bubble wrap. Protein: hard to come by, but we have an entire lost, living subculture of us that pretty much exists on nothing but urban guilt and leftovers. The Unhoused are ingenious. Never underestimate ingenuity and genius born of dire straits. The unhoused don't abuse what's given. We don't waste anything. But it's still like being kidnapped by Uncaring Gods. Never underestimate The Power of Ignorance and Stupidity. Prolonged economic deprivation of comfort and dignity left us as Urban Nomads, Post-Organic Mendicants, Neo-Industrial Aborigines; we live off the land; we understand the Vibe. Urban Alleys are my neo-fields and streams. Dumpsters are my buffalo. Society's Waste is my harvest.

It is what it is with turns and twists Potholes, fools and hypnotists

Check out the Bubble-Up Laundry bulletin board at Main & Ocean Park for our next meet.

*

PTSD

Fried Sal and I were recapping his war. So, I'm goin':

"If an infinite number of monkeys sat around a table they could figure out a deal amicable to both sides plus allow each pro-active and legal way to monetize their differences in less than ten minutes without a single shot being fired."

Sal goes:

"It was an infinite number of monkeys sitting around a table that agreed to the war in the first place. All they needed was a finite number of monkeys who saw financial gain somewhere along the line to buy into it. I was just trying to get through the day and kill someone before someone killed me and find a safe place to sleep when it got dark where I won't explode or get my throat slit. Nothing's changed now except the army kept me better-fed and they had solid medical facilities. All I want is a job and a family."

"Research says jobs and families work better when narcotics, Liquor, and or PTSD are not involved 110% of the time."

"Everybody's on something to keep 'em alive and help 'em cope just a little bit longer."

"Exactly. However, the particular drugs you're on were designed to solve particular and specific needs for pain, pressure, and/or pleasure or to perform a very specific public service, but not so much designed to be used while performing immediate, pro- active and unapproved safe judgement-calls while doing the right thing at the right time every day on time in a highly socialized and scripted environment, _nor_ to be used in the raising or nurturing of a vertebrate of any species.

It's a job spec, that's all. Nothing wrong with you, the drugs, nor the rules. It's the juxtaposition of life and death and great and lasting bodily harm based on statistical, first-person experience and objective observations that's all: Numbers. Keep the ego out of it."

"I'm self-medicating."

"Exactly."

"Personally, if I wake up tomorrow and I'm able to stand and walk by myself, I'm a winner."

"Got it."

"This is a war zone, B. So, get outta my face."

"I feel your pain."

"I got this."

"Got what? What do you _got_?"

"I got something going down in LA. I'm leavin'."

"When?"

"Soon"

"How soon?"

"Tomorrow."

"Where's--!?"

"HEY!!"

Sal yelled at a 16-year-old Chinese skateboarder that just zoomed past us heading down the street and took off after him in hot pursuit. Still pursuing, Sal yelled again: "HEY!" The skateboarder looked back, saw his pursuer, turned forward, pushed off hard again, took a low- leaning left, and disappeared onto a side street followed by Fried Sal full tilt. Sal is a Hard-Core, Old-School Survivor.

*

STANDARD HOMELESS BUSINESS LOSSES

I'm not just talking about losing a million dollars – I'm talking about losing a finger or being stabbed and robbed or losing everything you own even if it all just fits into one shopping cart and you're bleeding to death. As my mother used to say: "Everything is everything." My advice while unhoused: have as little as possible. My advice while alive: have as little as possible.

Sal told me that the oldest, most basic entrepreneurs are prostitutes, poets, clowns, and beggars: Sex, Art, Laughs, & Guilt. They have three things in common: Self-Supplier, low productions costs, and a seeming endless supply of product.

The upside of Survival is the stripping down, the sluffing off the gunk; the barnacles; the paradigms.

Fried Sal's PTSD Action/Reaction Philosophy was Old School: "Alert, Options-Review, Decide-React, TOOK TOO LONG." PTSD gets it down to one word: ConcludeReact! Safer. He figures if he's wrong, he's the one that's alive to apologize. In a war zone it kept him alive. As a citizen in a peaceful nation and city, it gets him arrested and committed. Not fun. They know him. Each time they try a different test. Drives him insane. Sal says It's a learned autonomic reflex. Hard to come by. Hard to unlearn.

It's connected to survival instincts: "ConcludeReact! No Option-Permutations, Moral-Compassing or Recognition-Processing. Mother Nature designed it to keep me alive, that's all. It doesn't keep me from making unhealthy decisions." PTSD is DNA's version of "Once bitten, twice shy" on steroids. However: One of its major side-effects is that it can also produce a quite wily, seductive, toxic, and paranoid worldview.

*

MYTH OR CONSEQUENCES

We've got to start thinking more about this "testosteronal edge" fantasy. It's a blessing, it's a curse. It's gotten out of hand. It's getting in the way. I'm for freeing males from expectations that males have about not being a Heroic Male. The Fairer Sex are just as brave even braver - just in a different way.

We Males have been sold a bill of goods by ourselves. "We're in charge" is backfiring because our strength is cool and needed but our consciousness of others leaves a bit to be desired. Which might be where the opposite sex's point of view can also come in handy - besides pro-creation - as to who does what and who knows which, when, why, and how.

The Better Way is usually the best way until there's a better way. It's not, "Better, best." It's: "Best, better." Fine, if both parties have all the applicable info on how it really works. But not in the classic male storyteller's world of The Male Dominance Theory at work. Dads teach your daughters to grow up to be cowgirls, leaders, and their own person would really help, not hinder, and that they'll be able to refuse or share mutual desires with a like-minded person more equitably (less hassle) (LIFE: The DNA-Driven Seeking of Less Hassle).

Ladies and Gentlemen, these pre-historic male myths must die a fair and honorable death – or die none-the-less. They served their purposes as best we mostly knew at the time. But that's all gone and we're here now.

Homo sapiens were argue _about_ evolution. Homo sapiens are now arguing _with_ evolution. It got us to where we are today, but now it's not far or fast enough. We can't wait (Free Will and Instant Gratification {Consciousness} are cool, but evolution takes too long).

We now can predict evolutionary and planetary problems 5,000 years ahead. A problem formerly only solved by surviving for 5,000 years. To Evolution, we say, "We can do it better, faster".

We've already proven we can change the weather of an entire planet and its fresh water supply faster than the planet could without us - evolution is simply looking for the way that works better than the present one - no best, only better. Time is for testing for failure- points and tweaking. Curiosity moves the universe but there's more revelations to it with A.I. (like the invention of the telescope and microscope). The things we invent tend to change us as much as our environment and food sources do. Thus, we will change us. Sooner than later. Not necessarily to our own liking, either. The universe is really into more layback, Let-the-party-just-happen-type scientific explorations. Work-It-Out-Amongst-Yourselves-Anthropology. Consciousness (ours) is way more impatient. At the moment, the universe doesn't work the way we think it should or fast enough or slow enough - the way we want it to. But we'll solve it. That's what Homo sapiens do - solve problems. Fix things. Make them Better. The universe is a Mess (God is Omnipotent but a Slob?). We're problem-solvers. There's always got to be a better way – one simple, obvious trick: The 3rd Way.

*

When one is unhoused and hungry long enough to learn the ropes and pretty much have shown how you can get at least one meal a day somewhere somehow and you're starting to figure it out just a tiny bit: your paperwork's finally done, you know where you can take a shower, where your bathroom is, you're getting a routine, starting to feel the vibe; to understand how this works. Where to go, The New Laws and Rules, who to avoid, who to ask, what to say to who, which law enforcement officers are cops, and which are policemen, which bulletin boards have quality temp job ads and which newspapers have good, permanent job/help wanted sections with Job Specs for jobs I'm qualified for - unless the economy goes all electric and A.I. on me which it has already.

If I were me and in charge, I'd start re-training the unhoused first. Eager workers = Free votes. Politicians salivate but follow The Money. People follow The Lesser of Two Evils.

At present I prefer to suffer a life living outside of society, but within a beach community with lots of water, wind, waves, dirty, unbroken windows, and alleys with dumpsters full of usable supplies – rather than suffer a life living inside a society full of dirty windows, geared to filling alleys and dumpsters full of great stuff and yearning to move to a community by the beach where there's water, wind, and waves; soup kitchens, friends, tourists.   Where the police have me down as a regular, elder street poet and windowwasher, panhandler, and generally try to ignore me and I try to stay out of their way. We get along like borderline sentries from opposite countries at a little used Road Gate between Finland and Russia.

*

BUSTED

Vagrancy, my ass. I got busted for Not Being in Possession of a Doorknob. The Judge gave me one-week whackin' weeds for The County. At the time I had forty-eight priors. I demanded a trial-by- jury. I got "a Hearing". which was exactly what I wanted: I use The Law to achieve personal goals - impossible and crazy as that may seem. In the Hearing Chamber, I was seated in a chair, my arresting officer was standing right next to me. I figured I already wacked enough weeds to start a dust bowl so, remaining seated, *I slowly raised my hand in a fist <u>in a non-threatening manner</u>*, bowed my head, and calmly announced: "I will not whack weed one, no more forever", grabbed my arresting officer's gun-hand and attempted to bite off his trigger finger. I felt a lot of hands grab me from behind.

When I came-to, my arm was dislocated, and it hurt when I breathed too deep. I had a bloody-hair-knot on the back of my head. I grabbed one of my cell bars tight, threw my weight back hard – and popped the ball over the hump and back in the socket and I gave out a yell could have rose The Dead Sea. Nobody paid attention. Probably thought somebody was bein' raped. I found out her honor the judge said I fell in my cell and ordered no medical attention plus, Solitary Confinement: Again, exactly what I was goin' for: No roommate.

My left, upper arm had teeth marks, and I was worried about rabies. Obviously, one of the cops bit me. But my arm was back in its socket, and I could use it. That night I dreamt I had a concussion and kept waking up because I didn't want to die in my sleep. I want to be awake when I die. It's not being alone; it's the walls.

They make me sick and paranoid. The food's full of drugs and poison. They're trying to make me look like I'm well-fed by making me fat so I can't run fast.

The ACLU got a court order to get me out of a jail cell and into the UCLA Hospital in Santa Monica immediately. I was black and blue. My face and head took a beating. They checked for concussion. None. I can take it, or they really know how to beat someone up so it can fool hospital machines. Whoever sewed me up the last time did a good job. I'll die on my feet. Nobody knows what happened to Fried Sal. Nobody's seen him in a week. Did he leave? Die? Get busted? Nobody knows.

*

Priest: "It's all going' to hell in a handbag. And I ain't no lily- livered, cross-eyed son-of-a-bitch in a garbage can neither. I'm president of Texas and the great-grandson of the Great Coronado of Spain and Africa, I am wise, and I ride alone. I'm a product of my environment: carcinogens, assumptions, and The Media. However: Whether you are Unhoused; Unsheltered, an Urban Survivalist; Independent-Entrepreneurial-Beggar-Panhandler-Saint, Cognitively Impaired, Disabled, suffer from PTSD or other Mental Challenges, or are simply Independent and Unaffiliated: *Proper Dress is <u>Non-Essential</u>.*"

*

Bald Gary: "You're not going for a job interview. You got the job: The Job is, "Get through today and find a safe place to sleep tonight". You don't sleep in the bathroom; you don't shit where you

sleep; you're on the clock 24-7. Keep it simple.
Eye of the Tiger."

*

There's a lot time to think when you're unhoused
with nothing to do except think of ways to get enough
sleep and nourishment to not get sick, fill out forms,
do interviews, wait, invent too-clever wrong answers,
weather stupid questions, rules, services, and bus
routes to transfer to. Even A.I. can't figure out how to
speed up and simplify the processes of poverty and
assistance.

Genitals and breasts must be covered, or they take
you away. Bam! Out of the game for a while plus meals,
shelter, drawn blood, bodily harm, and drugs that may
not suit your preferred temperament or comfort zone.
I have nothing against exposed breasts, genitalia, or
preferred comfort zones. It's just a matter of simply
staying in our lane, folks, that's all. That's another fight
for another day. Other than that, wear what you got.
You got rags? Wear 'em. You got a Prom Dress? Wear
it. You got a wheelchair? Use it. Got a one-eyed dog?
Bring it. If that doesn't work show 'em an open foot-
wound with live maggots. _Sell the sizzle_; you got to sell
the sizzle, folks. Remember who's your competition:
America's Got Talent & a Starving Kid in Africa with
flies in its face. This isn't chopped liver; this is survival,
folks: Focus.

Pop Quiz: Who's gonna get the help? A) A poor,
elderly, one-eyed, one-legged beggar; B) A starving
African baby with flies in its face; or C) Unhoused you?
If a starving baby in Africa with flies in its face can't get
a cup of milk, who-the-hell-are-you? Some schmuck

without a doorknob? Boo-friggin'-hoo. Figure it out. Ergo: We've got to up our game and pass it on. Here's what I need: (Me, personally) Does the Organization, Religious and Otherwise, ban these Eight, Now-Banned 'Curse Words': Healthy, Pro-Active, Positive, Furthering, Eco- Friendly, Worthwhile, Reliable Facts? Is there a bottom to the amount of "Don'ts" and "Can'ts" that a given religion, cult, person, company, Country, State, Neighbor, or Random Chaos can impose. What our species can't get our heads around is: We're a species. Homo Sapiens. Like Worms, Whales and Spiders. The whole planet's crawling with us. But talk to anyone anywhere, any time and you'd never suspect it.

Excuse a slight digression:

Question: Does my one little argument have a prayer against any all-powerful group or company representing an all-knowing God whom we worshipped dearly while He let us believe for centuries that the world was flat, and He knew it was round the whole time: Is this a God who pulls Celestial Pranks: or is He just another, uh-oh: Red Flag God?

His only son did stand-up: Yo-J: Story-teller: Told funny stories, true stories, but, unfortunately, he wasn't that funny. Some he wrote, some he just did off-the-cuff stuff. Anyway, he didn't disappear - he took his act on the road and one audience - Cathay, India, really didn't like his material boo'd, threw stuff -- but he wouldn't get off the stage. So, they nailed him to a cross -

Anyway, The Moneychangers got Yo-J's Disciples to become investors and printed a best-selling Self- Help & Self-Actualization Collection called J. Christ's Book of How to Self-Actualize Yourself and Rise from The Dead: "Like A Phoenix Rising from Its Own Ashes!" A genius platform to base a religion on: Man as A Real Human Phoenix Myth. Thank the Greeks. A genius use of The

Phoenix Myth all the way back in Biblical Times equal to or better than any Modern-Day Adman could ever come up with (many people believe the Bible stories are true, but the same people don't believe Aesop's animals could really talk, so I don't get it. Nothing against the writers in either case – Like Ripley said: Believe it or not).

However, The Disciples and The Moneychangers finally got Gutenberg to back printing bibles for general sale for 5% of the book's gross sales after expenses. He printed hundreds and hundreds of these allegorical, Self-Help and Self-Actualization Stories, and called it: The Book In Beatific, Lasting Epiphanies: "The B.I.B.L.E." And the rest of the Disciples and The Money Changers got their money back in spades. Made millions. Still do. The twist was, it was always printed in fancy, colorful, script so everybody could just look at it and conclude, "The book is fancy, expensive, full of Red, Blue and Gold printing, so the stories must be true." Those who were able to read at all translated it as near as possible to what they already believed or wanted to believe, plus a lot is unreadable to cover loopholes in the logic of the events or texts. The Disciple-Investors meant well - but the Money Changers were starting to push for more power. Belief started to flag; bible sales flattened. But Big, Gold Letters and Huge Colorful Pictures of Saints on the walls of caves, or indoors, through sunlit, intense Reds, Blues, and Yellows, Golden Halos, Pretty, Winged, Flying Women, Naked Curious Winged Babies: Chubby hands to chubby chins, looking down, playing, high ceilings - *all worked! Visuals!* But only for a while and then: The 3rd Way suddenly appeared: *Teach people to read!* It's got every story in there that ever was, Detailed, Logical, Illogical, Fantastical- Science-Fictional, Families, Miracles, Magic, Drugs, Visions, Life, Death, Heaven, Hell, Satan, Financial, Unpronounceable Names, Places, Dates, Habits, marriages, wars, intrigues, God, sons, daughters, How To, Who was really "The Swan", when, where, All You Need To Know, Nothing New, Needed, Nor Can be Added.

The Beatific Book was the #1 Best Seller of its time. Probably of All Time: Better than Movies, TV, Life Magazine, National Geographic, The Internet Siri, Wikipedia, Newspapers, Smart Phones, Tourist Guides, and Life Magazine of its age. Better than watching the bats do their thing on the ceiling of our caves or just staring into a fire for hours like it was a favorite looped re-run.

Meanwhile, the Moneychangers and disciple-Investors made so much money off their investment in Guttenberg and Their #1 Best Selling Book, they bought The Temple and all the real estate the churches and Temples were built on, rock, lock, stock, and barrel, incorporated – plus, #1: Got a tax-free business exemption and: #2: Got a court-ordered injunction personally barring Jesus from entering the premises in perpetuity. But I digressed:

Before the Industrial Revolution and the Ascension of the Middle Class, I could sleep anywhere. In a tree, on a road, in a barn - because there was nothing but grass and trees and woods and Barns - with or without animals. Who cared? Now? Try sleeping _anywhere_. I can't. not even in the street. Where's Habitats for The Unhoused Free-Range Urbanites? Gimme Shelter or I'll die on your doorstep and bring you bad luck.

Frankly, the only people I can really talk to anymore are dead people. A deflection? A cry for sanity? No: A recommendation! Dead people are the best listeners. No judgments, no interruptions. A dead person will never jump to a conclusion or finish your sentence. They don't assume, conclude, or over-react. Dead people are very cool that way. Dead people have listening _Down._

A lot of people ask me about Drunken Stupors and/or Fouling Oneself. Situational at best. I personally preach moderation in all things. There's certain points, places, and times where certain functions defeat their own purpose. There's a fine line somewhere between live maggots and actual bodily fluids. So, what works? Rags, A Prom Dress, A Wheelchair, A One-Eyed Dog, Tenacity, Brass Balls, Bullshit, Guilt, Hand-Puppets, Jokes, Open Wounds, Missing Limbs, Prosthetics, Prostitution, Hand-Lettered Signs: All Street Legal. Good Luck out there.

The End

(Theo: The following story is the one about the politician you mentioned)

LoopholesLand

Excerpts from the documentary
The Rise, Fall, & Resurrection
of
Ex-President Louis B. Loopholes

w/permission from unreleased
FBI Videos; Government Files & personal cell phones

*

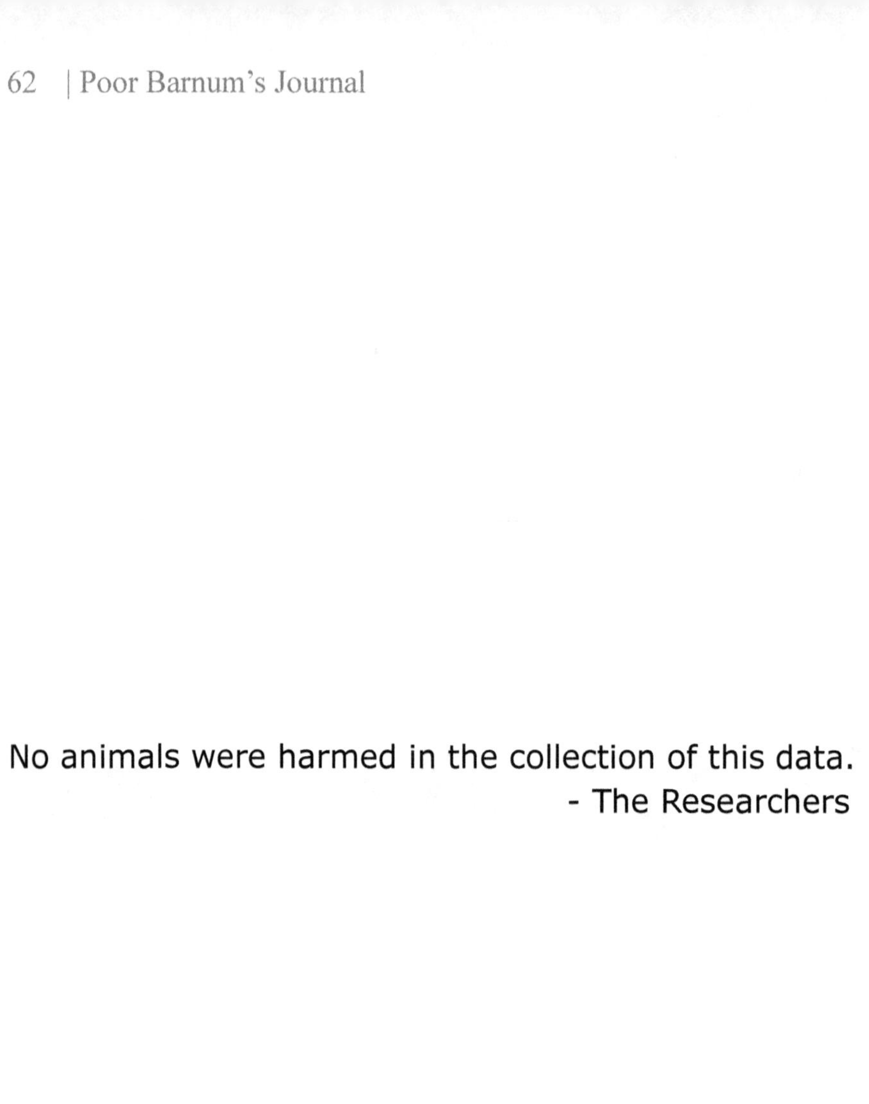

No animals were harmed in the collection of this data.
- The Researchers

Exhibit 1

5 Months Before the Election

Freedom of Information Act
Final Screening of Presidential Nominee 3-minute TV Pitches:

The room was a simple private screening room of the advertising agency, "Free, Now, & Best", in Washington D.C. There were four main participants in the viewing room. The rest were various guests of the judging panel.

The viewing had been going on for approximately a half-hour and the seventh Candidate GOP candidate's demo TV commercial filled the screen:

Candidate Demo TV Spots - Full Transcript

CANDIDATE 8: Tons of pounds are going be lost when I'm President. You're going to lose weight and be able to be eating ice- cream cake, fudge, and bacon tacos with fruit-flavored, buttered- popcorn and whip-cream-topped pumpkin pie, and -- (Sound, O.S.): *Click!* (screen goes black and switches to next candidates demo TV spot)

CANDIDATE 9: The lies I tell you to your face today may very well not be the lies I tell you tomorrow. The truth is a choice. *Your* choice. Is it a simple case of bubonic turkey surrealism or a plague of political- (Sound, O.S.): *Click!*

CANDIDATE 10: Facts cost money against the Bottom Line, and then nobody has a job. So, from here on out, we're all just going to low-ball it; use alternate facts, guesstimates, and ballpark--(Sound, O.S.): Click!

CANDIDATE 11: I will make America, 'America' Again.

And I have absolutely no 'Tell'. What do I do? I break balls and scramble brains. Born to it. A natural. Boom: In your face—(Sound, O.S.): Click!

CANDIDATE 12: Look at it this way: once you choose *someone other than me,* you are going to run into a Wall of Poverty, Doom, War, Disease, Death, Festering Pustules of--!(Sound, O.S.): *Click!*

CANDIDATE 13: The Question arises: what should we believe: The Facts or The Truth? The Pros, The Cons, me, or Your Lover's Lying Eyes? The World is a swamp with a forked tongue. We're going to do things the world shall fear nor long remember. Take that to the bank-(Sound, O.S.): *Click!*

CANDIDATE 14: I will get Congress to set aside 1.3 trillion dollars to build a large stadium in *every city in the United States.* Every city will have a huge stadium in the center of town. Many, many stadia and real games using real--!(Sound, O.S.): *Click!*

CANDIDATE 15: I would like to ignore everything I've ever said and deny everything I've ever done. God bless Me and God Help You. Thank you.

(screen goes black; title card comes on: "the end" – Light come up. One of the white-haired judges (#15) is asleep.

VOICE 1 (O.S.): That's the lot. Let's have a voice vote—!

VOICE 3 (O.S.): The last one.

VOICE 1 (O.S.): Yeah. He's very good. I like him. Yeah.

VOICE 3 (O.S.): Agreed. The last guy.

VOICE 2 (O.S.): Loopholes.

Judge #1: 3 0ut of 4 for Loopholes. Done (Gavel Rap!). Louis Loopholes's our guy.

*

Exhibit 2

Confessional-Cam* - Location: (Honest To God Church, N.Y.C., N.Y. (*used with permission of Pastor Schtaal Langerhans).

At 10:30. a.m. Presidential Nominee Louis B. Loopholes enters the booth and closes the door.

(Full Transcript):

LOOPHOLES: Father? You there? Anybody-!?

VOICE OF REV. NOAH LIDL (RNL) (O.S.): I'm here, my son. How have you sinned?

LOOPHOLES: No, that's okay. I'm fine. I just want to ask you a question.

RNL (O.S.): First unburden the weight of your misguidance, my son and confess your sins.

LOOPHOLES: Nonononono. I haven't sinned, Father. Never. I'm good. I don't mean I'm 'Good', good. I mean, I'm not good, I'm not bad. I'm me. I'm 'okay'. I'm 'good'.

RNL (sighs, O.S.): Fine: what is your question, my son?

LOOPHOLESS: A deal's a deal until it isn't, right?

*

Exhibit 3

5 Days After Loopholes's Election

as President of
The United States of America

MSCBC News Service - Full transcript available. Location, Dallas, Texas state fair: President Loopholes's Acceptance Speech as Newly Elected President of The United States.

PRESIDENT LOOPHOLES (PL): (Cheers from the crowd) - not only THAT - (more cheers from the crowd) – not only that, but also: I promise you on my mother's grave and every person who died defending this, whatever-you-wanna-call-it: country, republic, socialist republic, democracy, de-shmocracy, <u>whatever</u>! I promise you - PROMISE YOU! Starting tomorrow at noon, I will begin lying to you <u>All</u> <u>The</u> <u>Time</u>! *(cheers from audience!)* Now let me say one thing right here and now: when I say I'm going to lie to you all the time, I'm talking about lying to you on T.V., in the newspapers, the internet, on your cell phone; digital watch, Instagram, faxes, tweets: '<u>Media lying</u>'. Yes! *But:* if we're talking man to man, man to foreigner, alien, immigrant or - even if I have to – man to woman: a "Woke Woman": No, no, nononononononono: I would never lie to you off the record, outdoors, with no witnesses, to your face. That's also a promise. Thank you. God bless me and God help you!

*

Exhibit 4

White House Recording System

Freedom of Information Act
Location: White House, Oval Office,
2 Months Later

The president was in a private meeting with Doctor Schmocter, a chiropractic-proctologist sponsoring a bill to have his new plastic surgery procedure paid for by Medi-Care. The only one's present were President Loopholes, his wife, Leilani, and a film crew. Doctor Schmocter was ushered into the room. The President was seated behind the President's Desk.

(Full Transcription)

PRESIDENT LOOPHOLES (PL): Hey, Doc. How are you? Good to meet you. Sit down, make yourself comfortable. You know my wife, Leilani Leilani Loopholes (LL - nods appropriately): Good to finally meet you. I've heard and read a lot about you. Nice things. Very nice things."

DS: A pleasure to meet you, Mrs. Loopholes. Thank you, Mr. President.

Dr. Schmocter sits in a chair facing the president at a slight angle. The President was seated behind the Presidential Desk.

PL: So, what can I do for you? If I can.

DS: Well, I've developed a new procedure and I'd like Medicare—

PL: Whoa, whoa, there. Let's not jump into the deep end. Tell me a little bit about yourself. You, yourself are a certified plastic surgeon, yes?

The doctor reaches into his inside suit-jacket pocket--!! The President ducks behind the Presidential Desk!

Two Bodyguards appear (literally out of nowhere)

with outstretched, stiff arms pointing two handguns at Dr. Schmocter.

The Doctor calmly pulls a business card out and offers it to The President, who rises as if nothing happened, takes it, sits, placing the card casually in his suit-jacket's handkerchief pocket.

PRL: I'd rather hear it from you, personally.

The bodyguards have completely disappeared. There's nothing to disappear into or behind. The President remains casual.

DS: Yes sir. UCLA Medical school, Sloane-Kettering, into my own practice, over five thousand successful plastic surgeries, all successful, elected president of Alpha Omega Alpha twice--!

PL: Who was your first plastic surgery patient? On your own? How'd it turn out?

DS: My first patient was my mother. Eyes and chin. Beautiful job - I give her a tuck every three years on her birthday. She loves it. I'm a good son. Clinic's been open 15 years, I'm making more in a month than a politician can steal in a year...Little joke...Malpractice insurance is killing me: so, what else is new? But, more and more, I'm starting to specialize in male cosmetic surgery: Crow's feet, tighten your neck, restructure your nose, lower your ears, liposuction the old love handles, but even more: I find I'm concentrating solely on MFRs, Male Foreskin Replacement. Latest thing. The cosmetic wave of the future. I refer to it as MES: 'Male Empowerment Surgery': Think of a bald man getting all his hair back all at once in less than twenty minutes in my office on an outpatient basis for under 1K. If you have Medicare plus a second payer, you'd be covered. Which is exactly the reason I've come to speak to you today. A lot of Jewish men are having it done. Simple procedure: I just take a piece of loose skin from the tip of your elbow: snip-snip, stitch-stitch, a bandage and bingo you're back in business. I did my father. He loves it. At parties he can't keep it in his pants – your typical 'Proud Pop'. Hey: I'm a good son. A lot of nudist- colony men are having it done, too. But The Main Point is, it's *Empowering:* You might also visit #MaleEmpowerment. com.

PL: You know, I'm going to have to think about that. Not 'that', particularly, but I think Medicare is way, way over budget and frankly it's a hard sell. Really. I've got too many, so many irons in the fire right now -- but keep on keepin' on. I think you're on to a new era in the science of things that will be really nice for those who think that. And thank you for thinking of me - I mean them. All of us. With your idea. Interesting. Bye.

DS: Any time, sir. Thank you.

Dr. Schmocter rose from his chair, bowed slightly to The President, turned, and left.

*

Exhibit 5

Event: President Loopholes Speaks. Live, On-Air Interview:

Location: The Oval Office, W.H., Wash. D.C.

Interviewed by: Sperl Chartney of Channel 6 News, Wash. D.C.

PRES. LOOPHOLES (PL): Look, as a human being, of course I'm outraged at human rights abuses; but I'm sorry, I find it hard to sympathize with someone who hasn't taken a bath in two years. In a social economy based on need and lack, there are certain basic marketable skills that are required to deserve my

Presidential Attention. Making a sign that says: "Will work for food" and standing at a freeway exit with it, is not my idea of a BMA, Basic, Marketable Skill. My point is: If they don't want to help themselves, why should I?

SPERL CHARTNEY (SC): Don't you think--?

PL: I just want them off the streets. Sure, there's one or two that are worthwhile: an air-traffic controller or some aerospace engineer – but nine out of ten of 'em are alcoholics junkies, psychotic, pathological, diseased kleptomaniacs, gang-bangers, or rapists – on both sides, on both sides – *plus* lazy bums and terrorists - and they're all living off the money I need for The City Domes.

SC: "City Domes." What do you mean? What are City Domes?

PL: You know. Like in diners on their counters - over cakes on cake stands, to keep the flies off. Everybody loves it."

SC: "This is new. Flies? What kind of flies?"

PL: "Horse flies, Missiles, Immigrants, A.I. Drone Soldiers, bugs insects, prostitutes, drugsters, gang members, murderers, climate changers, dragonflies, Barflies, child molesters - I was being poetic. You also see 'em on the Cake shows. You bake a cake. Nice Icing. You put a dome on to protect it. I watch the cooking shows. Julia Childs. Great. She's Great. Classic.

SC: You mean the little glass covers for wedges of cheese?

PL: No. Gotta be cake. *'Khu'*. No 'Chee'. "Plosives": "K", "P", "T". Hard "C". A Super, *Super* Cake-*Kuh*... Cake Dome. Over every city. Like "Kake". Danishshsh: Shsh: Too quiet. I like sounds: KUH! Plosives.

SC: Sort-of like blisters on a landscape. Will each have a handle on top?"

PL: Blisters, handles, who cares? I'm living my dream. *You* asked to interview *me.*

(President Loopholes ripped off his lapel mike and left with bodyguards in tow).

*

Exhibit 6

White House Recording system: Freedom of Information Act

Location / Event: White House Cabinet Meeting Room

Emergency Cabinet Meeting

FIVE WHITE MEN, ONE BLACK MAN, AND ONE WOMAN WITH NOTICEABLY LARGE BREASTS ALL SIT AROUND THE CONFERENCE TABLE. All dignified, business-like, and in business attire. President Loopholes began the meeting by addressing those seated at the table: *(Full Transcription):*

PRESIDENT LOOPHOLES: Thank you all for coming. Now, I called you all here because I have a problem. It's nothing to do with me. I have nothing to do with it. So, we'll just refer to it as "The Problem". But, me: I have nada – <u>Na</u> - <u>DA</u> - nothing to do with it. Nothing to do with it what-so-ever. But we've got to solve it. So, let's all give me something to say. Whatever. Just a couple of words – not too long - and we can all get on with our day (to the WOMAN at his immediate left) There's an 'American Masters' TV Special on Julia Childs at two. She's the best. The best. So, how do we solve The Problem?

Answers: Go...

(The President folds his hands on the table in front of him and waits. There's a very long silence. Finally):

THE BLACK MALE: (BM): ...We...don't know which problem. What prob--?

PL: The problem is: everybody and everything is either poor, illegal, useless, stupid, white trash, homeless, drug-addicts, rapists, immigrants, fake foreigners; paid off; working for the deep state, or a disgrace; and they're all over the friggin' place. *That's* the problem. And all I need from you people - all I want to know is, what do I say about it? Because, if I have a problem, *you all* have a problem. Frankly, my solutions is : put them all in cages. Once upon a time it worked great: Murderers, Vermin, Kids, Animals. Worked great.

FIRST WHITE MALE (FWM): Okay, realistically, you're the president: You tell them, "It's good for the country, we're working on it, and we'll see".

PL: A start. This is a test, people. It's all a test. Anybody else? Something. Anything.

SECOND WHITE MALE (SWM): Look, here's the thing: If those are the demographics, you put them in stocks or stone them to death-- Now, wait, wait! Hear me out, hear me out. If that doesn't work, we can always tweak it from there, but at least we'd have a baseline.

PL: Good. Good one. One or two more.

THE WOMAN (TW): I think there's a bigger problem we're just not dealing with as far as helping--

PL: Folks, *I know what the problem is! And: I just told you the solution: Keep 'em out or put 'em in cages! Problem solved.* That's <u>not </u>why we're here. We're here to answer the simple question: What do I tell *them*?

(Loopholes gestures to the several News Media cameras and recorders quietly taping all this from their usual press places: facing the President, backs against the opposite wall, live, ten feet away. This was and is all being filmed and recorded; All in our group, including Loopholes, are used to it and them).

TW: Putting people in cages is inhuman. It's just

warehousing them.

PL: Exactly. But think who we'll be warehousing. What's wrong with that?

THIRD WHITE MALE (TWM): First of all it's not fair to punish people who don't have much, or have nothing at all to do with--

PL: Nonononononono! Look at them! Look:

(*The President holds up 2 exact-duplicate color photographs of several destitute and homeless children posing for the camera, all with unsmiling faces and no shoes. The difference between the two is: one duplicate has obviously been photo-shopped so that these malnourished children are now wearing brightly-colored clothing but still, no shoes. "Smiles" have also been photoshopped over their unsmiling mouths.*)

They don't need much: celery, Ketchup, chicken gizzards, a reflector blanket and they're happy. I remember, in school we read this short story by a very famous writer, it was called, 'Old Manny, The Good and Humble Beggar'. Great story. This was way back in the Old Country, back in The Old Days. Manchester Bog was an old homeless beggar in the old country. He was known as 'Old Manny-the-good-and-humble- beggar-who'd-been-around-for-so-long'. The town kept him alive with spare change or odd jobs and leftover food because Old Manny was so good and humble.

"And to prove just how good and humble and deserving Old Manny was, when he died and went to heaven, The Lord God met him personally at the Pearly Gates, welcomed him and said: 'Old Manny, you good and humble beggar: At last: we've waited for you for so long because you are one of my deserving. Since you never had much, yet remained good, kind, and honorable all your life, always gave always shared and helped and was always humble when alive, I'm going to offer you a gift only offered to those who are unique and special: I grant you one wish for anything you want in the Universe. Anything you ever wanted, wished for, or desired, while you were alive, you can have now as your heavenly reward. Go for it. No guilt. No Blame: fishnet stockings; whatever. This is what heaven's all about, Old Manny.' And all the old, humble beggar, wished for was a nice fresh, hot-from-the-oven bagel with some warm butter melting all over the top.' Beautiful, right? Humble. People should remember that. It's a story for our time.

TW: I know that story. It's a wonderful story.

PL: Yes. See? And she's a woman. Even she knows. Tell 'em. It's a great story.

TW: Three times God gave him a chance at whatever he wanted, and three times Old Manny took the hot bagel and butter.

PL: That's right. That's the story. Always humble.

TW: Well, the writer was very perceptive about how the long-term homeless think almost permanently in terms of short-term, day-to-day survival behavior. It causes the same damage as being on the front lines in a war over time. Any overly-long-term stress situation: 'Battered Housewife Syndrome'; 'PTSD'. The writer was saying Old Manny was showing such acute symptoms of highly advanced 'PTSD' that not even God found it easy to break him of his short-term survival-thinking by offering him his best and wildest dream, not once but three time--!?

PL: Excuse me, Miss: thank you. Thank you, everybody. 'American Masters: Julia Childs. Sorry. Gotta go.

(Everyone was immediately ushered out. The President stood, walked to the still-seated Woman and stood over her):

Wrong move. Your breasts aren't gonna save you this time, honey. Stick a fork in 'em: they're done.

President Loopholes turned and exited a door near him, followed by his people.

*

Exhibit 7

Official White house recording:
Oval Office – Freedom of Information Act (FIA)
Location: The White House, the Oval Office
1 month later
Event: Normal Day – Oval Office – White House

President Loopholes is sitting behind the presidential desk talking on his cell phone. His attention is divided between the call and A Bank of Eight Cooking Shows on Large TV Screens set up in middle of The Oval Office facing the presidential desk with no sound.
(Verbatim transcription from original WH voice recording):
PRES. LOOPHOLES (PL) *into cell phone:* I'm interested, but here's the prob--!... I thought everything was settled?... Horseshit... HEY! Look: I didn't get where I am by taking bullshit from you... Really?! Fine, and you're a two-bit hooker--!? (He hears a noise - spins to it – relief - It's Doctor Schmocter) Be right with you, Doc. (Back into his cellphone) None of your beeswax, Sweetie.

(The President covers the cellphone's mouthpiece with his hand and whispers: "My daughter", to the doctor). "Sit" (into his phone): It's nothing. Never mind. ... And you're a cunt just like your mother, honey, so go cry on your boyfriend's shoulder; I'll move it without

you… Love you, too. Bye, sweetie. (Disconnects. re: his cellphone): 'How sharper than a serpent's tooth' or 'A chip off the old block', right? She could teach politics to Machiavelli. She's been doing those Bony Dobbins Money DVD's and, lemme tell you, every time I talk to her, I learn something. Remind me: why aren't we talking on the phone? DS: You said you don't want to talk about replacing your foreskin over the—
PL: 'Procedure'.

DS: Sorry: Replacing your 'procedure' over the phone.
PL: Thank you. But, I'm definitely interested: The problem is, I have a very tight schedule; travel-with-the-limos-in-the-city, bodyguards, waiting rooms: too much trouble. It's a problem.
DS: Actually, It's a simple procedure. I do it on an out-patient basis. I can do it right here; takes a half-hour, tops.
PL: You know what? I have a suit-jacket fitting on Tuesday afternoon; tailor's coming here at two. Why don't you come at 1:30 and set up? When my tailor arrives, I have the remote; I'll stand facing the TV's, he'll work on the top half, you work on the bottom half, I can watch my shows. No wasted time. One-Thirty, Tuesday?
DS: My pleasure.
(They shake hands across the desk and Dr. Schmocter leaves.)

*

Exhibit 8

From: various, personal smartphones and local news footage FORMER-PRESIDENT LOOPHOLES'S MAR-A-GO-GO MINIATURE GOLF COURSE, Miami Beach, FLA. (w/permission)

Event: President Loopholes's birthday. Sunny Afternoon.

President Loopholes sat at a large round, outdoor table on the patio of a small, miniature Golf Course right off the main boulevard in South Beach, Miami. President Loopholes "Holds Forth" at his own birthday party with several American-business scion-friends and their wives. All were in Florida-golf-course-mufti, each with some kind of tiny umbrellaed drink nearby. A couple play miniature golf through a miniature Windmill in the background as President Loopholes is just finishing the punchline to a joke he's been telling for the last several minutes.

PL: --and she says, 'That's not the point', and eats it! (polite laughter and applause).

GUEST (G): But, seriously, "Loop": what's that got to do with the question?

PL: what I'm saying is, there's a special kind of pressure that goes with The Presidency of The United States that I don't find anywhere else in the world. Completely missing in totalitarian states and dictatorships - and there's something very warm and relaxing about the fact I can bring another color to the pallet. There's something strangely comforting about dictatorships and totalitarian states. 'No Surprises', 'Complete Control', 'Total Transparency'. Yes, it's like a king, but there's no comparison, really.

G: Hold it. "Total Transparency"! That's a lie or you're joking.

PL: Okay, look: As President of the United States, you're supposed to cover everything up. Hold it in. All that does is: it makes you constipated. I speak of _Fresh_ Air and _Don't Dick with Me_ Air. Before Me: Before I suddenly appeared on the social and political media scene – before me: the masses, The People, the eyeballs, the asses, fish, marks, hits, rubes, customers, voters, investors, wacko's, prostitutes, child-molesters, whatever you want to call them – they get very upset if you lie to them. They take it personal. In totalitarian states; dictatorships: Not-A-Problem. Here, as president, I keep on having to come up with more and more devious or weird things to say or do to _distract_ - _but_ - get the attention of The Media: Not easy, but Outrage and Lie Sell, Baby. What can I say? Social, Government, Left, Right, Tik Tok, podcast, internet, Twitter: <u>Media</u>. Because without media, I don't exist. All the famous people don't exist without Media. So, it's a tough call for me to attack the media. But what can they do? NA-<u>DA</u>. Their hands are tied: They only print the "truth". Schmuckos. Still: Sometimes lying's not as easy as it looks. Other times there's just not enough lipstick. So what else is new? That's life.

G: What's with the tweets or whatever? Do you really --!

PL: I don't tweet. At _all_. Anymore. Used to.

G: What do you mean-?

PL: I haven't sent a tweet in at least three years. G: Then who--?

PL: My youngest son, Whatchamacallit, does most of the tweeting. 90-95% of them, anyway. Sometimes he lets his Nanny or his bodyguards send a couple. They seem to enjoy it. But, listen; all those tweets add up. People become used to them, a slight drumbeat of chaos every day. It's good for them. Solidifies them. It's mesmerizing; attention-focusing. Like a cool, driving, bassline. I don't like jazz. At all. But they talk great, don't they? Boy. Uptight Bullshit is completely missing in totalitarian states and dictatorships. One person in charge: No one can tell me what to do. I don't want to start a war or hurt anybody. Just: what I say goes: end of story – or, end of *your* story. (Laughter).

(Points around to each man) I make you and you and you – everybody here - a huge ton of money. More money than you could've imagined. Was that a foolish dream? I don't think so.

(Approval of group).

PL (cont.): But, to answer your question: Complete and total power and control is a very warm, relaxing, comfortable feeling. Once that happens, I'm a completely different person. Like Jekyll and Hyde.

*

Exhibit 9

5 Months After His Impeachment

TV SCREEN: TV Breaking News – Ch. 6:

<u>TV TALKING HEAD</u>: Hello again with more Breaking News: 5 months after his impeachment, and only 2 months after his extraction from the Oval Office by the U.S. Marines and some very brave government aides, Ex-President of the United States, Louis Loopholes, showed up for his first day on his new job yesterday, finally fulfilling his sentence of twenty-five hours of community service.

*

Exhibit 10

Excerpts from Documentary:
"THE MAKING OF
"THE RISE, FALL, & RESURRECTION OF LOUIS B. LOOPHOLES"
(PROD. CO.: BBC Productions: w/permission)

Backstory: The documentary team (BBC-TV) had received sole rights to accompany the ex-president on his first day on the job of serving his sentence of community service by agreeing to allow the State of New York to use the footage to make a visual and oral historical survey of the Permanent Homeless Population of present-day Lower Manhattan. This was a coup of sorts as the ex-president's assigned location for his first day serving his one-day sentence was never released - nor discovered by any of the other major news services.

Rumor has it that BBC paid dearly for the privilege, rights, and secrecy.

<u>Clyve Benefield, Documentarian:</u>

We were told to be at a particular place and time in lower Manhattan: the mouth of an alley south of 8th and Houston Street at 10 a.m. At precisely that time a chauffeur-driven stretchlimousine arrived and dropped off Ex-President Loopholes and two bodyguards. He stepped out of the back dressed in a nicely tailored black suit, white shirt, gold tie, and a brand new, gold-initialed mailman's pouch hanging from one shoulder full of gift-wrapped boxes and bags of who- knows-what. He wore a white-tufted, red Santa hat jauntily cocked on his head, bobby-pinned and taped on just so.

He immediately entered the alley with his two bodyguards on alert, and the limo drove away. The question that came to mind was: Is he going to take stuff out of the pouch and give it away or has he been picking stuff up and putting it in? He was also carrying a clipboard with a gold, Montblanc fountain pen attached to it. He'd lost weight. He looked very trim and healthy. His body language seems extremely positive.

The ex-president approached an old, grey-haired, homeless man sitting on an empty milk crate next to what appeared to be his sleeping bag and gear. The old guy was quietly contemplating an empty liquor bottle.

EX-PRESIDENT LOOPHOLES (XPL): Pardon me, sir.

OLD GUY (OG): You better believe it.

XPL: I do, I do. Really. If I may: I'm personally doing an oral history on the Permanently Homeless down around lower Manhattan, and I wonder if you'd mind if I asked you a question?

OG: Are you askin' me a question about whether or not I'll give you permission to ask me a question? Yes or No? _BUT_: Without my permission to ask me if you can ask me a question? Right? Or "Not"?

XPL: Well, "Yes", but–

OG: What's in it for _moi_?

XPL: Great question. I'm going to offer you three choices, and you can keep any two of them you choose. That's it. That's all. And I'll leave you to your jam. Promise. Deal?

OG: Go for it.

XPL: Thank you. Okay: you can have any <u>Two</u> of the following Three Choices: please hear all three choices before choosing. Choice One: You can have an insured, $500,000 Government bond in your name, locked in at 19.3%, compounded quarterly starting on the first of next month with an automatic rollover to a straight annuity at 25% after six years and continuing for another ten. That's choice One. Choice Two: One ounce of pure heroin and a quart of cooking sherry. Wait, wait, you promised--Choice <u>Three</u>: Two bags of Nachos. That's it. Okay, choose which--!

OG: Two and three.

XPL: ...You're sure?

OG: Sherry, Nachos, and heroin, right?

XPL: "Right on, dude".

The President reaches into his mailman's pouch, pulls out a clear plastic bag of white powder, a bottle of wine, two bags of Nachos and hands it all to the homeless old guy.

XPL: Thank you. Nice meeting you, sir. Louis Loopholes. Call me Louie.

OG (shaking his hand): Manchester Upton. But everybody calls me Old Manny.

*

Exhibit 11

Also w/permission: NYC Community Visual Services Division

Time: 9 p.m. / NYC Welfare & Social Services Office

Event: Ex-President Loopholes reports back.

Documentarian: Clive Bonefield:

CB: We filmed from outside the glassed-in-but-sound-proof office of Ex-President Loopholes's Superior Officer, Captain L. Cosgrove, as The Ex-President stood gesturing to the captain who remained seated behind his desk the entire time. However, all conversations in Cosgrove's office are automatically recorded by the office monitoring system as policy.

Full Transcription:

XPL: Let me tell you something; social programs are a waste of time. 98% of the permanent homeless chose the heroin, cooking sherry, and nachos. 3% knocked me down and robbed me, and 1% raped me. They're animals. And they wouldn't help fold up the chairs after we fed them. They just walked away. I had to fold up the folding chairs myself. They have no social skills, and they don't have a "thank you, masked man" – Nothing. They knocked me down, stole my credit cards, and raped me. I told them if they didn't take my shoes, I'd write them a check for two hundred dollars. They took my shoes, my wallet, and my gold Montblanc fountain pen! That was a goddamn sacred blessed gift from my father. You know how long it takes to get another Driver's License? You gotta answer twenty questions! <u>I don't answer questions:</u> I <u>say</u> things. Words. Incredible Words. Numbers. Massive, Mean, Powerful, Meaningless Gold Bullion Numbers. That's me. That's what I do. You don't like it. Sue me.

HIS SUPERIOR OFFICER (HSO): Mr. Loopholes, sir: first-of-all, they're homeless, not stupid. They know you. You were president: that's why you're here. They know that as soon as you got home, you'd stop payment on the checks.

XPL: Nonononono. No; that's just my point: me being a liar has nothing to do with respect. I was president of the United States of America. Respect must be shown.

HSO: So, thieves and rapists should believe a liar just because the liar used to be president?

XPL: Yes. I was El Presidente. If the El Presidente says it, it cannot be untrue. I'm a conduit. Like the Pope or a Pharaoh or anyone else who has the green light. Otherwise, there's chaos: you have immigrants, druggists, rapists, locusts, measles, bird-dropping from the sky, flying fish, omens and harbingers up the ying-yang. Obedience must be paid. Plus, attention.

HSO: Whether or not you were lying to them?

XPL: Absolutely. A priori. Listen: I lie, sure, I lie. But I hate it when somebody doesn't trust me. That's

<u>different</u>. It's an insult. A disgrace. Because it's an insult to the country and a disgraceful disgrace to gracefulness in general. And a shame.

HSO: But you're an ex-president now.

XPL: *FORMER* President.

HSO: *FORMER,* FORMER PLAIN ORDINARY CITIZEN.

HSO: Fuck you.

HSO: Sir, have you ever told an intentional lie?

XPL: No. Never.

HSO: You just said: "I lie. Sure, I lie": You're a liar. You lie.

XPL: I don't lie.

HSO: That's a lie.

XPL: No, it isn't. And no, I'm not, and no, I don't. But sometimes I have no choice.

HSO: The truth is not a choice.

XPL: Bullshit: All Truth is a bunch of *Loopholes*! That's my last name, or didn't you think I noticed?

*

Exhibit 12

5 YEARS AFTER

Location: "America's Truth TV Studios," NYC, NY.

Event: 'Book Prefaces on Video' - Promotional Programming ©

Ex-President Loopholes wrote a book about to be released. He sat in a TV studio, in a comfortable armchair on a comfortable living room set, his book-in-hand, a fire in a fireplace to his left behind him while soft music played in the background (with permission). *(Full Transcript* - The following TV graphics were shown while spoken by a V.O.:

"*"Streaming Book Prefaces" presents Former President Louis B. Loopholes Reading the preface to his soon-to-be-released book:* **'PRIDE of LIARS'**, How I Became The Alpha Liar among a Pride of Liars."

The Ex-President put on his reading glasses and began reading from his own book, to camera from memory or by referring to either of two teleprompters:

EX-PRESIDENT LOOPHOLES (XPL): First of all, I don't think lying is a bad thing. But then, I don't think evil is a bad thing either. When I think of lying, I immediately ask myself the question: 'Which is better: The Whole Truth, or A Great Lie?' Very few people know or realize that lying, as President of the United States, is actually quite easy. Much easier than lying as an ordinary American citizen or legal immigrant to the police. All you have to do as President is do it: Just lie. Lay it out there. Either it sticks and you get on with your day – or there are people paid to back it up or *walk it back for you*. But, frankly just telling a Bigger, Different Lie works just as well. However, having someone else walk it back for you has one advantage: accusing someone of lying about lying about somebody not lying raises such a quagmire of government-called witnesses and committees that it's just not worth the trouble or money to bring it up.

However, having someone else walk it back for you has one advantage: accusing someone of lying about lying about somebody <u>not</u> lying raises such a quagmire of government-called witnesses and committees that it's just not worth the trouble or money to bring it up.

We all know that every president has lied at one time or another. Take George Washington; The Father of our country: Remember: "Father, I cannot tell a lie. I cut down the Cherry Tree." *Bullshit!* And I can prove it. I have proof he lied. He used it to cover up the fact that he was involved in a Godless sexual relationship with a man 40 years his senior. A stranger from Sussex, England. For money. Yes: The Father of Our Country: "Lyin' George" Washington. I have people researching it and we're turning up a huge amount of proof about all his lies – things" I can't tell you, but believe me, lyin' George is a dead man.

There's "The Truth, The Loopholes, & The Lie": and I say this with all the wisdom of hindsight: If I had to do it all over again, The first thing I'd do is sign an executive order stating that-- (he reads directly from his book):

"--it's perfectly all right to lie anywhere, anytime, under any circumstances, to, and including *but-not-limited-thereto,--* I got that one from a legal document--

(directly to camera):

"Or For No - Freaking – Good - Reason. And Only I am Exempt!" (To off-camera personnel) We'll clean that up, it was a joke.

Back to reading from his book:

"—For no good reason whatsoever, with one exception: <u>There</u> <u>shall be no lying, in person, to one's face."</u>

(To camera) So, I'll just whisper it quietly in your *ear. The ear* is *not the face:* 'The-Truth-The-Loophole- & The-Lie. Buda-bing, buda-bang, buda- boom. Easy-Peasy.

INT: Interesting. Now with this book coming out, what are you thinking about as a next project? Or you just want to rest. Take a break. I'm doing hands on research into my next book best-seller: My own personal memoir printed on grains of rice. A grain a page. The New Book is called, "Nothing Matters".

INT: In What Way?

XPL: Well, if nothing matters, you have to <u>make</u> <u>it</u> <u>matter</u>. The book can serve several purposes: Read it or simply add water, cook it and eat it with some shrimp and soy sauce or buy several books and make a Bean-Bag Chair. My Dad taught me: "Nothing really matters to begin with: You're here. And then you die. The hard part is, 'And then', so, you have to really make it matter to yourself before even beginning to make it matter at all to anybody else, anytime, anywhere. Revenge, for instance. It has a good body and bite to it, lasts almost as long as True Love, some say. Revenge sticks to your bones and has a long shelf life. But it could be any good, solid emotional foundation for your reason. Hate is a waste of energy and unsatisfying in its conclusions, but I don't knock it. Whatever rows your boat."

Learning how to write my memoir on a grain of rice-a-page changed the way I saw the world. I found out the real reason why Homo sapiens lie. It's <u>not</u> because of a deep-seated power grab – or some sinister, father-driven ego-trip or greed, paranoia or even survival. Homo sapiens lie because *The Whole Truth is just too frickin' long and involved.* Believe me. Telling the truth means you've got to have facts, references, all videos, recordings, tapes, corroboration, verifiable research, witnesses, gravitas, time, money, lawyers -- it just goes on & on & on. The Truth never stops.

But with a lie, it's just: "What do you want to know?" Budabing! And you get on with your day. It's not brain surgery. Little kids can do it. Little four-year-olds are Black Belt Masters. No sweat. A lie is quick, it's easy, it's serviceable; it's a quick-flick-of-a-paradigm whenever you're confronted with Facts and/or Proof that doesn't fit your side or situation.

Fact: when confronted with facts and/or proof that doesn't fit into your world-view-paradigm-puzzle-picture: you only have two choices:

1. Ignore (Deflect): Facts and proof play havoc with budgets, plans and foregone conclusions) or:
2. Lie (Do The Math): Lying saves time: time is money: lying saves money.

At this point the subject of "Truth" is always brought up as a third choice. You miss the point. Lying is not about *Truth*. Lying and Truth have nothing to do with one another.

Personally, I've never seen myself as a liar - *Per Se.* I'm simply saving time and cutting to the chase: Look, I was President of the entire United States of America plus, I had Real Estate all over the world, I had kids, a marriage, I had Lawsuits, delays, people to sue. And all the press needs is a 10 second sound bite - so I make it up. Much easier. Improv. I studied with Violent Spooling in Chicago back- in-the-day. The press needs news; I need to "Look and sound Presidential": Look like I got moxie, mix-it up, cause a tumult. Money Follows Power. Evil follows Money and Power (as does other money, other power, politicians, corporations, beggars, mortgages, Real Rich People, and Media. *However!* There are those of us who simply get on with our day & BE HAPPY. And if you're not happy: GET HAPPY. Let Me, Us. Let me, Us - and the people I designate - *do the* thinking. Let *them* deal with Logic and The Deep State and let me worry about the other stuff. Biddah-bing-bidda-boom-bidda-bang. I have always considered anyplace outside the Continental Limits of The United States, as Terra Incognita: A dark street's back-alley. A Black Hole. People disappear. As do we all.   No body, no crime. But I'm not a lawyer.

Let me tell you something about "Facts" and "Proof". Some of my best friends have Facts and Proof. No biggie. Let me tell you something about Facts and Nature: If you have Facts and Proof *You Don't Need to Lie!* Hey, if I have the facts and the proof and I'm right morally and according to the law, I may be a liar, but

I'm not stupid. I'll tell the truth; and if I'm 'Il Duce' of The United States and I don't have the cards? What-am-I-gonna-do? <u>DUH!!</u> What I'm saying is: Lying is simply a political tool to level the playing field, that's all. Lying simply gives you a little breathing room: a second shot; time to regroup.

Here's a tip for For Being-in-Charge & Staying-In-Charge: Presidentially or otherwise: Hire solid dimwits for all leadership positions. That way, you're always The Boss, and your word is to be worshiped in front.

Also, with lies, there's a simple, finite number of answers you have to know - basically, 8. The Golden 8: Yes / No/ Maybe / I don't know but I'll get back to you / I know but I can't tell you / You look great in that / I can't talk now / That's not mine.

If it involves Quantity, it's even simpler: *a reasonable number, plus a topic-related category: e.g.:* if you're talking about scrap metal: 97 tons not 97 ounces. If you're talking about money not 'hundreds', not 'thousands', Millions, Billions, throw in a Trillion every once-in-a- while. Milk: 97 *gallons* of milk. 97 *ounces* of milk doesn't work. But even so, as President, somebody else *will walk it back for you*: i.e.: lie to cover your lie – and you can get on with your day. In conclusion: Here are my three Personal Cardinal Rules for Leadership Lying:

a.) The bigger the lie, the better the lie (proven classic; ref.: WWII)

b.) On the Down-Low Side: Lies work like bug killers, fossil fuels, asbestos, tiny particulates of plastics, and cancer: Their toxicity works mostly <u>sub-rosa and over time</u>. You hardly notice the toxic effects day- to-day, and by the time it shows, the toxicity has already won, plus the liar is already The Leader and you, personally are slowly dying and you haven't noticed. Thank God for Science.

c.) As President, if your lie is not believed, someone else
  will walk it back while you tell a different, bigger lie.

INT: Any Last words before we go?

XPL: It's a lot of work. It's not easy thinking up things
to do and say to the press. I make it up. Wing it. I see
something in the paper, I'll use it somehow – Something
new every day, day after day. And the weekend Golf
games, plus the golf in between – After a while, a toilet
bowl is a just a toilet bowl. It's tough.

INT: Thank you very much Ex- Former President Louis
Loopholes. Any last words?

XPL: Always be closing. I'm Louis Loopholes. You need
this book.

_____Addendum to: Exhibit 12_____

3 recent undercover videos: Current Loopholes
properties

Location: "The Strip", Miami Beach, Fla.:

Video #1: Looking down the neon-lit "Strip", busy
Miami Beach Saturday night.

Video #2: a bright neon sign on the façade of
a miniature golf course proclaims: "Welcome to
LoopholesLand!" A Recording /blasts-a-spiel as we
slowly ride by in slo-mo:

> "It's Former President Loopholes' Loopy Miniature
> Mar-A-Go-Go Golf Course! Sink a Ball in any
> Loophole! - Win A 'Golden' Loopholesburger! FUN
> GALORE! BRING THE FAMILY!"

Video #3: we drive passed bigger, brighter yellow and
orange neon letters on a bigger façade proclaiming:
"Loopholes' Studio 55! A Private Club! Topless is Back!!!"

*

Exhibit 13

6 YEARS AFTER IMPEACHMENT

With permission: BBC Doc. Prods.: Full transcript
Location: Patio of Former-President Loopholes'

Magnificent Miniature Golf-Course: LOOPHOLESLAND. Ex-President Loopholes was being interviewed by the BBC from England, for a major BBC documentary chronicling his political life: *"The Rise, Fall, & Resurrection of Ex-President Louis B. Loopholes"*. The setting was the dining area of an Upscale Miniature Golf-Course featuring Fine Dining, Burgers & Tiki Bar Overlooking a Large, Genuine-Safe-Simulated-Green-Irish-Grass-Putting-Surfaced-and Miniature-Golf-Range ("The Pro's Practice Here!"), featuring Genuine, Pure Moroccan Sand in the miniature traps. FUN GALORE! BRING THE FAMILY!". Both participants were seated comfortably as they saw fit, ready for a discussion.

INTERVIEWER (INT): you're the Ex-President of the United States and yet your book didn't sell. It never made one Best Sellers List, World-Wide.

EX-PRESIDENT LOOPHOLES (XPL): *Former* President of the United States. It sold a million copies.

INT: Excuse me, *Former* President, sir: You went into significant debt buying up the entire first and second additions of your book. You've been giving them out as Christmas stocking-stuffers for the last three years to anyone who wears shoes.

XPL: I'm a winner because I'm a risk-taker.

INT: And you've landed on your feet every time: I get it. And we're here because this latest may be your biggest deal yet. Isn't that true, Mr. Loopholes?

XPL: Former President Loopholes. On more than my feet. A major deal. Massive. I landed on every other miniature-golf-course owner's syphilitic dick.

INT: Wow. Well—Okay. We can-- Right, so, then after running for president, winning, being the president; becoming impeached; serving a minimal amount of prison time--

XPL: Community Service.

INT: Community Service, writing a book, selling your nightclub--

XPL: It was a very, very minimal amount of time. Almost no time at all. And, Miniature Golf _Czar._ Like in Russia. Like A Russian Czar. But a World one.

INT: But miniature-golf.

XPL: And Fine Dining.

INT: Which leads me to this question: What have you taken from the presidential experience that has served you so well in these, your so-called Golden Years?

Reaches in his jacket pocket and pulls out a THUMB DRIVE.

XPL: The White House Rolodex. On a thumb drive.

INT: What's a 'Rolodex'?

XPL: Phone numbers: The U.S. governments personal digital phone book on a thumb drive. I can call people all over the planet. Without a question. I can call anybody: A king, a prince, a ruler, a president, anyone who's ever been the lead story in The Enquirer or NY Post or on Fox News, CNN, MSNBC; anybody. I could probably call your girlfriend.

INT: I'm married.

XPL: Sorry if I gave away any secrets on national television. Is that your nose or are you eating a banana? Look at this.

Loopholes touches the interviewer's tie-tack. The interviewer looks down to his tie-tack, Loopholes lifts the tip of his finger up under the interviewer's nose, flicking his nose as his finger flies up and away.

XPL (cont.): Gotcha. Old public school shtick. Still

works. One of the major perks of being president is you leave with phone numbers. World-class.

INT: Let's talk about the deal you've just made.

XPL: Yes. Incredible. Rule-breaking. A mind-boggling deal.

INT: In what way?

XPL: I got a ton – I swear, a ton, a huge ton-of-money off the top, in front, in cash, plus beachfront property <u>after-sea-level-rise,</u> computed-by-satellite for the next 100 years. Sweet. Very sweet piece of land. I made out like a bandit; I must say. Saved my ass, frankly.

INT: In what way?

XPL: You have to understand, I was being sued by a particularly deep, serious, organization that doesn't write letters and doesn't take threats, checks or words if you know what I mean.

INT: You were being threatened by a foreign entity.

XPL: Threatened, sued, entity, country, a girlfriend, a spy: it was a simple conversation in an elevator about death, and a gun was involved.

INT: My God. what did you do?

XPL: I lied.

INT: Of course.

XPL: I had to, to get out of the elevator.

INT: Of course.

XPL: You'd do the same thing.

INT: Of course.

XPL: I was running out of options, I threw the dice: I put out the word, a representative of an investor contacted me – in the end - guess what?

INT: You worked out a deal.

XPL: Thank you.

INT: Russia? China? Near East?

XPL: Well, whatever you want to call him, her, them, 'it': I say, 'an investor'. I'm not in politics anymore, remember that. Anyway, we sealed the deal.

INT: Nice. What did the investor get?

XPL: A bargain. He got a great, great deal, is what he got. Terrific deal.

NT: In what way?

XPL: My daughter and her boyfriend what's-his-name are worth twice-the-price. More. By an astronomical amount more. A strongly, large, huge—

INT: Wait-wait-what do they have to-what are they going to do? What's their duties – how does the quid pro quo work? Did you sell, lend-?

XPL: A <u>fee</u>. I got a fee. A big, big fat fee - <u>Up front</u>. So, there was quite a quid pro quo there.

INT: But are your daughter and her boyfriend part of a diplomatic service, or is it political, social,-- I mean, one's mind imagines all sorts of – criminal…, um, sex trade, porno-you know--

XPL: I can't say: I had to sign an NDA: Non-Disclosure Agreement. Let's say: I'm good; I'm very good. That's really all I can say. So—But—it was a very good-nice-solid-huge-tremendous amount of cash and Coastline Property above the future-high-water mark. Crypto, Air- tanks and oxygen: Next big thing. Gonna be huge. I'll make a ton.

INT: Enough to deal with the 'elevator situation'.

XPL: Exactly. <u>*Plus.*</u> I told you: I made out like a bandit.

INT: But, again, what does your daughter and her boyfriend have to—what are their duties – I mean…in return for this - incredible amount of money you seem to say you've made?

XPL: Honestly, I don't know. I haven't read the contract yet.Obviously, I read where to sign my name and how much was involved in front. I'm not stupid.

INT: Presidential thinking.

XPL: Thank you. I hope. But, from what I hear, the "Investor" (makes "air" quotes), got both for two years or until the prime investment is paid back in full. So, we'll see.

INT: You just said you got a massively huge amount of money in front. My guess would be, you'll never be able to pay it back. Ever.

XPL: Finally! …You're pretty slow, you know that, right?

INT: My God. What did your daughter and boyfriend think? Or his parents?

XPL: They loved it. Everybody loves it. Eye on the Prize: what's the goal?

INT: Money. World Dominance.

XPL: The Art of Getting Out of The Elevator Plus a Taste. You're small-time, you know that, right? Plus, after all my debts are paid in full, I'll have enough left over to keep the Miniature Golf Course Franchise and take it world-wide. Why? From now on it's <u>Former</u> President of The USA Loopholes' Humongous Golf Course & Fine Dining. I eat At 6:30 P.M. promptly. Come buy me a dinner and sit with Me and Leilani, or just come watch me eat: $100 a couple through the soup course. You can also practice your putting. "You bring the Club; we supply the Balls". "*We have the Balls*". Because, why?

INT: You have the White House phone numbers.

XPL: And <u>you don't</u>. But you're a little wiser.

(At that point A COUPLE and their TWO TEEN KIDS entered the miniature-golf-course's patio.)

XPL: Again, and still: Even when I'm losing, I'm winning - excuse me (to camera, then turns to arriving Family): "C'mon down. Play some golf: Three-putt the

"Loopholes Maze" and win a free Loopholesburger. Prime beef, my own brand of cattle. My genes – No, we never meet. The cow never knows who or what. It's separate. and I'm a vegetarian. (He rises to meet them) I hear it's the best, "Best Burger" in the Universe: Known-- !(SOUND: RI-I-I-P!)

The Ex-President's suit-jacket lapel is partially ripped-off-but- holding as the solidly attached lapel-mic is pulled taut by the wire's other end dragging the back of his tipped-over director's chair. He forgets it and assumes the WELCOMER'S demeaner, walk towards them, the director's chair dragging. "Welcome to LoopholesLand!"

The End

THE 7 FABLES

OF

SOMETIMES JONES

(This is the other story you liked - the runaway kid - BJ)

The mighty tiger is big, beautiful, and powerful. And after all the big, beautiful, powerful tigers are gone, alley cats will continue to do their thing.

1. Sometimes Jones & The Magic Credit Card

The Ballad of Sometimes Jones

Now, this here's a story 'bout Sometimes Jones
Blood, guts, skin & bones
All he was, was just a thief
But the things he stole were beyond belief:

Born in Chicago on Avenue "B"
Learned how to steal on granddaddy's knee
His daddy sent a message from cell block "C"
Said, "If you get caught, kid, don't depend on me.

"Learned how to steal on his grandaddy's knee...."

Steal the pennies off a dead man's eyes
Swear to the truth on a stack of lies
All dressed up in his disguise:
Jeans, high-tops & big brown eyes

Steal your stool at your favorite bar
Steal your woman & your guitar
Eight Ball, Straight Ball, spot-you-ten
One hand, blindfold, & do it again

He knows the moves & he moves real quick
Keeps a real loose tool, shoots a cool pool stick
Steals the wheels offa' police cars
Lives on women & candy bars

Gonna steal the statues from the park
Steal The Cross from Joan of Arc
Steal the crown off a King Tutt's head
Curse your God & rob your dead

Liar, cheater, lock defeater
Break your pants & steal your peter
Practiced hard & watched his health
Got so good he stole from his self

Deals from the bottom with his back to the wall
Throws his money to the wind & the finger to y'all
Wheels by day & he steals by night
He's the alley cat's shadow & the ladies delight

Hocked his grandma & sold her brace
Steal the gold out of a grinning face

Gonna get into heaven, don't bother to lock it
Gonna talk to the Lord & pick his pocket

*

His real name was Lawrence Bartholomew Pittsburg and he never got along with his father, so on his 15th birthday he ran away to San Francisco and lived on Market Street with all the other runaways and bikers and pimps and hookers and winos and weirdos and geeks and freaks and geezers and wheezers and funky junkies, lookie-lou's, and lonesome losers. He was fifteen, tall, thin, with big ears and a big nose, and he changed his name to Sometimes Jones.

He wore this really cool, black baseball cap with no markings on it at all which he wore mostly backwards, and he was the best pickpocket on Market Street. As a matter of fact, the story was that if Sometime Jones got close enough to touch you, your wallet was gone. I'll give you an example of how good he was:

The President of The United States of America was up for re- election, and he had this big, get-out-the-vote parade down Market Street and the president got out of his limo and started shaking the hands of the crowd along the curb. The Secret Service freaked, but just through luck and timing, Sometimes Jones got to shake the hand of the President of the United States of America.

So that night back at his pad, Sometimes Jones went through the President's wallet. Inside was a valid driver's license, credit cards, some cash, a Social Security Card, pictures of the family, and a strange white, plastic credit card with the inscription "2 for 1" written on one side and on the other was: "The Agreement: Be it known that Whosoever or What shall be Prime Mover In Perpetuity Throughout The Known and/or Unknown Universe but not limited thereto, shall grant to the bearer of this card One Other Life Beyond Suspicion. Registered Card Number 3434343434.68.

Sometimes Jones thinks it's a pretty cool card to have and he feels so good the rest of the day, he doesn't mind losing all the President's money in a very close game of nine ball with his best friend, Sal. After all, he figures he's got another life in his back pocket.

That night, on the way home, Jones takes his usual shortcut through an alley, and he's held up by a desperate man with a gun. And The Desperate Man with A Gun sez, "Your money or your life." And Jones thinks: "Wow. I got this covered." So, he very slowly reaches into his back pocket, pulls out the plastic two-for-one card, hands it to The Desperate Man with A Gun, who takes it, reads it, gives it back and sez, "This is bullshit. I want <u>money!</u>" And Jones goes: "I lost all my money in a very close game of nine ball with my best friend, S--!" "Shut up! Okay! ...Gimme your hat."

And Sometimes Jones goes, "No, no. Not my hat. This is a good black hat, I stole this from a very important person, the cops chased me for blocks, I worked very hard to steal this hat. If you want a hat like it, go steal your own." And the desperate man with a gun sez: "That's exactly what I'm doing, putz", and grabs Sometimes Jones' good black hat and Jones grabs it back and they pull, and BANG! The gun goes off! Sometimes Jones grabs his chest and looks at his hand and its covered with this thick, red, warm blood.

And as he sinks to the ground, he sees the desperate man with the gun run out of the alley with his good black hat.

*

That night – suddenly, the alley is filled with light and an angel appears. But it's a punk angel with long hair, no shirt, baggy, old jeans with holes in the knees, he's got wings, but he's molting, so there's pinfeathers floating all over. Jones, sneezes in pain because he's allergic to feathers as The Angel stands him over him.

The Angel goes: "You may exchange your death at this time for your two-for-one card or you may keep the card as a souvenir and have your name placed in the 'Who's-Who in History' book, placed there posthumously'."

Sometimes Jones didn't want to die so he reaches into his back pocket, pulls out his two-for-one card, hands it to the angel and he stands up in perfect health: no wounds, no blood, no nuthin'! The Angel puts the card in his back pocket, sez: "We've fulfilled our obligations. You're on your own. Good luck". "No hard feelings?" They shake hands. The angel leaves. Jones has his card back. The angel suspects nothing.

Now, knowing the secret of the card, *having* the card, and knowing it works – gave Jones some options. So, now he starts taking any chance, any dare, any risk. He starts off slow: picking cops pockets. He's got the card. He's totally cool. Breaking and Entering: he's cool, steady, climbing fire escapes, ropes from roofs. He's cool, successful, and popular. Any dare.

Ladies are taking notice. He starts wearing Bling. Any dare. Any risk. Older Guys are impressed. So are their Wives. At sixteen-and-a- half, Sometimes Jones is shot in the back by a jealous husband.

As Jones lay dying in a pool of his own blood… just as he hoped and prayed, The White Light and his Guardian Punk Angel with the now bright yellow, "Mohawk 'Do'", dressed in white jeans but now the knees are aesthetically blown out, wings are still molting, feathers everywhere, two more mini-eyebrow-rings and a nostril piercing have been added. Still no shirt. Jones sneezes.

The Punk Angel stands over Jones and goes: "If you wish you may exchange your death at this time for your two-for-one card or-? Haven't I seen you before? Hey, did you date my sister that time!?"

Jones has no idea what the angel is talking about; he just reaches into his back pocket, pulls out the magic credit card and hands it to the punk angel…

The Angel puts the card in his back pocket, says: "We've honored our agreement. You're on your own. Good luck."

And, when he turns to leave, Jones picks his pocket and gets the card back.

Unfortunately for Jones, you can only fool a real angel once. This time, as Jones turns to leave, *The Angel picks Jones' pocket!*

Thinking he still has the card; Jones starts taking riskier risks and chances: He becomes known as The Fearless Crazy".   Kids in the neighborhood want to meet him.

Breaking and entering, ladders, roofs, ropes. Fearless. Crazy. More successful, more popular, till he became known in all the nearby 'hoods.

Which gets him invited into a very badass gang. Just to show off, Jones holds up and robs their neighborhood police station and gets away with it. He was so fearless and crazy the gang elects him their leader.

Now Jones has a posse. Now they're stealing cars with people still in them – crimes involving risk: heights; danger; and on and on: he's got the card and he's Beyond Suspicion. No problem.

And Jones is never afraid of any of the members of the gang because if anyone of them ever challenges him he always calls for "A Fight to The Death", because either way he'd win, either win the fight – no real chance of that - or blow their minds by rising from the dead. It would be *so* cool.

At least, he thought he had that card until one day he tried to find it, to make sure he had it – but he couldn't find it anywhere: not in his pockets, not in the closet in his jacket, not in-between the couch cushions, not in the kitchen drawer, not in the refrigerator, not in the cat box or sock drawer – Nowhere.

Jones thought: "I lost it or somebody *stole it*. The Gang!"

So, now, the fearless and impulsive Jones becomes fearful and cautious. And he starts making mistakes, which makes him paranoid, so he becomes suspicious, which makes him self-righteous, so he starts treating his gang badly, so they become confused, so he becomes angry, so they become obstinate, so he becomes vindictive, so they just get fed up and challenge him to A Fight to The Death.

Well, Jones tries to talk his way out of it, make excuses, make jokes, make accusations, but the gang isn't buying it.

And then, when Jones sees that they see the fear in his eyes, he pulls a gun. And while his best friend Sal is trying to calm him down and talk some sense into him, another gang member, Terry, sneaks round behind Jones and shoots him in the back.

As Jones lay bleeding to death on the cellar floor the gang just stands around him looking down and all agreeing that Jones was cool but, "You messed up, 'J'."

Jones decides to confess: "See, I wasn't who you thought I was. I had the magic credit card. I couldn't die. I'd just give it to the tattooed angel with the green hair and I could live forever." The gang didn't know what the hell he was talking about: Can't die? Angel with green hair? Magic credit card? What? Terry said it was the babblings of a dying Jones. He felt sorry for Jones.

Terry sits and cradles Jones's head in his lap. Jones just keeps on babbling: "See I'm just a thief. A pickpocket. Pretty good pickpocket. Not great, but pretty good."

Terry looks down into Jones' dying eyes and goes, "Jonesy, you're an <u>asshole</u>."

With his last bit of strength, Jones slowly raises his

hand and offers Terry his wallet back: "Pretty good for a dying asshole, huh, Ter?" The gang laughed; "Jonesy's dyin' an' still pickin' pockets: friggin' funnyman messed up!" But then Jones goes: "Yeah, but, no: Terry's right. I *am* an asshole."

And as Jones says those words: the room fills with light and Jones' guardian punk angel with spiked hair appears. Only this time his wings are all grown in, he's got on a clean, white pair of jeans, still no shirt, a couple of new 'tats', and he's looking good.

The gang sees the angel, freaks, and splits. Jones' head hits the cement floor with a dull, 'bonk!' as Terry stands and books out after them.

The punk angel stands over Jones and goes: "No Jones. You're not an asshole. What you are, is a poor fool. Here's how it works: Ultimate power has two lives.

Cats have nine. But Poor Fools live forever." "But I lost the card. I lost the card." And the angel goes: "Dude, you never had a card. We don't give cards to poor fools. They lose 'em, they sell 'em, the dogs eat 'em, they get stolen, who knows what: they're fools. But we already know that, so we keep their cards. Besides: we know you, Jones. By the way: Everything you got with the President's card has been confiscated. We were just messin' with you. Yeah. But, anyway: here's ten bucks", hands Jones a ten dollar bill, reaches behind him and pulls out Jones' good black hat.

"Here's your good black hat back. But, remember: You can live forever as long as you don't use that knowledge for fame or fortune. We've honored our agreement; you're on your own. Good luck." And, POOF! the angel disappears.

So, Jones goes back to the pool hall happy in the knowledge that ultimate power has two lives, cats have nine, but poor fools live forever. Plus, he explains to Sal, "I got my good black hat back and ten bucks. So, obviously it's better to be a poor fool; It's just a lot harder, that's all. An incredible amount of sweat equity goes into it." Back at the pool hall, Jones bought a candy bar for two dollars and lost the rest of the money in a very close game of nine ball with his best friend Sal. The end.

*

2. SOMETIMES JONES & THE GREAT EARTHQUAKE

Okay; so now it's spring in San Francisco, and Sometimes Jones is takin' a short cut through an alley behind some stores – because, mainly he doesn't want to run into several of his closest friends and associates – a sizeable segment of whom he owes large portions of cash money – and to a preponderance of which he has told he will repay tomorrow – when all of a sudden, out of nowhere – or from behind one of the dumpsters – Jones is stopped by an Insurance Salesman who goes:
"Hey, you got insurance?"
And Sometimes Jones sez, "Why?"
And the Insurance Salesman goes, "You don't take your pants off in earthquake weather, do yuh?"
"Why not?" asks Jones.
"Because," goes the Insurance Salesman, "You never know. So be prepared."
"I guess," sez Jones. "How much does it cost?"
And the Insurance Salesman goes, "A lot. Way too much. Much more than you can afford or probably have or could even get in time." "Wow. Yeah, well, sure: that IS way too much", goes Jones.
And the Insurance Salesman goes:
"Unless'."
"'Unless' what?" goes Jones.
"Unless you get The Deductible."
"What's The Deductible."
"The Deductible," goes the Insurance Salesman, "Is how much we take off what you have, and that's how much we don't have to pay. And all the rest is all yours. That way, the more the deductible, the less you pay. Simple, really. The deductible saves you money."

"Well, I guess: BUT:" goes Jones, real cool, "How much deductible are you going to deduct – and how much is it gonna cost me?"

"Well, now, that," goes the Insurance Salesman, "Is an *excellent question;* and the answer depends on how much you have and how much 'How Much You Have' is worth. For instance: Say you have stuff worth – oh, say $1,000. Now, if you WANT: you can insure All Your Stuff against anything in the Universe known or unknown ever affecting it in any negative way, shape, or form, and/or any anti- positive manner: all of which is judged solely by you: your word is final, with NO DEDUCTIBLE. But we charge you $1,500 a month per $1,000 worth of stuff we insure. But THAT," emphasizes The Insurance Salesman, "Is what we call our Complete, Total, A-number-One Coverage. The Best."

"Wow," sez Jones.

"Or," goes the Insurance Salesman, "You can take a $200 deductible, and pay us only $900 a month."

"Every month," verifies Jones.

"You got it," confirms The Insurance Salesman (who was Salesman of the Month last month and the month before that, too).

"Yeah. I can't afford that," goes Jones.

"Well, then," goes Bernie - that was the Insurance Salesman's name: Bernie.

"Okay: With a $500 Deductible you pay us only $500 a month – but, then we only replace $500 worth of your stuff – or: you pay us only $250 a month, but there's a $750 deductible plus certain things are not what they seem plus the standard codicils and atypical provisos, plus certain assessments and riders, and, of course, the normal variable exceptions and fees. Okay?"

"Mmmm – lemme think about it," goes Jones, leaving.

"OR: you can take what I call my 'Today Only, Just

to Really Special People like yourself: The Simple, Plain Bernie Plan: which I personally recommend to you or anyone in your similar but particular situation".

"Exactly," sez Jones. "My similar particular situation. Perfect. You got it. Okay: what's the Simple Plain Bernie Plan like?"

"Well, what it IS," goes Bernie, "Is my simple, no frill, '100% Deductible Agreement'. You just pay us a flat, straight ahead, simple ten-dollar premium just once every thirty days and all your stuff is insured for its full worth for just ten-dollars-a-month--"

"Every month," confirms Jones, showing he's nobody's fool.

"Every month, plus you get the deductible every month included with that. It's a good deal. I sell a lot of them. Hell, anyone can afford just ten small ones every thirty days.

"To insure _ALL_ my stuff?", cagily asks Jones.

"Guaranteed: One hundred percent deductible. I must be crazy. I actually lose money on every one I sell."

"How do you stay in business?"

"Volume."

"Be prepared," goes Jones.

"You never know," goes Bernie.

"I'll take it, Bernie," sez Jones, and hands Bernie a wrinkled 5- dollar bill, and 1 dollar in small change and counted out.

Three years later, everything Jones has is destroyed in a 7.4 earthquake and, sure enough, luckily, he has insurance. But not for an earthquake, which is a separate policy altogether which costs extra and way more than he could ever afford plus a deductible that is stated in a very peculiar and specific way. But, - and again, luckily – since he loses everything and nothing is replaced by the insurance company because 100% of his stuff is deductible, and therefore – since Jones doesn't have any stuff at all now – he has nothing to insure anymore: so, he stops sending the insurance company his ten bucks every 30 days.

That's when Bernie shows up again – in an alley Jones is passing through – with a new idea. And he goes:

"Jones, everybody needs insurance because you never know so you gotta be prepared. I thought we agreed."

And Jones sez, "But the Devil's in the Deductible. The Deductible has more than one Loophole. I'm not stupid."

And Bernie agrees, "You're right. You are so right. Not many people know that."

"Know what?" sez Jones.

"Know they're not stupid," goes Bernie.

"And besides I don't have any stuff anymore," sez Jones.

"Okay:" goes Bernie, "Remember the $1500-A-Month Complete Total A-Number-One Coverage with No Deductible? The best?"

"Yeah," goes Jones.

"Well," goes Bernie, "Since everybody needs insurance and because you never know so you gotta be prepared: And--you don't have any stuff…AT ALL - right? Still?"

"At all," repeats Jones. "Still."

"Okay," continues Bernie, "I'm gonna write you a Brand-New policy with Absolutely No Deductible – just like the A Number One Best Policy – And: I'm only gonna charge you fifteen dollars every thirty days. AND: as soon as you get any stuff – at ALL – the policy is automatically Cancelled Null & Void. And you stop all payments."

"Automatically."

"Of course. We use A.I."

"Great," agrees Jones, but still confirms: "Any stuff at all: Null & Void."

"At all: Null & Void," swears Bernie.

"In writing," re-confirms Jones.

"In writing: 'Cancelled: Null & Void," Bernie confirms, "All for just fifteen dollars only once every thirty days. And, sometimes even, only once every thirty-one days. A savings of several days a year right there in front. Hell, any butt-hole can come up with fifteen bucks only just once every thirty days for the very, very best you can get at any price!"

"I'll take it," sez Jones, and hands Bernie five singles, six quarters, a dime, and seven pennies. "I'll give you the rest Wednesday."

*

3. MORGAN'S GIFT

The Crime

One-time Sometime Jones and his best friend, Fried Sal, were hitchhiking along a road on the outskirts of Santa Mamacita, a small- town on the coast of Central California, when Jones had to go to the bathroom.

They were hot and tired; hadn't had a hitch in over two hours. Jones is being tenacious: waving his thumb and flashing his "Ride To S.F." sign to cars and trucks and giving them the finger after they pass, while Fried Sal was seriously trying to explain how Free Market Capitalism works under a Laissez-Faire, Enterprise System based on Research, Risk, Acquisition Of Venture Capital, and Growth Potential. He's thinking himself and Jones should go into business together. Meanwhile, Jones has to move his bowels in the middle of nowhere.

They'd been living on the beach in Venice, California, but things were slow, so they decided to hitch up to San Francisco to attend their 65-year-old homeless friend, Morgan Yu's 65th birthday party and also see what the temp-job situation was like up there.

They were totally broke, except Jones has $75 cash in his pocket which They'd both saved-up specifically to buy Old Morgan a pair of real wool gloves and a light, portable, army-surplus, fold-up tent as a birthday present from both of them. Morgan's stuff had recently been confiscated by the S.F. police or stolen. Either way, they both swore by the blood of their eyes that nobody touches Morgan's gift.

It was obviously something he ate; but, whatever, Jones had to go really bad. Jones is eyeing the bushes along the roadside, trying to remember the tell-tale leaf-design of poison ivy, and Sal points out there isn't any poison ivy on the west coast (yet) and spots a small Trailways Bus Station about 1,000 yards up the road.

So, Jones hurries not-too-fast right into the Men's Room and tries to open one of the stall doors, but it's locked-shut with one of those old coin-operated locks. A quarter or a credit card would instantly open any one of them. Neither Jones nor Sal had any change or a credit card or cash – except for Morgan's gift. Jones strongly believed that his good buddy Morgan's birthday gift shouldn't be compromised or threatened just because Jones had to move his bowels and somebody was trying to charge him money to do it. So, right now, Jones is really getting pissed at the idea of having to go to the bathroom becoming way too complex. "This sucks", mutters Jones. But Sal saw it as a teachable moment.

"Jonesy: don't you see? That's exactly what I was just telling you about: the whole genius of a capitalistic, free market system, which is incarnate in pay toilets: We can make money on anything."

"Yeah, I guess," said Jones trying to pay attention, but Mother Nature was losing patience with him.

"You guess?" says Fried Sal.

"Hey, listen, Jonsey, do you realize the monumental technological- entrepreneurial-marketing leap the guy actually made? I mean, first this guy invents a lock that can be opened with *money instead of a key*. It's frigging mythological, dude."

Jones was trying to remember back where that good spot was.

"He doesn't stop! inventing a lock that you can open with A Magic, Mythological Coin is okay. Nice! But to then put a lock on toilet bowls and charge people to take a dump: Genius! We can make money on anything. There're only two things you gotta do in this life: and one of them is taking a dump. And it doesn't matter what the other one is. Monetization-wise, there's more upside in toilet bowls than there is coffins and candy! Pay <u>toilets</u>! Capitalism. Love it."

"I'm not using Morgan's money."

"Then shit in the woods."

"Bears shit in the woods. It's demeaning and dangerous."

A "*Free the Toilets!*" bumper sticker flashed through Jones' mind. "I'm going under," he muttered, got down, and went under. Jones heard Fried Sal say, "I'll wait outside," and heard the main door open and close. Silence.

Jones quickly lined the toilet seat with the convenient toilet- seat-liner, dropped his pants, sat down – and heard the main bathroom entrance-door open and close. From his seated position, Jones could look under his stall door to see two Black, Shiny, Payless Shoes step in front of his stall and knock three times: "Knock-Knock-Knock". And an official voice goes:

"Come on out of there. I saw you on the spy-cam." Silence. Getting caught sneaking under a pay toilet door is stupid AND embarrassing. Knock! Knock! Knock!!

"Hey! Come on out of there. Let's go! I saw you on the spy-cam! This is the police!"

"I'm not coming out!"

Jones made his stand (From a seated position – Irony).

"You want me Copper, come in and get me!" So, the cop borrows a quarter, comes in and gets him.

The Trial

"All rise."

All in the courtroom rose. Judge Sneiderman entered, took his seat; rapped his gavel; all sat down.

"Bailiff, read the charges."

Sometime Jones watched Ralph Waldo, the beady-eyed, beefy bailiff with a big black belt of bandoliered silver bullets attached around the back, and a big gun with a neat handle in a holster at his side as he stood and addressed the courtroom:

"Hear ye, hear ye: Court is now in session: The Honorable Judge Zalman R. Sneiderman presiding. The People of the City and County of Santa Mamacita, California vs. Sometimes Jones, to wit: breaking and entering a private facility for the express purpose of committing malfeasance, damage and mischief, therein."

"Hey, I just wanted to take a dump," goes Jones.

"Another outburst like that and I'll hold you in contempt, sir!" said Judge Sneiderman, and rapped his gavel: "Call the first witness to the stand."

Bailiff Waldo: "The first witness is the defendant, one Sometimes Jones being accused of malfeasance, resisting arrest, destroying public property, and breaking and entering."

"Swear him in."

Ralph Waldo stepped up to Jones with a big, thick, black Bible and held it out to him.

"Raise your right hand, place your left on the Bible."

Jones did as he was told.

"Do you; will you?"

"I Do, I will."

The anal Santa Mamacita prosecutor, Casper Ort approached Jones with his thumbs hooked into his suit-vest pockets.

Jones sat calmly and folded his hands neatly in his lap.

"Mr. Jones, Why were you in the Santa Mamacita Bus Station?"

"I wanted to go to the bathroom."

"Yes. Of course – we've all heard that one before, Mr. Jones. Were you there to see a friend off?

"No."

"Were you there to catch a bus or meet a loved one?"

"No."

"MM-hmmm…Mr. Jones, how much money did you have on you at the time of the arrest?"

"$75; exactly."

"$75 _cash._"
Casper Ort leaned in.

"Enough, in fact, Mr. Jones, to go the bathroom _300 times._"

Ort wanted this one so bad he could taste it.

Jones' trial went on for two more weeks and cost the taxpayers of Santa Mamacita County $15,000. Charts were shown, experts brought in, witnesses were cross-examined, Santa Mamacita's very own Sperl Chartney of their Local 5 o'clock Channel 6 News Team and his camera man, Dave, attended all of the last eleven days of the trial and reported live from the courthouse. But it was the afternoon of the thirteenth day of the trial that people still talk about.

The gallery was packed; Sal was flossing his teeth in a seat near the door, the jury was still passably attentive; and the judge was pretending to listen. Ralph Waldo, the Bailiff, was standing right next to Jones, who was at his court-appointed table seated next to his court-appointed lawyer, Brandon Tutoot.

The D.A., Casper Ort, was questioning the bus stations' Police Patrol Officer, J.D. Hummer, on "Direct", and everyone, including Sometimes Jones, knew it didn't look good. Officer Hummer had seen Jones sneak under on video, while previously, Casper Ort, in a brilliant display of prosecutorial pyrotechnics, had totally exploded Jones' story about looking for the quarter he dropped by producing, for the jury and the world to see, the video of Jones sneaking under, and hearing Jones' voice calling the arresting officer a "Copper" and refusing to come out. His attitude was clearly hostile and obviously didn't play well with the Santa Mamacita jurors (the next day the Santa Mamacita

Tribune would report it as "...a brilliant prosecutorial moment that Ort had played for all it was worth." Immediately, Tutoot claimed the video was a fake-!!!!--?

"FREE THE TOILETS!"

Was heard! Jones was standing on his table, shouting:

"FREE THE TOILETS! SISTERS! MORE STALLS FOR WOMEN! WOMEN: KICK OUT THE JAMS! STEP OUT OF LINE. USE THE MENS ROOM! BREAK THE CHAINS OF MONETIZED ALLEVIATION! FIGHT THE TYRANNY OF THE TOILETS! GIVE ME A BATHROOM OR GIVE ME The judge hammered his gavel several time--!!

"CLEAR THE COURTROOM! CLEAR THE COURTROOM!"

*

The Cub Reporters Article
by
Joshua Zukeeny
with permission of The Santa Mamacita Press

"When the jury, Sal, Sperl Chartney, his cameraman Dave, other guests, observers, and this Tribune cub reporter filed back in, they saw the defendant, Sometimes Jones sitting calmly at the defense table, both wrists handcuffed to his chair with his mouth duct-taped shut. The trial seemed to go downhill for Jones from there.

"Though Casper Ort's summation was too long and not funny, it was more than adequate as Jones' lawyer, Brandon Tutoot's summation didn't make sense.

"The jury deliberated for less than ten minutes before returning a verdict of Guilty on All Counts – at which point the judge excused Brandon Tutoot to pick up Jaso, the youngest of his nine children, at Day-Care. You could hear a pin drop as Jones sat handcuffed and alone at his defense table.

"With much gravity, Judge Sniderman said he took everything into consideration before coming to his decision to invoke "Special Circumstances". He sentenced Jones to the maximum The Law would allow: Jones was banned from urinating or moving his bowels within the city limits of Santa Mamacita for two years.

*

Three days later, in San Francisco, after presenting their friend Morgan with al warm pair of wool gloves and a collapsible, portable, army surplus tent; Sal and

Jones agreed to become business partners in a business venture to be designated at a later date because, as Fried Sal explained to Morgan: "With Jones' chutzpah and my knowledge of demographics, we can't lose. All we need is venture capital."

4. SOMETIME JONES: QUICKSAND HERO

Sometimes Jones stepped out of the cool darkness of the bar and into a blue-sky, yellow-hot, summer day. He just couldn't keep it from creeping in: The Blues. He'd just broken up with his latest girlfriend of two weeks and three days ago and he needed another place to sleep. He wasn't going anywhere and had no money. Feeling sorry for himself, rejected, alone and hungry, Jones took a walk out in the country. He hadn't eaten in two days because things were tight, his self-image was shaken, and he was bluer than Medusa's eyes.

As he's walking along this road out in the country, he sees some wild blueberries growing near a stand of trees in a meadow about 40 yards or so from the road; he's feeling really hungry, nobody's around, no fences, he steps off the road and heads for the food.

As he nears the blueberries, the ground got softer and softer and he starts sinking as he stepped but so what, there's blueberries the size of grapefruits--? One foot goes down over his ankle and he can't pull it out. ...Quicksand! Jones is stuck in a quicksand bog! The thick muck was over both ankles and he very slowly began to sink. Inch-by-inch. Jones quickly calculates he has at most 20 to 30 minutes before the quicksand will be completely over his head.

Over the next few minutes (and as Sometimes Jones slowly sinks up to his mid-calf), a couple of joggers, bicyclers, hitchhikers and cars passed on the road 40 yards away and he called to each for help. Some people didn't hear him; some people didn't see him; some thought it was a trick, some people didn't care, some thought it served him right, some would like to help but not right now, and some even thought it would be very good for his character if he got out all by himself.

All of which left poor Jones to slowly and inexorably sink, and after about fifteen minutes he found the quicksand was up to his waist, he wasn't getting any help, and he wasn't liking it at all. But he didn't like the passing people more. And as he sank another inch, he started hating them and cursed them while he called to them for help. He'd call out: "HEY! Dumbass: help me!" Or, "Help me or go 'F" yourself you stupid shit-for-brains!"; or "Hey Schmuck!" You get the idea. But, when the quicksand was up to his chest, he had an amazing epiphany: "Maybe that's counter-productive." And that's when he had his second epiphany: "I could die here."

It was just then that a Good Samaritan happened by, saw Jones up to his armpits in the quicksand and voluntarily decided to help him. So, The Good Samaritan immediately made a sign, that read: "Donations here to help The Guy in the Quicksand", with an arrow. And he held the sign, so it faced the road while the arrow always pointed to Jones, who had, by now, sunk to his shoulders in the quicksand.

Miraculously, and in a matter of minutes, just from passing bicyclers, joggers, three passing cars and one bus, The Good Samaritan collected five thousand dollars (the Good Samaritan also happened to be an incredibly Good Fund-Raiser). He then took a thousand dollars for himself as a commission (Sweat- Equity: 'Pay yourself first'; always pay yourself first), but, being an Honest Samaritan as well as a Good One, he put the remaining four thousand dollars in a leather pouch and threw it to Sometimes Jones (it landed right near his earlobe), and wishing Jones all the luck in the world, The Good and Honest Samaritan went down the road to do more good deeds.

As Jones feels the cool muddy sand creeping up around his Adam's Apple, he sees a Thief come running in his direction from one direction while a white-mustached gentleman dressed in full L.L.Bean hiking attire (Shorts, alpine high Socks, boots, backpack, hand-carved, ivory- handled walking stick), comes hiking briskly along from the other, and both pass each other right in front of the sinking Jones' eye-line. So, Jones calls out for help. Both hear, stop; see Jones in the quicksand, look around to see it's not a trap, they both come down, and stop not- too-near the edge of the bog. With quicksand just below his Adam's apple, Jones goes: "Gentlemen, if either of you rescue me, I'll give you the four thousand dollars I have in this purse floating by my ear." And he turns his head and indicates the wallet with his nose.

The thief goes, "Throw me the money and I'll get the rope out of the trunk of my car parked around the bend, come back, throw you one end, you grab the other: and I'll pull you right out", and Jones yells back: "You misunderstand: I appear stupid, but I'm just unfocused."

Jones asked to talk to the white-mustached gentleman behind him. The thief agreed, went over to a grassy mound by the side of the bog, sat, and watched what happened next. The white-mustached gentleman stepped over to the same safe spot as the thief and said, "Throw me the money and I'll pull you out right now", and he took off his backpack and pulled out a coil of sturdy, climbing rope.

"I'll throw you the rope-end and pull you out. But first throw me the purse. I drive a hard bargain, but I stick to the agreement, and my word is my bond. Do we have a deal?" Jones goes: "How about: 'Pull me out and I'll hand you the money in person?'"

The white-mustached gentleman goes, "Men are funny: They lose their memories when they're safe and warm. I'm a rich man because I drive a hard bargain, but I stick to the agreement and my word's my bond: After I have the money in my hand, I will pull you out to safety within three seconds if not sooner. Do we have a deal?" Sometimes Jones had no Plan B, no Fall-Back Position, no leverage. He just felt the cold, clammy mud creep a half-inch up his neck.

With difficulty, he pulls up one muddy arm, grabs the floating purse, and throws it onto solid ground. The thief immediately runs over, scoops up the purse before the slower elder gentleman could get to it, and runs away. The rich, elder gentleman turns and starts back to the road. Jones yells: "Hey! Where you goin'?" The rich man turns back and says, "'After-I-had-the-money-in-my-hand'. I never got near it. I never touched it. I drive a hard bargain, but my word is my bond, and *I stick to the agreement.* That's why I'm rich and you're stuck in quicksand. But good luck with that. Chin up"; and heads back to his morning constitutional.

The quicksand was now up to Jones' lower lip. Sometimes Jones was spitting sand. He looks skyward: "Okay, Dude: 'Uncle'. You made your point. Look: if you let me die, it's pointless, right? What you want are converts, right? I just need a miracle to get me over. I'm *that* close." And Lo and Behold (Luck? A Sign?), A Priest, an Imam, and a Rabbi come driving by, see Jones and, realizing he's just seconds away from the Warm, Soft, Breast of Death, they quickly stop, run down to the edge of the bog and administer Last Rites.

"Hey, God damn it!" goes Jones, "Form a daisy chain and pull me out! Help me!"

"Hush my son," the spokesman goes, "The Lord moves in mysterious ways." "Then damn you all and screw your Father in Heaven!", screams Jones.

Thunder Cracks!! The Sky grows dark, lightning flashes. Wind blows dry leaves and whips dust into the holy men's and Jones' eyes. Fat raindrops start splattering and plumping into the dusty road and muddy quicksand; faster and faster, and more lightning and thunder! The Three Wise Men hurry back to the safety of their manses and minions. Jones figures this is it – and yes, it is: Lightning strikes a nearby tree which falls across the quicksand bog right near Jones, who grabs onto its trunk and pulls himself out onto the safety of solid ground.

Sometimes Jones thanks the storm with a confused, shy shrug and swears he'll kill the first person he sees for all those that left him there to die.

He takes shelter under a stone ledge and, before too long, the storm subsides, the sun comes out, and a Lone Man comes walking down the road. As he passes nearby, Jones sneaks out and up behind him and smashes the man in the back of his head with a rock. The Man falls dead at Jones' feet. About ten minutes later, a policeman in a patrol car drives by, sees the dead man lying on the side of the road, stops, examines the body - and sees Sometimes Jones sitting on the nearby grassy mound still trying to figure out how to get those blueberries on the other side of the quicksand bog. When The policeman asks Jones if he knows who killed this person laying in the road, without hesitation, Jones goes, "I did."

The Officer says, "Great! Thanks", shakes Jones' hand, and informs Jones that the man he killed was J. Edgar "Mad Dog" Simpson, a cop- killing, terrorist-rapist wanted in ten states by the F.B.I. and the officer was in the midst of tracking him down. So, Sometimes Jones is taken down to City Hall where he was officially called a Hero, given The Key to the City, given a parade and invited to go, that night, onto, "The Nightly Afternoon Show starring Garry Festers". The interview is going very well until Festers asks Jones, "So, Sometimes, tell the folks exactly how you captured this cop-killing terrorist-rapist wanted in ten states by the F.B.I."

Jones reaches into his pocket, pulls out a rock, and smashes Garry Fester in the back of his head with it, knocking him unconscious or dead – hard to tell with so much blood. It's seen by 27,000,000 people just before the first half-hour commercial break. In the studio, pandemonium breaks loose. The live audience turns into an angry mob, charges the set, stomps Jones, the inert, bloody, Festers, the TV crew, the producers, trashes the TV station, sets it on fire, and it takes three days for the riot squad and fire department to cool things down. And to this day, there are still tons of people who don't understand why a real American Hero would kill a famous, late- night TV star.

*

5. SOMETIMES JONES AND THE NEW YEAR

It was New Year's Eve and Sometimes Jones was getting ready to celebrate by going over to his friend Howard's house.

And, as he was getting ready, Jones was going back over the best things that happened to him in the past year.

Well, first, and most important, he broke up with Sharon, his girlfriend of two years. That was, without a doubt, the numero uno, best of the things that happened all year. All they did was fight. They fought about sex but that wasn't really what it was about: it was really about money, which Jones knew she saw as a source of obligation, control & guilt, but, of course, that was really only a symbol of her not being happy with her low-paying, dead-end job as a lowly receptionist at a nowhere office, which was just another manifestation of her paranoid insistence that he was invading her space, which she claimed was a male-territory thing, but even that wasn't really it either, because, deep down, that was only symptomatic of her having a very low self-image of herself because of her extreme low self-esteem, but he knew that really wasn't really what it was about: because feeding that was him having no patience for her needs, but then, the Patience Thing was just a red herring for his not understanding what she really needed, but that wasn't really really what it was about, because what it was really really, about was the fact that she didn't know how to express her needs clearly enough for him to NOT get confused, but even then, Jones had to confess, he knew THAT really wasn't what it was only all about, because, when you got right down to the nitty- gritty, what it was REALLY was the simple fact that he didn't have control over his own life and couldn't keep his shit together or even get his shit together enough so that he'd even have some shit to keep together so he took it out on her by trying to get her to get her shit together because it's easier to tell someone else what to do than actually do it yourself – but even that could have been worked out if it wasn't for the fact that Jones was just feeling lonely and sorry for himself and thought he wanted to get married and have someone take care of him and Sharon had just broken up with somebody just like that right before she met Jones and she was looking for freedom and being single for a while and having time to herself as against Jones, who knew what he wanted to do with his life and she didn't, and so, consequently, they both had different agendas and timetables & perceptions of what "going together" meant. Or even "knowing what you wanted to do with your life" really meant.

Plus, meanwhile, on a whole other level, they were totally incompatible just because Jones knew that Sharon thought he was immature while the ironic part was that Jones knew that it was really Sharon that was really immature, and yet, ironically, it was just really both their father's emotional and psychological baggage & bullshit they were carrying around and not even their own – even though Jones knew in his heart-of-heart that he had to finally take responsibility for his own actions and life, but: so should she stop trying to be perfect and thinking of herself as a total loser and accept herself or him as is – but she wouldn't – or at least give him some time to learn how, but No-Way-Jose; so, even though he really missed her right now, he had enough self-esteem – or maybe it was pride, but he didn't think so – to not be the first to call and he knew she was so stubborn that she'd never call him first even though he was convinced she liked him even though she hung up on him the last time they talked, so the bottom line of it all was it was best for him in the long run that they broke up and therefore probably one of the best things that happened to him to him in all of the past year.

So, why didn't he feel happy?

Because he wasn't trying to think of the HAPPIEST thing that happened in the past year – he was trying to think of the BEST – "A totally different animal", he thought. "And it's a wise Jones that knows the difference. Think: 'Best'".

Like: both him and his best friend Sal getting laid off work at the same time so they could both concentrate on what they really wanted to do with their lives, which right now was to have time to think and set some goals and find out what they really wanted to do with their lives and really get their priorities straight and their acts together and really have the freedom and time to get a good running start at really developing pro-active habits and get some focus and stop procrastinating and finally write down their great porno-horror movie idea, find some investors and get the partnership thing going, and – oh: right – PLUS: the other-one-of-the-best-things-that-happened in the past year: his eviction.

He was always so worried every month about the rent and how much he owed the landlord; trying to sneak into his apartment every evening and sneaking out by climbing down the fire escape in the morning and all that debtor-renter-guilt baggage that he was carrying around to where he couldn't think straight. And now all that was gone. His head felt a hundred pounds lighter, and his mind was crystal clearer now that he was living in his car. And really and truly: what a relief to be able to just come and go as he pleased and have no landlord or rent problems anymore. And now, not having an address, his ex's lawsuit was totally on the back burner because her asshole lawyer can't find him: a true Benefit Gift from The Gods in Left Field.

But, then, Jones thought, maybe the Best-of-the-Best of all of the past year is gotta be the simple fact that he could finally follow his bliss and get his shit together and become an independent entrepreneur and get a really nice place to live instead of the rat trap he was evicted from – get a place with a view and an extra bedroom that he could turn into an office and get a new girlfriend and learn to cook. Hire a maid.

Sometimes Jones looked at his wristwatch as he stepped out of his VW bus onto the cement of Howard's driveway and he thought, "Great: I can tell it's going to be a Great New Year: it's already 10 p.m.: which obviously means I'm going to spend the last two hours of this year and the whole first three hours of the new year not having to worry about where I was going to go to the bathroom. Plus, food, drink, friends, leftovers for at least two days, and Howard already said I can stay parked in his driveway all day New Year's Day and probably the next. "Oh, yeah," thought Jones, "I can feel it. Next year's gonna be my best year yet."

*

6. SOMETIMES JONES SPEAKS W/GOD OR JOHN D. FILLIPPI

Now, exactly how it happened was like this: Sometimes Jones was sitting quietly; all alone in his apartment; staring at his favorite wall. All of a sudden, he feels this "Presence," & he hears this VOICE go: "GOD KNOWS".

Jones looks around, but there's nobody there, so he thinks he's just hearing things and turns back to his favorite wall, and all of a sudden, he hears:

"GOD KNOWS."

So, Jones goes:

"Who's that?"

And a Voice goes,

"It's me. God."

Jones looks over at Sox, his black cat with white feet that had been asleep over on the couch -- but now Sox's back was arched way up and his fur is standing straight up and he's looking all around the room like he'd lost track of a fly he was tracking, and he looks over to Jones with this: "Hey, man, that wasn't me," look. So, Jones figured: Sox heard the Voice, too.

Luckily, Jones' brand new pocket voice recorder -- which he'd found in his pocket -- but that's a whole other story - anyway: that voice recorder was right on the desk near his hand, and he figured, if Sox could hear that Voice, maybe a voice recorder could hear it, too. And it was right at that moment that Sometimes Jones prayed for the first time in his life.

And Sometimes Jones' first prayer ever was:

"Please, dear God, let the batteries be good & let them last." And then he pressed "record" just as The Teenager's Voice goes:

"You ever hear that, Jonesy? You've heard that,

right? 'God knows'?"

Jones is thinking: "I wonder if God knows that I don't believe in God. Not even right now. Especially since he sounds too young." This thought didn't seem to bother The Teenager's Voice in the least, because The Voice just continued:

"I mean, I must personally hear, 'God knows' about a billion times a day, at least. Right?"

"Yeah. Right. A billion, easy," goes Jones, looking all around the room like he lost track of a fly.

"Well, if the truth be told, I DON'T know. If you really want to know the truth of the matter: There's just too much to know. Who could know everything? C'mon. Get real. "God Knows" is a very human-child notion: remember, once, a long time ago, you really believed that your parents knew everything: Right? Of course, you did. But you got over it. Because they didn't. 9 times out of 10 they were faking it or flat out lying, right?"

"Where're you going with this?", goes Jones.

And The Voice goes: "'God knows'. See? No, I don't. I - don't - know. I set the table, I give you options and choices and I move on. Right now, I'm three Universes ahead of you at this very moment. I just happened to have a nano-second to drop in - in my Time, not yours, so forget it. But other than random curiosity, that's pretty much it vis-à-vis: where I'm going with this: Not a clue."

Jones peeks at the voice recorder. He sees it's little red light glowing; numbers whiz by.

"So, yeah, I mean, you adjust, I adjust, and we both learn a little more every day. But - Hey, I wasn't going for an Infinitely Expanding Random Inevitability plus Consciousness."

"What's wrong with Consciousness?"

"Haven't worked out the kinks yet."

"What, 'Kinks'?"

"'Expectations and 'Potential'. Who knew? Not me. 'The more you know, the more there is to know.' Nice concept: Perpetual Biological Manifestation. Very interesting. Who'd a' thought? Not me. But I don't know. See? I don't know. Sue me. I'm a kid. I was going for something else. It's an experiment. Never been done before. At least, this way."

Jones concludes God is just a smart-assed kid that rambles. The Voice continued:

"Yeah. See, what I did was, I thought 'keep it simple', right? So, I just started with the basics."

The Voice kept rambling, and the little numbers kept flicking by:

"I started with the <u>Most</u> Basic Thing I had at hand: Which, at the time was nothing. Which was all there was at the time, and the most there's ever been and what I brought to the table was *Pressure*. That was my idea - Pressure. Never been done before. But I mean a lot of pressure. And in the beginning, nothing happened. For a long time. I mean a really long time, so I added a lot more pressure. Nothing happened - I got bored, and I left.

"Frankly, I forgot about it. And while I was gone – all that Nothing & Pressure: KABOOM. It blew up. Sparks in the darkness. True. Go figure that one out. Who knew? Not me. By the time I came back it was all over everywhere, spreading, and starting to coagulate. Now, I gotta tell you: I'm curious. Everybody's got something. Some people are musical, some are mathematical, some people are double- jointed. I'm curious. So, I just let it go -- I left -- just for a little while. Why? I don't know. Curious. Non-judgmental. I let it go to see. Just 'to know', you know? So, anyway, when I come back -- in no time at all: Space, Time, Black holes, mucus, genitals, Wiley Coyote, Dental plans -- and that's just here. You should see--"

"What's your point, dude!?"

"My point is: I couldn't do this again if you paid me and my existence depended on it. It would be like me asking you to predict what's going to be in your refrigerator if the electricity went off and you didn't open the door for six months. Every refrigerator would be different, and it would be different every time you did it. I'm God, not a magician. That's not an excuse; there's no blame; I'm not sorry: 'C'est la vie, c'est la guerre, c'est la pommes de terre'. I'm just sayin'."

Now the fur on Sox, the cat's back is down; but he's still looking around trying to see what it is that he's obviously hearing. And Jones goes, "Can I ask you a question?'"

And The Voice goes: "You just did."

"Cute. Ha ha. But, really. Seriously—"

"Okay. What?"

"Is there a 'Hell'?"

And The Voice goes, "I know this is gonna sound like a vast over- generalization but Boy, are you all alike. No: there <u>is no Hell</u>. BUT - and this even amazed me -- as far as I know, there IS a Heaven." And Jones goes,

"Far-fuckin' out."

"Yeah, go figure that out, huh? But, as far as I know, it's true. And: Here's the really weird part: 'If you're good: after you die you go there - to Heaven. <u>*But:*</u> if you're *bad*: After you die you don't. Weird, right? I don't get it. And don't ask me what "good" is. That's your term. To me, "Good" is just another jar of mayonnaise in your particular refrigerator. Remember, I didn't plan to make a Heaven -- but there it is. Go figure. The next time; somewhere else, something else's refrigerator: who knows? <u>Not me</u>. But for here; for now: Hell: No; Heaven: Yes."

"What's Heaven like?" blurts out Jones. And The

Voice goes, "I don't know: I've never been good or bad and I've never died. See? I DON'T KNOW. And I'll probably never know. Those are your rules in your refrigerator." And then there's this very long pause.

So, Jones finally goes: "Um… Are you finished? 'Cause there's a couple a' points I'd like to discuss."

"Well, there is one more thing I'd like to mention", goes The Voice. And Jones thinks: "Fifty-to-one it's about me believing in him."

And The Voice goes, "It's about this whole business of believing in me."

"Believing in… You? God?".

"Exactly: believing in Me. God. Right."

"You're just a kid! You don't know crap!"

"Exactly, again. What did I just tell you? I. Don't. Know."

Now Jones is very worried because he still doesn't believe in God: it's still just a voice. But, he thinks - with his luck, if it _is_ God, and if God only knows one thing, it would be that Sometimes Jones doesn't believe in him. Even now. This second. So, Jones waits for it: The Wrath of God.

And The Voice goes: "Now, frankly, enough people believe in God. In me. Really. I mean believe in me -- don't believe in me. Who cares? Not me. Belief in me has never been a problem with me. Ever. I mean: believe in me? Great! I'm humble. And, in my humble opinion, enough people believe in me. The problem is, not enough people believe in what I believe in."

"Can I ask another question?"

And The Voice goes: "I can't stop you."

So, Jones goes: "What exactly DO YOU believe in?"

And The Voice goes: "Do, wow, swing, bow, and bow-wow."

And Jones goes: "Do wow swing, bow, and bowwow?"

And The Voice goes: Exactly. "For what it's worth."

And Jones goes: "Okay. But, how do You get enough people to believe in what You believe in -- whether or not they believe in You?" And The Voice goes: "God knows. And I'm here to tell you, I don't. And if the truth be told, it won't do any good for me to think about it, because, if the truth be told, I'm really not much of a thinker. Really. What I like to do, is 'Do', you know? I mean, if you think about it, I've always 'Done' way more than I ever thought about or said, put together. From where I sit, there's really nothing to think about. From where I sit, there's no right way or wrong way. From where I sit, there's either my way or the highway. I mean, wrong implies: 'Another Way', and frankly: there isn't. I'm It. I mean All of It. And when you're All of It, there's no 'Other', there's just 'This' -- and _This'_ is not how I pictured 'It' being. At all. I was totally going for something else. I should stop now." And Jones goes: "No, no, keep goin'. I'm listening. Really. You're fine." And The Voice goes: "No, no: it's not you; it's not me; it's your batteries. They're about to go dead. I gave you eight minutes. Times up."

Jones goes: "Hey: you answered my prayer!"

The Voice goes: "Well, technically, yes. But it's hard enough answering Regular Prayers – meaningful prayers. I figure if I answer seventeen percent a day, I'm doing great. But, whatever. First come, first served. But I consider, 'Please extend-the-life-of-my-batteries' prayers as 'nuisance prayers'. I mean, have you any idea what some people pray for? Blows my mind. I don't know how I cope. Really. I don't get to talk much: kind-of a work-aholic so, every now and again I just have to drop in and put cork in a lot of inbred buttholes out there. Sorry to bother you: no harm, no foul and thanks for listening. If you ever get to heaven, gimme a call. I'm really curious to hear what that's all about. Like what do they do? What do they talk about, right?"

Then Jones feels this amazing silence and he looks over at the voice recorder. The little red light is off, the numbers blank, and Sox is washing himself. And when Jones checks the batteries: they're stone dead. He immediately puts in two new batteries and pushes play: The recording is fine. Perfect. You couldn't ask for a better recording. There's Jones and God talking -- Both voices clear as a bell.

And it's all there. And, for the first time Jones notices that, actually God's voice sounded kind of like this bossy Maitre De's Kid, Sally DeFilippi in apartment 514.

So, then Jones plays the recording for Vinny, who owns the bar on the corner, and his girlfriend Trish -- and they don't believe it's the voice of God either. They both think the other voice kind of sounds like Sally Filippi.

"It doesn't sound anything like Sally."

"It doesn't matter—" goes Bananas Winograd:

"Because, basically, you got a recording of two people talking, one of whom may possibly be you."

And Vinny goes,

"See? Exactly my point: that's exactly what I'm sayin'."

"Never mind."

And Jones walks away.

Two weeks later, back at his pad, Sometimes Jones is recording himself practicing Jimmy Hendrix' original recording of "Foxy Lady" (electric guitar and pig nose amp) on his handy pocket recorder. He runs out of tape-space. Determined (for every reason he can think of), he records himself practicing "Foxy Lady" over his recording of him and God talking.

And now, if you listen to the tape real close -- in this one part, for a couple of seconds – Sometimes Jones sounds exactly like Jimi Hendrix.

7. THE MEANING OF LIFE
(A Shaggy Monk Fable)

So, this is about when Sometimes Jones didn't like the way his friends would disrespect him and belittle him, you know like, if he would say the wrong thing and they'd immediately go: "Hey, schmuck, what'd you say that for?" and stuff like that. So, finally Jones gets really tired of hearing this, so he decides to learn stuff and get a new point of view. Totally. Say wise things or nothing. Become Enlightened and say the right thing or nothing All The Time.

So, he saves and he borrows and temps and sells and trades and finally he scrapes up enough money to get some mountain-climbing gear and a round trip ticket to Katmandu and an address in the mountains of Tibet.

As soon as he lands, he starts asking around: "Hey, do you know who the wisest monks are and how to get in touch with them?"

And everybody in Katmandu points to the top of this same, huge, high, snow-covered mountain and goes, "The wisest monks are up there", luckily for jones, in perfect Katmandunese.

So, Jones puts on his gear and climbs and climbs up this huge, high mountain and when he's three-quarters of the way up, he's caught in a snowstorm. He's exhausted, he's ready to quit and as he turns back, he sees three old monks just sitting and meditating on this ledge in nothing but saffron robes in the middle of this snowstorm.

Cold and weak, he goes to them and asks: "Oh great monks, I have saved, borrowed, worked, spent all my money and climbed this mountain to ask: what is the meaning of life that I might follow my bliss?" and the first monk says, "Life is a fountain." And the second monk says, "Life is a tree." And the third monk says, "Life is a cloud." And Sometimes Jones get it! He goes, "Wow, I get it! Right on. That's so great. Thank you. Okay: I want to dedicate my life to your sect and wisdom and be wise just like you." The three monks point up the mountain to the snow-covered top where a huge monastery is built. "That is our monastery. There is our teacher. The Great Zen Master."

Exhausted, cold, hungry, but determined, Sometimes Jones climbs to the top of this high mountain and with his last bit of strength he knocks on the huge door and collapses. The door opens and he's carried to the Great Zen Master by acolytes who accepts Jones' request to become a student.

Sometimes Jones studies at the monastery for the next ten years. He learns to Meditate while his back is beaten with a bamboo stick; he learns discipline and focus. He learns how to dry a wet sheet with just the heat of his naked body while standing out in the snow and wind; and he spends one whole year in total silence. After ten years, the Zen Master comes to Jones and says, "You have studied and meditated well. Remember those three monks who you approached when you first climbed this mountain?" and Jones nods affirmatively. "One of them has shed his mortal coil and has passed on. We need someone to replace him, and I have chosen you because you are my number one student."

So Sometimes Jones, clothed only in a saffron robe, takes his place next to the other two wise, saffron-robed monks on the snowy ledge where they spend their days in silent meditation until, one day, Jones sees a young man climbing up the mountainside towards them much as he had done ten years before. And this Young Man stops in front of Jones and the other two monks, and he says, "Oh, great monks, I have traveled across the sea and climbed this mountain to ask you, - what is the meaning of Life that I may follow my bliss?" And the first monk says, "Life is a bird." And the second monk says, "Life is an ocean." And Jones says, "Life is a boat." And the Young Man says, "Thank you. You have eased my chaotic mind. I will now return to follow my bliss: thank you." The Young Man turns and goes back down the mountain. As soon as he's out of sight, the first monk turns to Jones and goes, "Hey schmuck, what'd you say that for?"

The End

T -

Those are the two stories you asked to be included. The following is a more, in depth bio. All In total 68,429 words. Almost 70,000 words. I'm willing to go to court. My lawyer tells me I have a case.

BJ

Barnum & Kaye by Barnum

I'm the Seventh Son of a Seventh Son
I got Second Sight and heart by the ton
An' I'll tell it and yell it till the cows come undone
A warm-hearted woman can be cold as a gun

-- Barnum Justice

I was born on Friday the 13th, June 1947. I grew up in Belle Harbor, Long Island, New York. I didn't realize I was dyslexic until I was in my late 40's. The War had ended and everything was looking Rosie. Mom and dad both had jobs.

As a youth it seemed like I had a learning problem, but according to my father it was only my Lazy Brain which caused me to not think quick enough. My father, therefore concluded I was stupid and treated me as if I was. He'd make demands that were always faster than I could follow or accomplish (his way of forcing me to "think faster"), which confused me, so I would ask what he meant - which only proved I was even stupider than he thought, and therefore was deserving of punishment by whacks to the head and beatings with a leather belt; logically beating curiosity out me while beating his rules into me. Beatings To Tow-The-Line. I was being taught to be stupid. And, like any good son of 6, I learned too well from and for this older, bigger, stronger person. I was voluntarily becoming less and less curious about anything at all as I absorbed a worldview that was weird (because it was and still is weird – Reality, not me. I was 'quirky': I liked art, reading and free speech.   I tried to learn his way, but it didn't work in reality – but the thinking became imprinted by the pain and buried deep inside me, manifesting itself as a habit and way of thinking about the world outside that did me no good. But the beatings stopped.

Stupidity has nothing to do with Dyslexia, but both can cause chaos. Alone or together.

Plus, my parents arranged marriage - caused by my father and mom's pregnancy with me - and the ensuing family dynamics and mind games were too sub-rosa and complex for a child under 10 to avoid or comprehend so I simply learned to shut off all connections to normal safety and rest: What others call "Home". In this way, Dyslexia is randomly specific to each individual so there's a lot of different weird things about a lot of different people with the same weird thing.

For my 13th birthday, my father's father and my father, decided I should have a real, old-fashioned, Orthodox Coming-of-Age, Religious Ritual in the Ancient, *Original Language* that didn't sound real and that it should be celebrated on a Holy Day – on a Saturday: Shabbos: a Super-Orthodox Weekly Religious Taboo Day of Rest: No keys are to be used, no driving, no riding, only walking till sunset. My mother went along to get along.

I was 13 and not ready to be a Man, forced to memorize an alien language I didn't understand and read a scripture on a scroll I had no idea what the sounds meant I chanted out loud for two months every day only to ask questions that I was told I shouldn't ask.

On *The Shabbos of My Entrance to Manhood*, my father parked our car three and-a-half blocks from the temple on a side street and my dad, mom, grandpa, and I walked the rest of the way so we wouldn't be busted by the ORP: Orthodox Religious Police.

13-years-old in a new suit, tie, and yarmulka, I was running a fever of 101, confused among bearded ancients speaking a different language: Old, bearded aliens dressed in black. Each hummed and swayed to his own inner music.

I concentrated on the ritual I memorized over the last two months in their alien language I didn't understand, to be presented to a sparse, orthodox audience who were all hundreds of years older than my grandfather at 10 am on a sunny Shabbos morning.

I searched the Temple for any other 12, 13, or 14-year-olds anywhere. Buddies who had my back. Nada. No back-ups till up around age 165 or 170.

They tell me I got through it. By the time it was over my temperature was 103 - my mom brought a mouth thermometer specifically for checking purposes. I woke up that morning, "with a slight temperature": my DNA was having none of this and my mind was going along to get along.

I had no idea about what I was saying, chanting, swearing to or off, in a language that was spoken by ancient people in some north- African desert, thousands of miles and years before I was about to become a man through the magic and blessings of a language massaged, bastardized, and ridiculed through Europe and Germany, and spoken around me by parents who, in my opinion, had abandoned me to a communal pod of ancient, bearded, droning, orthodox aliens- in-black and a few separated, Elderly Female Homo-sapiens being held captive across the aisle, some marked by purple hair. Obviously worst offenders.

Afterwards, my family group slowly strolled like we were going to walk all the way back, turned left three blocks down, got back in the car and drove home. It was over. I was 13 and officially A Man with a whole lifetime's worth of the world's toils and troubles resting on my shoulders ahead of me. Since that day, to me, the title "Authority Figure" or "Religion" is simply Lipstick on an Iron Fist.

Lately, I've started to have this reoccurring dream: Inevitably I come to the same fork in the road: Road A) The Lady, or Curtain B) The Tiger. No matter which I choose: Either fork ultimately leads to a wide, swift, cold, deep, black river that flows to a Waterfall of Salvation advertised to wash and cleanse. I jump in. Its swift current carries me to a waterfall ahead. The river's flow is too strong! I sense danger. How far will I fall? outstretched branch; my last chance. The lady is the tiger. I wake up.

I finally succeeded in running away at 15 for the last time. I changed my name to 'Barnum Justice' because I wanted to and could and because Mr. Hoover Clement Justice and his wife Mrs. June-Marlene Justice finally took me in after 3 weeks of thumbing and hiding: A new home. A new Mom and Dad.

I'd just turned fifteen. After months of planning and extensive research, checking out times, maps of the Southwest, Mexico, and watching Viva Zapata, Hondo, Zero for Conduct, Stalag 17, and lots of Prison Escape Movies, I slipped out of the house one night when my mom and father were asleep with 25 dollars, no-I.D.-on-purpose, and headed for Mexico for two days. The plan was to fake going south for two days then head north to Canada. Due Diligence.

I got as far as Flat Rock, Texas where I was nearly caught by a Deputy but, luckily, I was hidden and spoken for by this childless couple who owned *Justice's Flower Shoppe* on Main Street, Flat Rock, Texas. Mr. Hoover Justice and his wife June Anne owned it: Weddings, Galas, Flowers, & Sheep Dip. They vouched that I was their son. Mrs. Justice maintained the deputy had the wrong information. Flat Rock was a small town, no big deal, a runaway, happens all the time. June Anne Justice swore on her father's grave and gave the deputy a piece of hot cherry pie straight out of the oven. He took the pie and her word, and The Justices took me in.

I adopted their last name and through Mrs. Justice's town connections I got my very own new I.D.: I chose Barnum (after good, old P.T.). It was all Government-Official, tax number and all. That was a great gift from my new adopted parents - a completely new I.D., separate and unconnected to my given specs at birth. Hopefully, never Barny, Barn, or "B".

I helped around the place for a year-and-a-half, mainly delivering flowers, sheep dip, swept up late at night, and locked up.   The odor was not flowers, 50 to

1. They fed and clothed me, raised me like a son, and I delivered and swept and locked up and stood by them till a month or two after my 17th birthday.

The end of summer. 4 pm. Mrs. Justice - my adopted Mom - seduced me – I willingly submitted as it had crossed my mind - while Mr. Justice was out helping a neighbor's cow give birth. I don't think Mr. Justice was fulfilling his husbandly duties as Mrs. Justice seemed to be a starving woman and I was simply a young lad doing my best to help her out, but it was also definitely a signal for me to run again. Why? Because I wasn't going anywhere. This wasn't going anywhere. I was a middle-class, 17-year-old, East Coast run-away working in a florist shop in Flat Rock, Texas. All I'd saved was $100, I had no transportation, a new I.D., and had just had sex with my boss's and adopted father's wife and my adopted mother. A two-for-one sin. But to run where? And how?

To me, San Francisco seemed like the perfect place to disappear to, and far away enough so none of my 4 parents could find me. And then I thought, There're dirty windows everywhere; I'm all in, World. All I needed was a way to get there.

Mylan Oberman, an ex-hippy and now local volunteer fireman who lives down the road, offered to sell me his battered, old, green and cream VW bus. I didn't bring up the fact that green and cream- colored VW buses were "'60's" not "70's", but it gave me a hint as to why he only lived in it for two weeks. Every time Mylan and I spoke about the van his wife, Sarah would say, "It's been sitting in the garage ever since the fall of 1965 and we sure could use the space".

The insides were completely gone. "I used it as a delivery truck for a while. So, I sold the seats to an auto repair shop years ago." There was one wobbly seat for the driver. If you rode shotgun, you sat on a milk crate and the rest of the van was empty, no seats, all down to the metal. There was a thin foam mattress on the floor behind the driver. Mylan pointed out it also had a secret hiding place for stashing my bankroll, cellphone, jewelry, gun, drugs, or small, important items, whatever. Totally invisible. I didn't have a bankroll, cellphone, jewelry, gun, drugs, etc., but if I ever did, I'd have a place to hide them or it.

Sarah convinced him to sell it to me for five dollars, which I thought was an incredible gift (I was willing to go as high as fifty), I handed Mylan a five, thanked them both profusely, and I called my go- to buddy, Fried Sal, alias Salvatore Dentello. "Fried Sal" because he's always either high or drunk or both, and to differentiate him from Straight Sal: Jesus Salamanca, son of Fred Salamanca who owns Flat Rock's only grocery store.

Sal had just gotten out of the hospital from overseas from the war. He said he was okay, but he took shrapnel when his buddy stepped on an IED. His buddy died. He was okay and we hung out but there were certain subjects that were not welcome conversationally. Cool.

He suffers from PTSD: Wars cause most of it. Near East, Far East, all wars are exactly the same: People die, and the rest tell the story or go mad. PTSD: Battered Housewives Syndrome for Warriors. Plus, all wars cause an amazing number of fatherless children in foreign countries and the loss of millions of dollars in canceled bridal gowns and rental halls throughout the entire United States.

Me and Fried Sal – a better poet than I'll ever be - would hang out together a lot and talk about his time in the (Vietnam) war and how he got wounded, girls, females, women, football, movies, stuff like that. A lot of times we'd have these long discussions about Human beings and Homo sapiens as to which one is the real species, and which one is evolving, devolving or surviving as a species at all.

According to Sal, species sometimes just choose to get littler instead of going completely extinct, like the little elephants did for a while around Siberia. But they went extinct anyway, so, there's that.

But mostly we'd talk about getting published. Sal wrote too. I read some of his stuff. He's good. He just doesn't care. He's got other fish to fry according to Fried Sal himself. I also think he's just trying to help me keep moving ahead because he isn't. Also, we couldn't talk about politics or religion, so we didn't. I brought each up at separate times and each time Sal got real angry. Really: "*Hey man*! I told you! No!" So, I learned something: Fried Sal is weird just like everybody else, including me. A good thing to learn. Fine. As long as we can still hang out and it doesn't involve harm, pain, or jail.

Sal used his brother Caz's car to tow my VW van to Brody Stover's house because Brody, according to Sal, loved to work on VW engines for whatever reason. And it was true. A "'75?!" Blew his mind (Yes, they're out there). He tested it out and said the motor was still in pretty good shape, extremely low milage. Next day it was running like new. Also, for no reason anyone could figure out, Fried Sal disappeared. He didn't say goodbye to anybody. Just left. Even Caz didn't know if he was kidnapped, murdered, arrested, or really pissed off at something or somebody.

While the Fried Sal mystery went unsolved, I loaded up my new home- on-wheels with a pail, and the rest of my window-washing gear and paraphernalia, change of clothes, medical box, etc., etc., filled the tank, laid my sleeping bag and stuff neatly out on the thin, foam-mattress on the floor in the back, hung a crimson curtain across the inside of the bus right behind the driver's seat, checked the oil, turned the key - she started right up. Thank you, Mylan, thank you Sarah, and thank you Fried Sal-wherever-you-are, Caz, and Brody Stover for "Babe": My New Home Sweet Home-on-Wheels. I had no idea nor ever dreamt that my life would suddenly be divided into 1-or-2-hour segments of available parking space and time. Plus, there's always this nagging-possibility that my home could be towed away with everything I need to survive while I'm gone if I misread a sign or misjudge a parking meter: A haunting, scheduling nightmare; night or day. But it was all cool. It was either get out of Flat Rock or end up in a Texas/Louisiana Reformatory.

I headed north and traveled with the weather all over the Midwest for years: 2 years here, 3 years there, 1 year another it adds up, but I was hooked on the lifestyle. And I got rich relatives in Saskatoon, Canada. I could understand it, cope with it. Gas and food, Oklahoma City, Wichita, Lincoln, Kansas City, St. Louis, Paducah and back around. Zoos, motels, trees, monuments - Babe 'n Me: We worked the Midwest, but it was boring. The economy was in the toilet, A lady or two, I must admit - ships in the night, nothing assumed. Had to panhandle a bit, started getting the knack – the feel - the street vibe – very important; it's everything. But sales were slow to zero. I called my real parents in Belle Harbor and told my mom I was okay, not to worry, I don't need anything. My father only listened: "I'm here. I'm listening." I resolved to call as little as possible just to let them know I was alive and okay.

My curiosity grew about The Pacific Ocean, the number of cool women in bikinis who read books on blankets on the beach; the movie stars I could meet at the legendary Malibu Mall. I had a great idea for a book-to-screen story that I could sell to a big-time book publisher: "The Siren's Call". I'll start easy;

San Francisco: A simple, five-hour drive from L.A. & Hollywood.

Yes, there was major scuttlebutt among the 4-Wheelers and The Street in the Midwest that, "The Lord's Forgotten San Francisco." "The Streets are an Apocalypse of PTSD, Needles, Litter, Disease, and Homelessness." I didn't care. I needed West Coast, the Pacific Ocean, women readers, huge sales, and nothing was going stop me. I lead- footed Babe all the way. I only stopped for gas, food (burgers an' fries-to-go, ate and drove), roadside-bathroom pull-overs, one flat tire, changed it myself and pulled into San Francisco in two and a half days. Babe did fine. No smoking engine, no extra quarts of oil: Thank you Fried Sal, VW, and Brody Stover.

First, I just drove around North Beach. Plenty of plate glass storefront square footage so no problem there: Dirty glass is a worldwide problem understood worldwide: "How much to 'make-see-through'?" A few places looked like yesterday: Used-up-and-painted-over. Panhandling is passable, and the citizens seemed to be intelligent to a point around Union Square plus, lots of temp jobs available along the Bay and tourist piers. I see people reading books around Ghirardelli Square. Again, mostly women. But I'm not feeling it. Sales are slow to not at all. L.A.'s starting to look better, regularly. I sell a book: $5. I wander around, meet a nice woman - Marsha and her 6-year-old niece, Chelsea. Chelse's parents were killed in an automobile accident 3 years ago. He mom was my sister." They live on a small houseboat permanently attached to the dock of a junkyard on the shore directly across The Bay, right below Sausalito. She buys a book of pomes and invites me to her 52th birthday party in 3 days at 7:30pm, gives me the address and directions to her place if I ever get across the Golden Gate Bridge, and splits. I went back to panhandling. It pays better than hawking my books but it's not furthering my cause.

I drove down to Los Angeles for 3 days and checked out Venice Beach, 3rd street Promenade, and the Malibu Mall. Sold a total of 25 books in 3 days walking the beach in Malibu and met a lot of very famous people at the Mall. Guess who I ran into: Bryan Cranston. Gave him my business card, we talked, bought my book, and then I drove back to San Fran.

Sleeping in the back of Babe, I finally figured out my brain has been rewiring itself while I sleep – sometimes for a couple of days, sometimes weeks, or sometimes forever. Like, the way I go to sleep: Now, it depends on what secret sounds I accept; what's friendly or threatening? Near? How near? Paranoia? What am I willing to eat or not eat to stay healthy? Suddenly I fear getting sick. Where to go? How to pay for it; who am I willing to trust? Senses I never knew I had or needed are on constant alert, which changes the way I wake up and what I do next and why, and where do I go next and for how long can I stay there before a cop comes, or hopefully, a policeman?   How far am I from a legal, accessible bathroom? If too far, can I take a dump without being busted again and fined again for money I don't have, so I'm put in jail which is free shelter, care, semi-hemi-demi- food and possible rape, then get kicked out to repeat the process. I'm not sure about San Fran. I haven't sold a book in two days. Might be an omen. I'm thinking, L.A. I'm looking for signs.

Today I met Marcia and Chelsea at Ghirardelli Square again. We're friends but that's all. Relationships mystify me. I simply blame it on my own mysterious weirdness.

Or maybe because of my parents' arranged marriage - I can't recall witnessing any true love between them. No jokes. No laughter.

It's Marsha's birthday: 52. Party's at her place tonight. She invited me. Cool. Perfect Timing: In my mind it will be a secret going- away-to-L.A. party for myself that Marsha and Chelsea are throwing for me. Marsha and Chelsea will never know.

They were evicted from their apartment after Marsh's husband was deported back to Senegal. They had no place to live besides the shelter, which Marsha, because of Chelsea, was not comfortable with. A friend-of-a-friend let Marsha and Chelsea stay on his permanently docked boat: An old, hollowed-out, WWII Omaha Beach troop-landing barge permanently fixed to the dock. It can't go anywhere and just has basics: Large duckboards to flatten out the floor, a flat, wooden palette with a thin, flat mattress, two electric wires to the dock connection, a working bathroom, sink, electric stove, and running water. Home sweet home. They can stay three months for free and then they'd have to move because he has a couple coming in town with two kids and that's where they'll be staying and it just too many people for the people and boat to handle. Marsha and Chelsea have two and a half more months to go.

I drove Babe over the Golden Gate Bridge at Sunset. Marsha loathes going back to the shelter with Chelsea. I figure, get to the party sooner, leave early, get a good night's sleep, and leave in the morning. As I crossed the Golden Gate Bridge, I could see far out beyond the steep cliffs of Land's End to the gold and orange-red sun setting behind the vast, flat ocean's horizon. Mesmerizing. Total connection with The Ancients.

I brought a bottle of excellent chianti (cost: 4 book sales), Marsha introduced me all around, and about 10 or 15 of us gathered in the one room hull of an old, converted WWII Landing Craft, Birthday Houseboat: Candles, cake, gifts of great sentiment and humor, jokes, beer, wine, many bean salads of all colors in all kinds of improvised containers, pizzas, etc., Everybody brought something. That afternoon 2 of Marsha's friends, Roberta and Janice, had gone over to Janice's boss's house to bake the birthday cake. It was the warmth of spirit and just being together like nothing else existed in that moment in time. Something I'd forgotten about. Chelsea dug it the most, she even told a joke. Everybody shut up and listened. At the end, everybody applauded (that it wasn't any longer). Chelsea thought it was hysterical.

Marsha blew out 9 candles in the shape of a "5" and 7 candles in the shape of a "7" – thus Marcia blew out all 16 candles and the required 1 candle for every year. Marsh literally "blew out 52 candles in one blow. As the applause and cheers died down, she confessed: "I practiced."

We all sang happy birthday and meant it, led by Roger Flanders on guitar. Roger is the lead singer for The Redlegs, a local rock band. He was backed by a cool rhythm acoustic guitar and three females, a red- headed guy named Terry, and Marsha. All joined; a tambourine jingle- jangled in, a harmonica, and one old guy on pots, pans, and spoons. Plus, food & wine - a Birthday Party. Occasionally, someone of us or two would go out onto the dock to smoke a doobie or breathe some fresh, cold, S.F. Bay-Pacific Ocean air, and back into the warmth of the birthday boat hull. More wine and good pizza and bean salads mostly all delicious-to-great. I wished Marsha many more happy birthdays. Chelsea was now asleep on everybody's jackets and coats – I said my good nights and left around 12:30 am. No one suspected my going away party went without a hitch. So far so good.

I headed for a hill I'd found – a spot overlooking the Golden Gate Bridge and The Bay at night. A real steep San Francisco hill that I go to and just watch tankers come and go. It's always a grind but Babe always makes it up that incline. Something about a VW engine, maybe.

I park off the road overnight; a great view, semi-untrodden paths; secluded. No one's going to bother me. A great day; a great evening. A perfect way to leave. The city's lights, the lights of Sausalito across the bay, a Tanker slowly creeping along. Outward bound. All Good Signs.

Nights are colder up there, especially that night – a bit of a bite to it. But I was prepared. I pulled out my tiny hibachi and bag of charcoal briquettes, poured them into the hibachi, poured some liquid "fire starter" on, lit a match and threw it on. The liquid caught and, in a few minutes, it was toasty warm. I shut all the windows to keep warm in and cold out, took off my shoes and socks, got in my sleeping bag, and dozed off.

Unknown to me at the time, I had perfectly prepared myself to die in my sleep. Burning charcoal briquettes give off carbon monoxide, like what comes out of your car's tailpipe when you want to commit suicide by locking yourself inside your car and breathing the fumes. I even made sure my VW bus windows were shut tight. I had stupidly just turned Babe, my home-sweet-home, into my own, street-legal, suicide-coffin-hearse.

I thank the Universe for my Autonomic Body Responses. I woke up suddenly about two hours later with the worst headache any living organism ever endured. The head pain was humongous. Unbearable. I jumped out of my bag rolled open the side door and piled out into the freezing air thinking the headache was because of the charcoal's *heat!* I stood outside on dirt and grass in my bare feet, freezing and trying to get the pain out of my head, and *an Epiphany!* Burning briquettes emit very little smoke *and lots of carbon monoxide!* I was asphyxiating myself while I slept. If they found me in the morning, they would have marked me as a suicide, because any fool knows about charcoal briquettes.   My headache woke me up just in time. It Was an Autonomic-Physical-Response to Life-Threatening-Input (basically a minor form of PTSD): A Pile-Driving, Headache!   My Own Excruciating Pain overrode my Own Excruciating Stupidity: Irony. Or Luck. Or a Sign Received Loud and Clear: Get Out of Dodge.

I used the following day to say goodbye while not giving away that I was going anywhere, went to the Italian Bakery and bought a fresh- from-the-oven, whole, large, round, hard-crusted Italian bread. I went to the market and got two cans of bean soup and one of mushroom. As I drove Babe across The Golden Gate Bridge, the sun's orange ball was gulping for its last bit of air as it performed its daily evening drowning shtick. I pulled into the dock behind The Sausalito Bayside Junkyard - Marsha and Chelsea's place.

I figured torn pieces of rye bread from a fresh loaf would go good with hot soup and whatever leftovers were left over from the party. The idea was a sound one and Chelsea and I volunteered to cook two left-over hotdogs which I diced while Chelsea mixed a spoonful of olive oil with some leftover bean salad, my canned soups, torn pieces of bread, and frozen peas all in a big frying pan. We called it Fried Soup. Marsha set the table. There were tons of leftovers from the party, and it was going to go bad sooner or later, anyway. The fried soup Chelsea and I made turned out better than expected (we experimented with the seasonings), and the three of us sat down and had a nice big, hot meal together, I helped do the dishes, used their bathroom, and I remember, when I was about to leave - I said to Marsha, "Bye. I'll stay in touch." I had no idea what I meant.

It was chilly and dark outside, and I was stuffed and wanted to sleep, but no way: the adventure ahead was a shot of adrenalin. Marsha and Chelsea waved goodbye from the warm-lit, tethered, old landing barge, I waved back to two big grins, put Babe in gear and steered her out through the dirt truck-path that wound its way through piles of steel-structure-parts and wrecked-car junk to the main road below the majestic, mortgaged, Sausalito hillside homes overlooking the half-mile long junkyard strip along San Francisco Bay, drove back over The Golden Gate's Bridge-Over-Blackness, onto the 405 Turnpike's entrance South, and Babe and I plunged ahead into the distant blackness beyond Babe's headlights: L.A. Baby!

*

WHAT ARE THE CHANCES

MY 1965 VW BUS-VAN "Babe" and I jammed our way down to L.A., several bathroom breaks, no flat tires; we hit L.A.'s County Line in 4 hours and 35 minutes, stayed on the 405 till I hit the Santa Monica off-ramp and headed for the beach way at the end of Washington Boulevard, at The Venice Pier. Thankfully, it was a weekday so I could park in the Pier's parking lot for a couple of hours for free. I slept like dead wood.

When I woke up, I drove around Santa Monica and Venice. I suss out the Local Storefront Window Square

Footage Situation, parking spaces, available free bathrooms, and the cost of parking lots.

I start swimming in the ocean most every day as a shower (water's usually very cold – I can take it - and generally hung out at the Main Santa Monica Public Library or the beach for the bathrooms, spare change, and book sales potential.

Restaurants, bars, canals, beach, ocean, pier. Not as old-looking as the Midwest or S.F., with more people, and a lot less parking spaces convenient to my personal lifestyle.

I park in a coffeehouse parking lot, grab a coffee and a Bear Claw, book three storefront windows for next week, hop back in Babe and head down Ocean Boulevard to the 3rd Street promenade and the Santa Monica Pier. Half-a-mile, totally different crowd. Tons of Tourists. I circle around looking for a parking space. I circle and circle, over two and down one; make left, down 3, make a right, I've been here before a few minutes ago - I finally see a bar with a small parking lot and one open space beckoning me. "Dukes Bar & Grill". I park; Babe should be cool for at least a half-hour. It's a risk, I know but, I can't afford the gas I'm using up looking for a spot to park so I can stop using gas to look for a spot to park. I park Babe in the open spot, get out and hear Happy Hour noise and chatter, check my watch: 4:15 P.M., walk over to the front window (the front door is right at the corner). I look in and see it's a regular Happy Hour bar with locals playing pool, sitting at tables, at the crowded bar, loud, talking over pumping music with a beat. Two different live football games play on the bar's TV's.

Outside, right in front of the bar, attached to a

parking meter by a slack leash, there's a cool, white bulldog, tongue hanging out and a- flop (permanently it seems), with a red kerchief around its neck sitting on a very worn doggie mattress at the sidewalk's curb. A sidewalk sign outside proclaims: "Happy Hour 4-7pm! Come On In!"

*

"Blackjack" Duke's Bar & Grill

Happy Hour is crowded and seemingly happy (it's a bar). It's a semi- hemi-demi-dive as much as it was allowed to be by local laws, payments and noblesse oblige. After all it's in a very important square quarter-mile of beachfront and city income property. But, for whatever reason, Duke's was in a great location - one of those bars where all the imams, rabbi's, priests, off duty cops, pool sharks, off- duty Lifeguards and bartenders of the local environs seem to gather, drink, hang, and pontificate.

I notice a bartender chatting up these three guys in suits. It's a bar*maid*! A bar with a barmaid. Cool. Mid-fifties. Nice. I order a beer from a bartender and I'm watching the Barmaid. I see she's working each guy to out-tip the other guy. Each one is at least pulling in 150-200K-a-year and they're either trying to out-tip or out-bullshit each other. I'm watching modern Homo sapiens' herd instinct at work. I ask a passing waitress: "'Scuse me miss—!" "Jenny", fills-in a short, seemingly homeless gentleman of around 60. More of him in a minute. I repeat, to the waitress, "Jenny, what's the barmaid's name?" She throws back, "Kaye - she's outta your league, Sweetie", and keeps going.

And guess who I see sitting six places down the bar from me at the bar?! Fate! <u>Got to be</u>! *Fried Sal!* This is Sal's favorite hangout come Happy Hour: 4 to 7 pm at Duke's! Fried Sal disappeared from Flat Rock two days before I split for San Francisco. 4 months later I book six storefront windows in Santa Monica, California, walk into a bar and who's sittin' on a barstool like he's waiting for me? Fried Sal with a lady friend! And Sal's buying! He introduces his lady friend to me as: "Floe Motion" (Black eye make-up, black lipstick, black nail polish, mostly black apparel). Can't be more than 18 or 20. Fried Sal is 67. Her given name was Florence Dappledorf and she had it legally changed to Floe Motion. So, we had something in common: We named ourselves. Rare Birds. But she spoke very little if at all the whole time I was there.

I already had my recorder turned on and out of sight before I asked Sal why he disappeared so sudden from Flat Rock. *(Transcribed)*

"What was that all about?"

Fried Sal: "C'mon, Barnum: It was Flat Rock. It was time. I'd been panhandlin' that area for 6 years. Covid changed everything. It's still not back to where it was. Plus, you ever see anybody buy a book of doggerel poetry in Flatrock?"

"Nope."

"And you never will. Bill Dupperman was heading for Tulsa, so I hopped in. When we got there, a buddy of Will's - Tom something - money guy, health nut - needed somebody to drive his Porsche back to Portland, Oregon because he's flyin' back in his buddy's jet. I'm there: 'I'll do it for two hundred bucks, cash in front.' He agreed so, that's what I did."

"Delivered it to him in Portland.

Fried Sal nod.

"So, how'd you get here?"

"Portland street-drugs were amazing and I had two hundred bucks *cash* burnin' a hole in my pocket and damn, that street shit was Primo, swear to God. So, naturally one thing an' another: two months later The City Hall's hammer comes down hard. The cops bust both my connections. Friggin' withdrawal, dirty drugs, dirty cops, an' bullshit. Ruined the whole scene; I caught a ride at a gas station in a reefer truck headed for San Diego, got off in L.A. an' thumbed my way to Venice an' Santa Monica about a month ago an' started here at Dukes for various reasons. Waitin' for your ass to show up. You're 20 minutes late, Bro, but glad you made it. What're you drinkin'? I'm buyin'."

Fried Sal gets by. He's an Old School Survivor. Been living out of his sleeping bag on the beach here and various women's apartments, bridge underpasses, and shelters; been living on the street and panhandling all these years. Before that, who knows? Former marine. Couldn't hack "Civies" - Civilian Norms. He joined the marines fought in Vietnam, shrapnel: leg, chest, and arm. 2 medals and 3 hospitals. Great auto mechanic – got Babe running once or twice (there's some kind of Male Weirdness about VW engines) and a great abstract painter. Paints walls and draws great, colorful sidewalk chalk drawings. Very intelligent plus, severe PTSD, Alcohol, and Drugs. I tell him L.A.'s getting too crowded. Fried Sal believes the planet's shrinking but the government won't tell us.

Floe's a mystery. I was thinking she's too quiet. Like she was wearing a wire. Inscrutable wisdom: Mona Lisa. On the other hand, a lot of good the Oracle at Delphi did for the Greeks vis-à-vis Mt. Vesuvius.

Waitress Jenny shows up, Sal is buying our first round of beers to celebrate "our fated Re-Meet". We order, I throw a casual quick peek at the barmaid, who is currently playing Bar-Dice with the three guys in suits and stuffing her cash winnings down her blouse between ample cleavage. The elder, very short, shaggy-grey-haired, homeless soul who supplied Jenny's name for me, catches my eye, winks, and gives me a thumbs up. Sal explains him:

"He calls himself 'Priest' He's not a priest at all but he insists he'll only answer to that name: Priest. You probably saw the bulldog tied outside attached to the meter, that's 'Marly', Priest's companion- in-arms."

Clearly, Priest and Marley were 'Unhoused', 'Unsheltered' and 'Homeless'. Priest got beat up a couple of times, so he got Marley from the local pound a couple of months ago and now they both sleep together underneath random cars parked on used-car dealership lots at night, after closing, Marley on the doggie mattress and Priest, his shoes and crumpled newspaper pages for a pillow. It's so the night gangs don't find him anymore like they found me one time walking back to Babe in San Fran. She was parked in a cool spot, and I didn't have to change sides till the next day, 6-pm, so I could sleep late. They jumped me. Punks. Never mind - I'm talking about Priest: Old pajamas, old bathrobe, old slippers with a white priest's collar, and a 5-inch, silver metal circle on a chain around his neck. He answered Floe's question with: "A Peace Circle" and wanders off towards the Men's Room arrow.

I find out Sal hangs out at Duke's and spends most of his vet's pension there every week. He's also the bar's "Trivia Question Winner" for six weeks running so far. A record breaker, so I'm told.

Priest's like an orphaned savant, a hemi-semi-demi-Ratso Rizzo character; knows where all the free meals are, times they serve, what they serve, best cooking, bus routes, where to transfer; the works. He's one of the last of Reagan's psycho-dumps.

Sal told me Priest's real name is Marcus Adonis Pulopulous. He comes from a very old, rich family from Zimbabwe that disinherited him because he was too crazy and Unpredictable. He was a CEO of some public relations firm and then became the American West Coast Rep for 1,759 King Kreme Ice Kreme franchises all over the United States. And then he started to have visions and hearing secret messages. He claimed he was psychic, could predict the future. He had a vision of himself in The Bridgewater, Massachusetts State Hospital for the Criminally Insane (I never found out what that was all about), but Marcus could feel "The Warden" (his father) probing his brain while he slept, searching for where his ideas came from and selling the information to "Experts in the field of Psycho-Biotic-Tropisms. Somehow (obviously with help), he escaped and disappeared.

Turned up here at one of my seminars couple of years ago. So, he wasn't completely crazy or stupid. He's been out here for the ten years I've known him. He hangs around a lot with the older gentlemen out here - released back in the Reagan years. He sleeps in a cardboard refrigerator carton, walks with a limp. Arthritis, but he won't say. Probably. He'll sit on an unoccupied bench on the 3rd Street promenade for a little while, then moves on to the next unoccupied public chair or bench, sits awhile, moves, sits, moves. All day. Just him and Marley dutifully lolling by his side on a slack-leash and his doggie mattress. Sometimes Priest'll sip at a white plastic cup of coffee somebody bought him.

Remember when King-Kreme Ice-Kreme came out with this brand new "Push-Back" sales pitch campaign:

"Hey, People!! Sick and tired of being told what to like by corporate CEOs and their Bottom-Line CPA's?! Then GATH! Go Against The Herd! Buy King-Kreme Ice-Kreme's NEWEST FLAVOR ICE CREAM: Protein-Packed BROCCOLI-ASPARA-CICLES!" Crisp, Dark Chocolate Plant Protein coupled with Fresh Real Florets of Healthy, Natural, Broccoli, Spinach, and Asparagus Ice Cream! Delicious, Healthy, Fiber on A Stick! GET USED TO IT! Who cares what other people say! Think for Yourself: "GATH!!!"

After that, their K-K-C- Brand Rating went lower than whale poop. Anything with their brand on it couldn't get shelf-space at any of the big stores. Worst business decision King-Kreme Company ever made. Cost them millions. It's one of the reasons the brand never recovered. That was Priest's idea. But, other than that, he's a marketing genius. Everything I know about marketing I got from Priest. Crazy as lightning but hits the spot. X-ray ideas. He claimed his bloodline goes straight back to the Original Oracle at Delphi. She was nuts and babbled Parables and Truths. Or was that Jesus because it really is a man's world? (Jews, Greeks, Asians, Women, Men, Young, Old Black, White, Brown, Red, Yellow, Big, Little, Smart, Dumb, Stupid, Clever. One Species. Consciousness is Not a Guarantee of Survival (more further on).

Sal catches me staring at the Barmaid and the three guys in suits laughing at a joke. Sal points, mouths, "Kaye LaMarr", shakes his head "No", and mimes slitting his own throat.

That's when Priest comes back and plops down on the end of our half-circle. I asked him what wisdom his bloodline Oracle passed down to him about Women and The Truth? Priest concentrates ("receives"), and reports:

"If she says, 'It's not you, it's me', it's you."

"That's it?"

"Who knows? Doesn't matter: It's always you. Even if it's her, it's still you. You fell for her with a blind eye to the signs. "Hurts your heart and it's hard to heal." There's the first line of the chorus right there."

Sal gives me the skinny on the neighborhood and schedules: where, what, and how, introduces me to some more friends, all the LSD's: 'Longtime Street Dwellers'. They clue me into the L.A., Hollywood Vibe; the Beach vibe; police habits, where to park for how long, when: Standard New Guy clue-ins: good guys, good streets, bad guys, bad areas, bad cops, etc. I sat at their semi-circular booth. Acceptance. The first step towards Power, Narcissism, and Anarchy. Too much work, not enough down time. Not my jam.

Sal pointed out my barmaid was playing the three guys at the bar, and she was cleaning them out. Thanks to Sal, I also remember turning every topic into being about Kaye LaMarr, the cool barmaid.

    Blackjack Duke got 5 to 10
    His Lawyer got his bar
    His Accountant knew what moved the booze
    And her name was Kaye Lamarr
    Now it don't matter who you are
    In her menagerie
    She's the queen of all men's hearts
    At Blackjack's Beanery

    She'll hurt your heart, it's hard to heal
    Can night be day, can dreams be real

She'll pour me a shot and talk about
Her mom and last Old Man
She hides inside her long black hair
And does the best she can
And she just scorns the hungry hearts
That love her secretly
And want to take her home with them
And that's including me

She hurts my heart, it's hard to heal
Can night be day, can dreams be real

Lovely, lovely Lady K
She knows just who she is
And she's got all the answers to
Your stupid barroom quiz
But if you play the jukebox right
She'll dance and look real good
The magic number's A-13
"Hooray for Hollywood"

She hurts my heart and hard to heal
Can night be day, can dreams be real

OCD of the heart. It's a visual thing with males. I get over it. Last call. The three guys at the bar left. Bald Gary, and Priest left for somewhere, but we couldn't come-with, so Fried Sal and Floe escorted/steered me to my "home-on-*weasels-hic!*" (sic). Sal said that Jenny was right, the barmaid, Kaye was out of my league and Floe agreed totally. Boom!

Barnum: "A gauntlet has been--. A gauntlet has been--. A gauntlet has been—"

Floe: "A Gauntlet has been *Thrown*".
B: "Exactly. Seven-Come-Eleven, Raven hair / Hell or Heaven, I don't care.

If all things were possible, you could measure infinity. If you can measure infinity nothing is infinite. If nothing is infinite all things are not possible. If all things are not possible then some things are impossible. If some things are impossible then the impossible is possible. If the impossible is possible, the impossible is impossible. if the impossible is impossible then all things are possible.

*

Kaye and Babe. It's all a test. Just get through today and local legal parking places and times and sides of the street and where I can park, and sleep overnight is what's driving me nuts because I understand. I really do. But I'm not a stationary homeowner anymore. My home must change sides of the street during certain intractable hours for the gutter-sweeping machine or be ticketed or towed away or both.

Good Women and Parking Spots are hard to come by. Most nights thousands of homeless, unhoused, free-range urban Homo sapiens living in their vehicles, plus late-working citizen-Homo sapiens arriving home, slowly driving around their neighborhoods throughout Santa Monica, Venice, the Hollywood Flats and the East side, in major city after major city, all over America, cruising, slowly searching, praying, chanting; looking for a legal place to park overnight. "An Immediate Parking Spot Across The Street: A Cold, Rainy Night's Gift." But the night belongs to the unhoused. The homeless. The newbies. The orphans of the storm.

*

THE NEWBIES

The Newbies to the street are families now: Moms, dads, kids, pets. It's even tougher. You gotta stay in shape. Burn that stress off. Exercise. Something to do. That's why I hold a separate seminar on morning workouts: My random, movable, "Bullshit Seminars". Gets rid of the Shoulda'-Woulda'-Coulda's. Very important.

It's easy: you get up in the morning and you go to any nearby traffic intersection – one with a 4-way traffic light is preferable – an intersection with a 4-way traffic light is the sweet spot for your Morning Bullshits, but any intersection will do: Street Corner, Driveway, etc.

You approach the selected byway, intersection, corner (driveway, etc., the benefits are the same). And you stand there, and you just point at something - could be anything – *go with your feelings – just so <u>it's something specific.</u>* And you point at different specific things and go: "Bullshit!" Point: "Bullshit!" Point: "Bullshit! HEY! You! No, him! HIM! Yeah, you! Bullshit!" You do that for about an hour. Opens up your chakras.

So, there I am, I'm doing my morning bullshits – my chakras are wide open. Bullshit. Bullshit. Bullshit-- on an on. People are walking by, staring, people telling me to shut-up. This is my audience. It's a shout and response Mantra. "Bullshit! Bullshit!" "Shut Up!" "Bullshit!" "HEY, ASS-HOLE!! SHUT UP!" "Bullshit!" My Public. And what to my wondering eyes should appear, but short, bald, weird, old, homeless Priest, Marley's mattress under his arm, Marley, his Bulldog on a slack leash, tongue out and a-flop as usual, at his side: "We are living in the richest city in the richest country—" I hear Priest accompanying my bullshits: "-- in the richest time in the history of Homo sapiens wearing clean white underwear!"

He comes over, looks me right in my eyes and chants: "Do-wow- swing-bow-and-bowwow!" The crowd grows quiet as Priest pushes his thumb down into a small, uncapped blue, glass jar in his other hand. The crowd is amazed: This little man has silenced the a-holes shouting "Bullshit". The crowd is our audience, silent and curious--

PRIEST: Close your eyes and bend forward.

ME: ?...What for?

PRIEST: To bless you with my Holy Balm. I see hard days ahead for you.

M: What's in the jar?

P: Equal parts grass-fed cow's butter and organic, Hawaiian-grown, powdered sugar by weight, melted, mixed, poured and hardened at room temperature.

He pulls his greased thumb out of the jar-

P (cont.): A dot on your forehead to protect you from some harm but not others nor death.

M: Go for it.

P: Close your eyes, count to ten, open them and I'll have disappeared before your eyes.

YES; I'm attracted to people with real off-the-wall aberrations. Some say it's a death wish but I don't think so.   Priest sends out good vibes.

I close my eyes, bend forward, I feel him thumb-print my forehead with a greasy thumb. I hear him say, "Count to ten". I count: 1, 2, 3, -- I opened my eyes: "5, 6-" and see him and Marley duck behind some parked cars. Eyes open, I finish the count: "7, 8, 9, 10!" I go along: "Wow, where'd Priest go--!?"

A police siren's WUP-WUP (O.S.) A Black 'n' White Cherry Top jerks to a stop, two cops pile out, the crowd backs off, but still curious. a young officer piles out of the driver's side pulls his gun and aims it over the car's roof protected by the car. the older cop aims his gun at me, yells, "stop!" Now everything is pointed at me: Cops, fingers, guns (Street Hat-Trick). "Freeze!" I pretty much froze from the time they drove up so, without doing a thing I completely complied while refusing to stop what I was doing. All for my own good and safety. I didn't feel safe at all as I calmly let them put me in handcuffs, I announced to the Looky-Lou's that I was a citizen of the United States of America and I am being arrested for Existing Illegally, which isn't a crime yet." "You're gonna get hurt out here", announces the Older Officer, "It's for your own good".

"HELP! POLICE!! I'm being _Helped_! I'm being _Helped_ by The Police! Help!"—

The back door opened--"Please Help--!?—He heaves me in and slams the door shut. The younger cop slid into the driver's seat and locked my door from his dash. The rest of the Cop Car's back seat cage was filled with Large, White, Angry, Black, Doberman's Canine Teeth attached to a big, muscular, Doberman Dog: A Nightmare- Come-True: Handcuffed and trapped inside a police car's cage with two Old School Cops and a Dog with a Rep and all I'm tryin' to do is get through my day. The dog is lookin' at me, and I hear a very low growl. The car rocks as The Older Cop gets in, slams his door shut and throws back: "Don't mind Charlie". The two cops bust out laughing. Charlie growls low and moves closer, eye to eye. I freeze. Charlie comes sniffin' up to my face - and starts lickin' my forehead. I don't move. Charlie looks up: "A-A-ooooooo" and goes back to lickin' my forehead. We're bonding.

Ten minutes later, we pull into the stationhouse parking lot and Charlie is asleep in my lap. The two cops were pissed. This did not bode well for me, as Charlie got chewed-out for sleeping on duty and not tearing me to shreds, and I got bad vibes from both policemen my whole check-in time. I was just prayin' Charlie didn't lick off all the sugared butter.

*

THE DUES

Next stop was the usually unusual FBCS (Full Body-Cavity Search). And while this police officer, to whom I have never been formally introduced – while he's lookin' up my asshole, I have an Epiphany: "Eye of the Beholder!" I am _not_ an Unhoused Bum: I am an Independent Entrepreneurial Beggar-Panhandler-Saint. Paradigm shift. Easy-peasy. I felt better about myself and my situation almost immediately. Charges: Interfering with traffic, resisting arrest, vagrancy, causing a disturbance, and attempting to coerce-and-or- poison, Attack-Officer Charles Doberman.

They took all my possessions including the recorder I'm using now. I got it back once I was released but I don't know what they erased. Second: the Santa Monica County Holding Cells are uncool & too cold all at once. I wanted out. I was released after 3 days to be recycled.

*

THE ODDS

Choosing to become an Independent Entrepreneurial Panhandler Beggar-Saint and Urban Survivalist, also carries an instant aura and panache of survival longevity, sustainability, street smarts, wisdom, trustworthiness, and acceptance. Yeah, the mind's an amazing, adaptable, creative organ, even when not in species-furthering modalities. After too-long exposure to stress it *normalizes to the sustaining reality* – a cool survival-mechanism as far as it goes but it goes wacky-weird-sideways under too much stress for too long.

Being unhoused, on a poor diet, with random sleep patterns, stressed every day with no bank account or pre-determined, knowable, foreseeable light at the end of my particular tunnel for over a year, my brain's choosing mechanism has been slightly altered without my permission or conscious knowledge due to extensive, constant, mal-nourished, & stressed living conditions. Demanding I get a 9 to 5 job after spending a couple of months or more living on the street is like shouting swimming instructions to a drowning person. You're throwing words to a grasping hand or offering a beggar whose fingers are black with frostbite a job darning your socks.

After a certain critical duration of random sleep patterns, dreaming of drowning, being hungry and unhoused, the only thing I trust is muscle-memory, adrenalin, and shelter. Everything else is insult or bullshit. I'm working on my attitude.

What we're going for is something salvagable. When unhoused and hungry, tenacity, attitude, and location are all tools of the trade: Procrastination is not conducive to Survival. But combined with tone- of-voice, approach, age, attitude, believability, circumstances and/or situations: these tools vastly increase the odds of a meal or a safe place to sleep tonight.

My publisher called this morning. He wants me to enter my last book of pomes, "Tomes of Pomes" in a literary competition. The first prize is $3,000. He thinks it's good enough to enter but not good enough for him to pay the $35 entrance fee. Artistic decision: Publicity or food. I sent in my application and "Tomes of Pomes", my latest book of stories and pomes and wished me (and my publisher) the best luck possible under the prevailing circumstances. I've only sold 10 books in the last week.

*

Kaye & The 3rd Way

Back-in-the-day, this Cavewoman named Kaye and those of her sex, weren't allowed to own animal skins and tools, no less a business, spear, bank account, or anything else - until she and a couple of her unhoused and hungry panhandling cave-lady friends figured it out. First: they didn't like being unhoused and hungry and not being allowed to own stuff or have money. And Kaye also didn't like living in a cave owned by a male who thought he owned her, so she went to The Chief of her clan, Ollie Oop, and said: "I want stuff and money too." And Chief Oop said:

"Sure. Got any money?"

"Nope."

"Got any stuff?"

"Nope."

So, Ollie said,

"Well, you need money or stuff to get stuff or money. I got lots of money and stuff. I want more stuff. I'll trade you some money for some good stuff." Kaye had to admit she wasn't allowed to have stuff or money. Ollie pointed out that it was because she didn't have any money or stuff that was the cause of her not having stuff or money and visa-versa. "But if you have money AND stuff, you can have more money and more stuff and if you have a lot of money and enough stuff then you can have anything you want and do anything you want and nobody's gonna do or say squat."

"Lemme think about it."

Kaye goes back to her two cavewoman girlfriends, Oona and Nagena, and explains the problem and the three women focused the energy of their desperation & anger on their challenge:

"The Chief says we can't get money or stuff without stuff or money", says Kaye. Oona, her BFF, goes, "We're screwed" (there were so few people back then there wasn't even a need for last names yet). Nagena, Oona's BFF, chimes in,

"Right. Like always: they're screwing us."

"That's it."

Goes Kaye.

"What's it?"

Says Nagena.

"The 3rd Way."

"What's that?"

Asks Oona.

"Sweet-potato pie."

Says Kaye, and lifts the hem of her deerskin.

At the hemi-semi-demi-annual solstice meeting it was brought up for a vote. Chief Oop (also The Caveman-in-Charge, Pro-Tem) loved the idea because, back then sex wasn't like Doves Mating: it was like Sharks Mating.

Bottom Line: it would take a lot of the hassle and scar tissue out of the act on both sides. But what to call the transaction? Chief Oop asked, "What did you have in mind name-wise for your endeavor?"

"The Sex for Money Company."

Said Kaye, proudly.

"What name did you have in mind?"

"We were thinking, 'Prostitution'"

Said The Chief.

"That's an awful, ugly name."

Said Kaye.

"Exactly: so ugly, my females will never believe I'd have anything to do with something with such an ugly name. See? The loophole's in the name. Boom, right outta the box."

Chief Oop put it to a vote before the Clan's Council: all the cavemen on the council voted for "Prostitution" (there were no women on the council in the cavemen and cavewomen days even though there were cavewomen back then, too). Three cavewomen who came with Kaye also raised their hands for 'Prostitution' but were later discovered to have all been women belonging to Chief Oop, so their votes were disqualified and still the vote was unanimous: 'Prostitution' it was (and still is). Meeting adjourned.

But Kaye and her cavegirls made it work. Even with its stupid name, Prostitution flourished. Women started getting their own money and their own stuff. And then: The Inevitable Unintended Consequences arrived. Prostitution worked too well. It made much Money and Stuff and Stuff and Money for the cavewomen-panhandlers, cavewomen-beggars (and even more money for Caveman Pimps, Doctors, and Gravediggers).

The unhoused, hungry, cavemen panhandlers and

beggars were no dummies: they too, used the energy of their desperation and anger to *also proactively* help them solve their challenge: it forced them to also think outside the box: and they came up with an equal and just as brilliant, lasting solution for getting stuff and money without having money or stuff: They called it "The 4th Way": Which their Sons' Sons cleverly renamed, "Seeking Venture Capital". And that's how, between Beggars and Prostitutes, Big Business was born.

*

FIGURING IT OUT

I didn't have a seminar or any windows to wash, and I found a parking spot for the next two hours, so I figure, why not pop in and check out Miz LaMarr? I park my bus on a neighborhood street where I can leave it for 6 days if I find the spot Fried Sal told me about, which amazingly I do, and walk into Duke's an hour before Fried Sal and Floe show up, sat at the bar, and start chatting up Kaye between customers.

I find out she really wants to be a hairdresser/stylist and hands me a business card: "Katherine Anne LaMarr - Women / Men / Hair / Stylist / Cuts / Color", and tells me she's saving up, working part time, and going to the Vito Visante College of Hair Styling in Brentwood. She starts telling me she's going to open her own hair salon in the next two years and starts feeding me this baloney about I need a haircut.

I noticed she kept glancing at my hair; an un-cared-for, salt-and- pepper mop I occasionally comb with my fingers--!

"...What?"

She felt my hair.

"You have great hair. You should let me cut it."

"No, it's okay. It's fine. I like it like this."

"Your ends are splitting."

She tells me if I let her style my hair it could change my mind and my whole self-image. I tell her I don't like people standing behind me with sharp, pointy, steel implements cutting things near my brain. She lets it slide and says she cuts hair at her apartment or goes to your home.

For a long time before then I've always thought there was something weird about me. The way I think or interpret what I believe is going on. And more than a few times I've been awkwardly wrong about what someone did, or was, or said-or-didn't. I've also I've been awkwardly right too. Plus, I have a hard time focusing on any one thing for long.

Around this haircut conversation time at the bar with Kaye, I was hearing about a thing called "Dyslexia" – a new phrase among psychologists and psychiatrists. Which started me thinking that what I think is going on sometimes isn't really what's going on. And, that sometimes and if that's true, Sometimes I see what's really going on subconsciously, even though everyone's ignoring it. Which means I probably have been a functioning ADHD and dyslexic all my life. There are workarounds, but I still misinterpret messages or don't get them at all.

So, I've become very careful when it comes to Homo sapiens of the female kind and perceiving their actual sociological or sexual intent. But I'm also human and curious. I call the number on the business card she gave me. She answers. I keep it very formal. _I_ don't want _me_ to get any wrong ideas. I make an afternoon appointment for a haircut being careful not to use the word, "Trim".

*

I spent the rest of the afternoon at the beach recording Fried Sal's skinny on his adventures since last I saw him in Flat Rock:

"I left Seattle, lived on the street up in Portland until it got too freaky and split for S.F.: Same old, same old. Ran outta' friends, had to get outta' town. Came down here. You?"

"Little better. Not much."

Sal would help me with my Random Seminars & Rants up in Golden Gate Park, or around Ghirardelli Square or The Coffee & Beer Bar in North Beach. If we were outdoors, he'd set up a microphone and amp if we could get either or both, or things for people to sit on, beanbag chairs, boxes, junk chairs. A lot of people stood. I could draw a crowd with a story or two. If I have notes I bring a music stand. The sound system is my voice or a mic and a simple mic-on / mic-off switch - loud or low, run by Sal.

Indoors, I've done seminars and rants in the S.F. Library conference rooms, in living rooms, Parks, bus stops, wherever I can get a room or a stage for an hour or so, depending on me, the people, the crowd, the mob, the nuts, the cops, the place – up north I'd post the times, dates, and places for my Random Seminars on the bulletin boards in the Italian Cafe on Columbus Avenue in North Beach and some of the laundry machine centers & Beer Bars in Noe Valley.

"What's going on in poor old Portland?"

"I had it with Portland *and* S.F. Got out both times right before the shit hit the fan and The

Big Clean-Ups began. The planet's too small for our species to comprehend. Consciousness is the downside of evolution."

*

The Haircut

Kaye's apartment is low rent. Her living room is set up for cutting hair: hemi-semi-demi salon-like. She greets me and sits me in a director's canvas-backed highchair in front of a large oval mirror on the wall in front of me. Kaye puts a nylon apron around my neck that covers my chest and lap. Small talk. Hair stylist's scissors. Serious, professional, my-hair-talk, barber/ salon tools. I'm quiet. She washes my hair and scalp in her kitchen sink, but it's set up with towels to wrap my head in, so I don't drip on her kitchen floor back to the director's chair. Almost a pro. She towels my hair and starts snipping away.

As she's cutting my hair, I don't make a move. First: I'm afraid the move will cause a badass hair mistake and second, is she a hooker? Still: Is she a hair stylist *plus* a hooker? Is this a front? Suddenly, I'm paranoid. Out of nowhere, I start telling her about some story from my childhood to impress her because I'm beginning to be impressed by her. I think I can trust her. I tell her about Kenny while she snips away:

"A month before I ran away for the last time, when my friend Kenny and I were around 15, I heard Kenny had a 27-year-old girlfriend named Regina. He was madly in love with her. Both our friends and I were jealous and curious as hell. Our questions were mostly about sex. What they did, when, where, and how. And then she told him that it was over; she'd been seeing another older guy for the last two months and they're going together now so goodbye.

"When I heard about it, I stopped by Kenny's house to buddy him through this obviously traumatic time. Kenny was there, alone. His parents had gone for a drive and were going to bring him back a Big Mac. Kenny took me upstairs— "Oh no, you're gay." "No, no I'm not. Just c'mon." Fine. He leads me into his parents' room, goes into their clothes closet and takes out a hidden box, opens it, takes out an expensive, Black Leather Case, and inside is a silver-plated, Colt .45 Military Police Service Revolver and a small, soft deerskin pouch. Kenny's father had been a Military Policeman, an M.P., and had obviously done something brave enough for the Army to present his dad with a Special Services Award: A beautiful hand-tooled weapon with Kenny's father's name and serial number engraved on the pearl handle. It was fully functional, with six highly polished and suitable bullets safely set aside in the small deerskin pouch. Kenny takes one bullet from the pouch, places it into the gun's chamber, lines the bullet up to be next, closes it, put the nose of the gun-barrel to the side of his head and pulls the trigger, blowing his brains and the other side of his head all over his parent's bedroom wall."

Kaye stopped cutting from behind me and studied the top of my head in the mirror on the wall in front of us:

"Is that supposed to be a parable?"

"Nope. Really happened. Messed me up for a while. My take- away being, true love doesn't

work, and the one or two that claim it does
are just the basic, normal aberrations of any
meaningful biological sample."
I watch in the mirror as Kaye considers her work and is
pleased. Done. She whisks my shoulders and takes the
apron off.

"A famous person once said, the greatest
cynics were once the greatest romantics."
"Or somebody just grew up."
She hands me a mirror; I look at the back of my head.
She's serious. It's good. She whisks my neck with a real
barber's soft brush. I look in my hand mirror. It's a pro
haircut.

"I didn't take off a lot. I just gave you a trim.
You clean up pretty well."
And that was it.

"How much?"
"For you, $10."
I paid her 15 (three times the price of a VW bus/van
slightly used.

"Thank you, Barney. See you at Duke's."
I played it cool. I misinterpret things so I show respect.
Pretty good haircut; really. But I don't know if it
changed my mind or my self- image. She probably says
that to all her male customers.

Nobody calls me Barney. 'Barnum' or 'B'. Cool,
respectful, but also distancing. I'm not your run-of-
the-mill Homie. I'm a Doggerel, Socio-Anthropological,
Rantist-Pome-ist and Squeegee Enthusiast. My Business
Motto is, "Invisible Panes." I write pomes: Neal Cassady.
I got that part from him. Blame him. Yes, I'm ratting
out Neal Cassady. I'm not him. I sell my doggerels and
rants for anywhere from $1 to $5, or a donation, Tomes
of Book is $5, Rants and Seminars, me and Sal would

pass the hat. Whatever. Plus, I wash easily manageable, see-thru, shiny, flat surfaces. I also deliver packages for a fee, no questions asked. There's a bit of a risk, but it's money. I only do it if I haven't eaten for 36 hours or more and, what you want me to deliver must be able to be concealed on my person without using my hands.

*

LAST CALL

1:30 am. Right before last call and I found a good parking spot near Duke's where I can leave Babe overnight till 10am. I just finished my last window for tomorrow morning and was looking for Priest or Fried Sal. As I'm about to go in, Kaye comes barging out with a towel sopping up the wet spots all over the front of her jeans and blouse.

"What happened?"

"Some A-Hole at the bar knocked over his drink while I was serving a customer next to him, and he spilled it all over me."

"Oh... You going back in?"

"No, no, I'm finished for the night. I was leaving anyway. Would you mind walking me home? It's just 2 blocks."

"Sure. Yeah, I wasn't-- (I automatically checked my wristwatch for no reason), Okay. Yeah, sure."

We start walking down the sidewalk--she stops. I stop.

"??...What?"

"You're not weird, are you?"

"No. No way. Why do I look--?"

"No, no. You look fine. I was just asking." We start walking again...She says:

"You know, I notice you keep looking at me when you're sitting in your booth with your friends."

I stop. She stops. I ask:

"...You're not a guy, are you?" "No."

"Cool."

We walked in silence for a bit.

"...So, what do you do?"

"I'm kind-of rethinking my career options."

"What was your last job?"

"I was in charge of a nursery."

"You worked with kids?"

"I worked with plants, trees, flowers, and sheep dip."

"Oh, nursery."

"I used to play pool for a living, but I retired. It got too weird."

"I used to live with a Brazilian drummer. He played with Geo Gilberto. I met him in Rio. God, he was *so* weird. Crazy. Took all my jewelry and sold it so he could buy a stereo system. I heard some woman stabbed him in New York."

"Whoa. Why'd she stab him?"

"Who knows? He was crazy."

"Well, c'mon, she doesn't sound too cool either."

"You ever been married?"

I checked my hair in a passing shop window. Looked fine.]

"...Uh-uh. No. You?"

"No. How come?"

"I don't know. My lifestyle. Never met anybody. You?"

"Same: never met anybody."

*

Billiards

I was hanging with Fried Sal in Maury's Pool Hall this afternoon. Me, Sal, Maury, and a couple of others were watching Eddie Dalsimer playing 9-Ball for 20 bucks a rack with Dewey Morrison, a 17-year-old pool hustler. Dewey sets up, shoots the five ball which misses the pocket while the white cue ball drops into a side pocket. Scratch. Eddie's turn.

Eddie is a one-armed pool shark from Vegas who paints houses now. He always wears his spattered house-painter's cap for luck when playing for cash. He's only got one arm - lost it in a car accident a few years back – but a total shark. Never seen Eddie lose money at pool or Lori Mitumba lose money at chess-in-the-park. But Eddie is a straight-up phenom.

How he does it is, he uses the table brush turned brush-side-up, lays it on the table's edge, places his cue stick in the hairs as a bridge and holds the back of the cue stick with his good hand. Wins every time. Beautiful stroke - like a well-oiled piston. I love to watch this guy play. His opponents think it's going to be like stealing candy from a baby and he cleans their clock every time. Fried Sal is a big Eddie Dalsimer fan. We both love the casual way he chalks his own cue stick: He stands his cue stick up straight, butt end on the floor, grasps it with his armpit and what's left of his upper arm, and chalks the tip with his good hand across his face as he circles the table looking for his shot.

"You score?

"She stopped in front of her apartment building, said, 'Thanks for delivering me safely to my destination; see you at Dukes."

"You didn't score?"

"I didn't try. I just walked her to the door and went back to my van."

"See, I make sure I never have too much on my mind at any given moment. And there's a perfect example of why."

Eddie shoots. The cue ball hits the five ball which caroms off the six ball and drops in the pocket. I call it what it is:

"Slop."

Eddie quickly and smoothly sinks the six and leaves the cue ball set up for the seven ball.

"You still see what's her name? You know, with the mole?"

Eddie's cue ball sinks the seven ball and stops all set up for the eight. He sinks it, leaving the cue ball set up for the nine.

"Sandy. Nah. She got married."

"What happened with Shock Therapy?"

"Sheila. She went back to her parents in Connecticut."

Eddie aims -- Bam! The last ball on the table caroms off a rail and into the Side pocket. Dewey pulls out a thick wad of cash and throws down several bills on the pool table's green.

"Again?"

"Nu-uh. I'm late. Yo, Barnum, Sal; later."

Dewey swoops upstairs. Eddie scoops up the cash with his good hand.

"I got time for one quick game, B."

And expertly folds and stuffs it in his pocket like he's done a thousand times.

"I'm just about to leave."

"Sal?"

"I'm with him."

Eddie unscrews his pool cue by holding the bottom half under his armpit tight, and his good hand unscrews the top half. All his moves are as quick, smooth and natural as passing the salt.

"Evening, gentlemen." And leaves.

I set the cue ball and the nine ball on the empty pool table, pick up an old, pool-hall push-broom, chalk the top of the handle, and using the back end of the push-broom handle as a pool cue, I set – stroke hard - bam! The cue ball strikes the nine ball which caroms off three cushions and into the corner pocket. I head for the door before the Cueball stops slowly rolling. Sal follows me out.

This afternoon, Maury maintained the cue ball continued to slowly roll into the left side pocket and scratched. The shot didn't count. I maintain there was no "game"; I simply planned to sink both balls with one shot. And I did.

"Fine. But, don't use my name. I'll deny the whole thing: I wasn't there, and I can prove it in court."

*

Though we have the moral high ground: we are, *in fact,* unhoused, unsheltered, undernourished, hungry, and sleep deprived. However, the public has only four choices as to *how they interpret these facts on sight:* Humble Beggar, Holy Ascetic, Impossible Dreamer, or A Threat. each as real as Santa Claus, Happy Clowns, and Granfalloons' Gold Balloons.

*

Fried Sal was walking me to Benny Benito's fresh fruit and vegetable store on the corner of Clune and Washington when this beautiful female walks by us at a much faster clip and Sal is immediately focused on watching her walk ahead. He points.

"That, my fine feathered friend, is a magnificent ass. I must bed that woman."

Yes, she has some class and a well contoured behind, but even I was stunned by his sudden, So-I-say, so-it-is-done, old, Black & White Movie Pharoah-isms. We both watch her approach the newspaper stand on the corner in front of the market. She picks out a particular magazine, pays, and starts talking to the news vendor. Sal informs me: "Definitely", excuses himself, and makes a beeline straight for the female with the magnificent ass.

It was a bright, sunny afternoon. I gave full attention to whatever was going to happen next by pretending to be interested in many things while clocking every move the vendor, Fried Sal, and the female with the great contour made.

I couldn't hear what the three Homo sapiens were making sounds about, but they all seemed to be enjoying each other's company. To me, Fried Sal was another person. Now, suddenly he's cool, gentlemanly, amusing, while completely dressed like he always is, like he permanently lives on the street which he is and has been for years: an egoless, social chameleon with no tomorrow but takes two showers a day no matter what, and which is not as hard as it seems depending on one's definition of how much water is needed to be considered "a shower". Plus, I'm not a joiner. I waited a while, till Sal finally peeked over to me, smiled, flicked me a good-bye and went right back to his goal. I turned and went to another market.

*

LSD

One of the lifeguards gave me a dose of LSD. I'd done it once a long time ago, but it was with supervision – an American Indian Sacred Ceremony. It was very spiritual and interesting, especially because in the middle of it I had to go to the bathroom.

I was totally wacked out on peyote, the Indian chanting, and drummingchanting-drummingchanting-- What if I don't come back? I don't remember what's outside anymore!

I really dug the fact that this simple act had been worked out way back; centuries, when we were real Homo sapiens: How, where and when to relieve oneself during a high religious ceremony in a huge Teepee, wacked out of one's mind on religious drugs, chanting and drumming? How many people didn't ever come back before they started to figure out, they had a problem?

The Problem:

One gets high on drugs, chanting, and drumming, one has to alleviate oneself. You remember enough to *know it's a Big No-No to do it in the ceremonial tent.* You alleviate yourself somewhere outside. You leave the drumming tent on peyote and, once outside, one is confronted by the Entire Universe all at once. Amazed, one wander off and is never heard of or seen again.

Back-in-the-day, some were eaten by animals, some fell off a cliff, got lost, or disappeared down a ravine. Even some very fine drummers never came back plus, some barn of the guys who handed out the peyote. Something had to be done. The simple solution:

When it came my time to leave the drumming, chanting, and drugs to alleviate myself, an Indian brave handed me an ornately carved tent peg – yes, like a regular boy scout used to use. *Because,* when you leave - for some strange reason beyond anyone's ken or control - the tent peg in my hand was like a psychic string back to the tent. When I tried to find my way back to whatever I was doing wherever I was: I just followed the tent peg's "pull". I also impressed the Indian Chief who was wondering if it really would work on a white man. But it did. And this was an Indian Ceremony with midnight drumming and peyote peace pipes in the woods in a Large Teepee with two other white guys and our Indian brothers chanting for a good harvest.

But not this time. This was a Venice Beach Acid Trip alone in my legally parked van. I took the "tab" with some orange juice, got down on my foam mattress, got under the covers and waited. I grabbed the edges of the foam mattress on both sides and didn't make a move lest I be murdered if I fell asleep or moved. It turned into a Paranoid Trip. Alone. It freaked me out so much I finally barreled out of Babe in my underwear, slippers, and rumpled bathrobe, and walked the streets of Venice, California at 3:30 am till I found myself standing in front of the first-floor street apartment of Jenny, our booth's usual waitress at Duke's Bar – Fried Sal pointed it out on one of our walk-and-talks.

I knocked lightly on her apartment door. A few second go by and she suspiciously opens the door a crack – chain still on - and peeks out in her p.j.'s and bathrobe, recognizes me from the bar, and whispers, "Hey, B. What's going on? What are you doing?" "I lost my tent peg."

Jenny, being not only a pretty good waitress, but also a naturally fearless and worldly female Homo sapiens, checks out my attire, the hour, my answer, my body language and attitude, I'm not a stranger, immediately senses my psychotropic trip vibe and that I will present absolutely no threat to anyone what-so-ever. She very kindly motions me in and whispers, "Be very quiet because my boyfriend is asleep in the bedroom." I nod and follow her handhold into a small room with a single mattress bed – no covers, no sheet, just the mattress. Jenny motions me to lay down, then sits beside me, curls up next to me and whispers in my ear, "Let's be very, very quiet", and we made love. Seriously. Intensely. I was on acid and she knew it, guessed it, or hoped it, and all I wanted was shelter but discovered I was also incredibly open to suggestion.

After our intense (gentle as a feather, she put one hand over my mouth and the other over hers) we each strained to silently climax. Quiet, major physical entwining, and it was incredibly, quietly...over. Peace, calm--Jenny whispers in my ear, "You have to leave now", and indicates the bedroom where "He" was sleeping.   Guileless as a newborn foal, I silently nod, put on my torn tighty-whiteys and robe and, finger-to-lips, she tiptoes me to the door, invites me out, smiles, waves goodbye, and slowly and quietly clicks the door closed. I walked back to where Babe was parked as the sun was just coming up. The beach was empty, the sea was flat, the morning sky went from darkened purple to light blue into the sun's bright orange and the morning breeze was filled with fresh sea air.

*

A NORMAL DAY

10:30 a.m.: Met Sal for coffee on my way to wash 3 storefront windows on the 3rd street promenade. We talked and I finally got around to the inevitable Basic Male Ask as I turned on the recorder under the table:

"How'd it go?"

"How'd what go, when?"

"How'd it go with La Notre Damme De La Gran Derriere? Last Tuesday."

"...Not quite the way I was expecting it to go. I'll get over it."

"Wow. What happened?"

"When we got to her apartment.... The deal was, she wanted me to do it in front of her husband who was a Marine Sargent, paraplegic. Syrian War Vet."

"Whoa."

"I wish."

"What happened?"

"It wasn't what I had in mind. She had to help me get it up enough to put on the condom."

"Wow. What was going through your mind?"

"I kept thinking, this was what I originally planned on doing, but somehow it wasn't at all. When she came, they both looked at each other and he approved. Mission accomplished. I pulled up my pants, flushed the condom, they both thanked me, I saluted him, he returned the salute, I was dismissed and left."

"Pretty Weird."

"Too weird."

*

A VERY SLOW NIGHT

10:30 pm. Found a spot near Dukes. Parked. Fried Sal was there but he had an appointment and split. Jenny smiled a cool smile, but otherwise she was just Jenny. I thought it was a very nice way to tell me it was a one-time thing. I'm a big boy. Guys seem to do it a lot or at least talk like they "Love 'em an' leave 'em" a lot, so fair is fair, and I regarded it as an early birthday present that I was going to get around to wish for, but it came true before I could think of it. LSD can be very cool sometimes. Sometimes.

Duke's, 12:45 am. Slower. I was sitting at the bar talking to Kaye in between her taking care of an empty bar.   Nothing heavy: I was talking about advertising her haircuts and publicity and she's telling me about what's wrong with men, my friends, or me.

"Some. Not all. What about local newspapers?"

"Nope."

"Why not?"

"Too expensive— we were talking about you."

"I was talking about Advertising. Branding."

"I was talking about men who are normal and men who aren't.

"Normal like Normal, Norman Rockwell? Raise the money and open your own hair salon. Five chairs: Four you rent out; the fifth chair is yours.

"What's wrong with Norman Rockwell?

"He's a man. Maybe you're afraid of becoming Vidal Sassoon.

"I'm not afraid of anything.

"Anything except everything.

"I give out business cards.

"Extremely local. Not the same as newspapers or late night TV."

"Too expensive. It doesn't matter. It's not a good match."

"You and Vidal?"

"You and me."

"What's that supposed to mean?"

"Nothing. It just slipped out."

I mentioned the conversation to Priest. All he said was: "Normal" to "Evolution" is anti-evolutionary.

*

Transcription:
(SOUND: Male pissing into a toilet bowl):

B: It's...3 a.m. I'm in Kaye LaMarr's bedroom bathroom taking a piss-- ! to someone in the other room): Be right there! I'm Pissing! (into smartphone) More later (Pissing sound continues-- Tape goes dead).

*

UNINTENDED CONSEQUENCES

I woke up wrapped up in my sheets and covers on my mattress in the back of my van. It wasn't a dream. It's 2:30 in the afternoon. I left Kaye's place at eight this morning. She was still asleep. Maybe faking it, I don't know. I'm writing this now.   I was at Duke's last night about 10 minutes before last call, Kaye asks me to walk her home again. I walk her to her apartment building. We talk. She invites me up for a drink, a little wine; she comes on, a little weed, into the bedroom where The Impossible Dream came true. I must have gotten somebody else's Karma. She said she's been watching me watching her at the bar for weeks. I'm not complaining, just explaining, and if it's really a gift from The Gods, only they know what for. I don't kiss and tell, but I been known to embellish a bit, so all I'll say is, if I don't play this right, I could fall in love with this woman.

> Her passion is boundless
> And deep as a well
> Thighs of white satin
> And tongue that won't tell
> Her lily-white breasts
> Are ambrosia to smell
> The drool of my lust
> Could quench fires of hell

*

POTSO

Raymundo "Potso" Alverez is a hard guy to figure. First: He's a genuine Peruvian. A real descendent of the Incas. Second: he's six foot six inches tall and he works out. And third: He speaks and understands fluent English. Six languages all together. The guy contains more multitudes than Walt Whitman in a room full of Rubik's Cubes. One minute he couldn't care less and the next minute he's in a uniform on a high horse defending Truth and Beauty.

We were in Elysian Park, sitting on Whale Hump Rock (because it looks like the rounding hump of a huge, sounding whale diving back into the earth). It sits at the edge of a green meadow surrounded by mild, green woods in three directions. The trees grow thick, deep-in and carpet the hills behind them. The trees also hide some interesting caves and cool streams. Potso nudges me and points to the sound of anger. Somewhere a guy is really pissed and doesn't care who knows it.

Potso points: This Hiker Guy wearing huge backpack comes cursing and raging out of the trees dead ahead. He's ranting; he's all in a big huff about his missing wallet and comes marching across the meadow, obviously towards the park path behind us. He seemed to be raging at nobody who was behind him about his missing papers and money, credit cards, his I.D., his "... fucking driver's license, social security card, etc." Then, a female, similarly backpack-burdened, also comes out of the trees and that's obviously who he's blaming for his situation. He's ranting that she is somehow responsible for this monumental tragedy that she's caused to be visited upon him – all this, while they both are aware that Potso and I are quietly, calmly interested, but couldn't care less. The more she whined or cowered, the more he demeaned her. It's becoming a grotesque reality theater; an over-the-top relationship for our eyeballs and edification but so far, Potso and I were both unmoved. The guy turns his back on us. When they got about 10-15 yards away, I watch her prepare her arms to defend a blow from anywhere at any time because the Hiker Guy is verbally working his way up to hitting her. She's yelling "Look again to dtal what was coming.

The guy stops, still cursing and blaming her for his lost, brand-new cell phone-watch while he busily searches and re-searches his pockets.

Dropping behind him, The Female childishly mimics her partner's searching himself for our amusement - and her partner *turns - catches* her comic imitation of him and unloads: *"You Think This Is F**king Funny!!?"*, straight in her face.

"Ridicule to anger is gasoline on a fire, Barnum." My mom told that to me about me to my father.

Blind rage explodes into a clenched fistful of her head-hair – I felt Potso leap--

The Hiker's fistful of his companion's hair pulls her around—*Potso's fist grabs The Hiker's poised Striking Fist in mid-air in an unclenchable iron grip,* and using both his hands, he slowly begins to twist the Hiker's arm out and down. Firm. Unemotional. Calm. Relentless. The Hiker's other fist lets go of her hair. He slowly sinks down trying to lessen the twisting pain, unwavering. Potso is strong, slow, focused. The Hiker's body buckles-under in silent-screaming pain. The Hiker collapses to the grass. Potso lets go. The Hiker stays down, breathing in pain. Potso walks back towards me.

Behind, him The Hiker, red-faced and breathing hard, struggles to his knees in the grassy meadow holding his shoulder-socket with his good hand as his formerly twisted arm hangs unusable for a while. The girl says something to him we can't hear as Potso steps back on the park path and kept going away. I followed. I try not to question his every decision but I can't help it. When I caught up:

"Why are you leaving?"

"Because it wasn't over, and I got things to do."

I looked back: The Hiker Guy was unpacking his backpack in the grass with his one good hand and arm and his Female Hiker Companion was helping him with his search.

I think Potso's some sort of genius. Maybe because he's also got the Perfect Zen of animals. He's always in

'Survival-Ready Now' mode, and just a couple of milli-seconds faster than any vertebrate in his immediate vicinity.

*

Dukes Bar, Happy Hour: In between bartending a busy bar, Kaye drags me into a discussion about marriage: She wants to have

"A normal life. A home."

" Your ideas are all ripped from a 50's Norman Rockwell magazine cover. It doesn't exist except on his easel in Connecticut. White Bread Art."

"You're just running away from growing up."

"Sometimes running away _is_ growing up."

"Having a safe place to run to is growing up. Just running away is escaping. Victims do that."

*

Santa Monica Public Library - Room 2

Eight homeless people of various ages, ethnicities and backgrounds are sitting around a large, long table listening to me:

"…Which is why I really don't think we understand exactly what we're becoming now that we've become aware of Choices-Have- Consequences. It's called: Evolution. As a wise man once told me: 'Normal" to Evolution is anti-evolutionary'." About a week later, Same dance: Right before Last Call Kaye asked me to walk her home, I walked her home, she invites me in, wine, doobie, couch, thigh, bedroom, second time.

She's funny. She paints black wolves, incredible clouds, and sinister angels. She dances around, wants to live in Malibu. She's amazing. What does she see in me?

> She wears Garbo's garters
> Got a Lady Pope's nose
> Got Mona Lisa's smile
> Wears Charlie's Aunt's clothes
> She got tiny claws
> At the end of her toes
> She's been around
> & She knows she knows

Left her apartment at 10:07 a.m. In the van at 10:20 am. Hour and a half to spare. 12 noon they sweep this side of the street. I'm in love with this lady. I know I'm skating on a thin bridge of dynamite. Definitely red flag territory. Plus, I'm into her for 100 bucks. On the other hand: best sex ever.

*

BALD GARY

n his book, "On Being & Nothingness", Jean-Paul Sartre contends that, "Man is an infinite, ongoing, historization of useless passion." Bald Gary claims Mr. Sartre is an infinite, ongoing, historization of useless passion.

*

MAN BITES DOG

There was a documentary double bill playing at the Aero theater in Santa Monica and one of them is my favorite: "Man Bites Dog" by three German Film School students who made it as their senior thesis. All three wrote, directed, and played the three main characters in the tale. Yes, it's a staged "Mocumentary" but it's perfectly done and a shocking story, well told, that could happen. It's great. I figured maybe Kaye would like to go on her night off, so I stopped by Duke's after her shift started and when she got a second alone, I asked her and surprised the hell out of me, she said yes. I say I'll pick her up at her apartment at 6 pm Thursday, her night off. I ask if she'd mind using her car as mine was in the shop. She said, sure, she'll drive us. She agrees, I leave. Easy-Peasy.

*

Thursday eve arrives. I make sure I'm not gonna be late. I take the elevator up to the 6th floor. Going passed the 4th floor I check my wristwatch: 5:55 pm. 6th floor. I get out and walk down the hall to 622. I check my wristwatch: 5:59. I wait. ...6:00. I knock. I hear "just a minute" from inside the apartment and finally the door opens, and she looks like she's going to a Hollywood Premiere.

My first thought was that if we walked down the street together, she's gonna get both of us beat up, robbed or worse. My mind racing, I scanned the presentation and gave it my best shot.

"A little too much lipstick."

She accused me of body-shaming and told me to leave, which I thought was okay because "Man Bites

Dog" is on first and I didn't want to miss the beginning, so I wasn't ready to argue. The film's got a great opening scene; great camera work with the three film school students playing the three main characters in their own Faux documentary about two film school students who meet their third student playing a great, strange, young, drunk business guy in a bar.

As I turn towards the door I hear:

"Chickenshit."

I stop. She goes,

"Just don't tell me how to dress."

"Don't listen to me."

"Fine."

She goes to the door--

"Where're you going?"

"None of your business!"

Steps out into the hall and slams the door behind her. I sit down on the couch, her couch, grab the TV remote-- The front door swings open and Kaye stands there looking pissed and hits me with:

"You're gonna let me leave?"

"Yesterday, I would have tried to stop you, but I was explicitly told – *but moments ago* - it's none of my business".

Kaye steps in, slams the door behind her, marches into her bedroom, and slams that door shut.   I plop on the couch and click on the TV.

I figured this is a relationship test. She's testing my commitment. I'll give her 20 minutes. It's a battle of wills and I'm not missing the beginning of "Man Bites Dog".

Fifteen minutes later I'm into the fourth quarter of a tight Lakers – Golden State game, Kaye comes out of the bedroom dressed in jeans, T-shirt, a jacket, and sneakers. Tight. I won (but even then, I knew: 'Too soon, Grasshopper'). Even as I waved the Gold Victory Trophy to the cheering crowd, I suddenly knew what Yogi Berra really meant when he said: "It ain't over till it's over." How right Yogi will ever be.

The agony of her driving and me in the shotgun seat as she stopped for stop signs and let people pass— *encouraged* pedestrians to pass - my stomach was churning. I was straining my seatbelt. I was trapped in a car. Time was not trapped. Time was moving onward.

It seemed like she was driving slower than everybody else. She drove, parked, and we finally got inside the movie theater. Her timing was perfect; just in time to miss the first twenty minutes of "Man Bites Dog". How'd she even know? So, she won. But we had breakfast together at her apartment, so I call it a draw. But I know she really won. I'm not getting a good feeling. I don't understand. There's something more going on. I think it's me and I don't know it.

*

SHIT HAPPENS

Two days ago I woke up in a three-bed hospital room. Curtains around two beds but not mine. I'm nearest the door. Everything hurts. I can lie on my back, but I have to favor my right side.

I was beat up and stabbed with a penknife a couple of nights ago. It happened fast so I don't remember much. I woke up in the hospital. Some kind of blade, sharp but luckily not very long. The docs say it missed one of my kidneys by a quarter of an inch. Most of my body hurts every time I cough. If you visit, don't make me laugh or cough.

I'm also hooked up intravenously to a clear plastic bag of 'Tequila' (saline and nutrition solution) and a heart machine.

Everybody came by to see me cleaned up, bandaged, and hooked up to a bag of 'Tequila'. When Kaye came, she kept referring to the skirmish as my stupid beating and stabbing.

"My Attempted <u>Robbery</u> and <u>Murder!</u> Plus, All Penalties, Fines, And Medical Fees!"

I was walking back to the van around 2 AM. I took a dark shortcut: Unwise on a lot of levels. I don't remember, they must have knocked me out real fast and kicked the shit out of me while I was out. Cracked a rib. (coughs) Ah!! Ow. I'm okay. See? I told you: "Don't make me cough". They just jumped me. I didn't do anything. No reason, just me. I'm enough. I measured up to their standards: Homeless. Who else you going to rob? The Rich? They'll rob you right back and call the cops. Rob the least among us. Easier; amazingly easier. If I had money, they would have taken it. But I didn't have any. Luck? Coincidence? God-Given, Lucky Poverty. So they beat me up instead. Why chance robbing the Protected Rich when it's so much easier robbing the Less Protected Poor? And the poorer we are the easier it is.

Knives are the worst. Not bad ass enough to kill me first strike, but it'll sure stop me for a second or two plus, there's a chance of infection. Something else to worry about. Missed my kidney, no infections developing, Doc told me I was stabbed with a small pocketknife, no concussion from the blow to my head. I must thank my assailants for their thoughtful carelessness on my behalf. I'm also a healer. The Doc doesn't care; I can't laugh or cough for another week. So far, no blood in my urine for a while. The kids probably beat the kidney stone right out of me so, thank you, kids. Just don't let me catch you, you little punk-assed spunk junk. I told 'em.

That night I dream Kaye has a large, razor-sharp, pointed, killing- knife in her claw and she tells me to look up, high up, higher, and I do, and she could just slit my throat and murder me right then with her razor-sharp, pointed, killing-knife; or come up behind me unknown, and stab me in the back, heart-high, and stand back and watch me twitch, gag, and bleed out till I lay still and dead. She stops, stoops, scoops up my dirty socks, and throws them out an open window.

I spend a week at Kaye's while she helps me with my bandages, stab-wound, stitches, and anti-biotic salves. She thinks my knife wound is smaller than she imagined (my ego?). My stab wound and stiches, "…are gross" (her words, not mine). She calls it Tough Love and drove me to doctor appointments. Or got someone else to take me and she'd pick me up. We got along great except Kaye doesn't like being a nurse or maybe I'm a bad patient or enjoy the attention a little too much. I'm back in my van now.   Real Dependence is a frighteningly unfamiliar ego-scape with dangerous access to manipulative means, real and/or un-intended.

*

Fried Sal came by my van – luckily, Patso got the driveway of a house on the block where his kids and ex-wife live, and that's where I was parked for two weeks until I was able to drive like other, normal Homo sapiens. Potso's ex-wife's new, live-in boyfriend, Murray, brought me out some hot oatmeal and raisins, had me over for dinner one night. Nice people.

When Fried Sal and Priest came by, Priest wore his long, Harpo Marx coat. When he opened it, Priest revealed off-the-shelf medical supplies from the local pharmacy's kids' section, so I have gauze bandages held on by band-aids with Colored Stars, Daffy Duck, and Pluto. The Doctor said the wound is healing okay so I can stop using the bandages and salve. Just treat it kindly for another week or two.

My back wound is healing fast and well. I'm doing fine. My Doc tells me 80% of the people he operates on or sees that are seriously ill, are simply where they are because they waited too long.

Plus, again I was lucky: I was in the process of bleeding to death when help arrived so, as my luck would have it, I got listed as NDBE: Near-Death, Bleeding-Emergency which automatically put me at the head of the ER line. Or I would've died. Pretty Lucky. I have a weird angel with a very dark sense of humor on my shoulder.

I can't laugh for a while because of my two bruised ribs. I'm in a chest cast so no one was allowed to make me laugh or even try for two- weeks, minimum. Of course, everyone tried, and Emmy Lester scored and set my healing back at least two weeks. Doc thinks I just passed a kidney stone which could explain the blood in my urine again plus I was clear yellow this morning, so I think I'm going to be okay. Kaye bought me a pair of slippers. They look stupid but I wear 'em because they work.

*

I'm healed enough to drive or take the bus to the doctors on my own. I was starting to feel guilty about how much Kaye's helped me, but I wanting to get back to Babe. Too much, 'being cared for'. Makes you feel Old, Useless, Helpless, and Forgetful. But, if you really are in a bad, impossible way.

I'm feeling a lot better. I'll be able to wash a window or two by next week, but I've lost a lot of momentum and a few customers. No worries. Most of my customers told friends to tell me not to worry. Worry is something to do when there's really nothing to worry about. If there's nothing to worry about, that's the time they get you, and that's something to worry about.

I've cruised and scoped out various places around Santa Monica and Venice where the parking would be favorable depending on where I had to be or wanted to be that day or the next four hours, or overnight, depending on everything else including my astrological sign and how the buses were running in my green zones. I just have to keep track of parking spaces, parking days, sides of the street of several streets all over Santa Monica, Venice, downtown, business hours, bus schedules, plus working out whose bathrooms I can use when and where (clothing stores, restaurants, etc.) and/or various other, public, available, usable, bathroom facilities and walking distances. It's a one-way ticket to The Happy Asylum, and I'll swear to it on my death bunk.

*

Evolution is merely The Universes attempt at Natural Cosmic Deflection: Evolution and Consciousness are a new thing in the universe as far as we can tell. Not common – like weird and not quite got it together yet.

"I know you want to fly. You need wings. Fine and okay. Come back in 350,000 to 700,00 years." For the first time Consciousness comes along and says: "Never mind: I'll build an airplane and invent Sky Diving in less than 100 - It began to rain-!"

I woke up to a drunk pissing on my right front tire. I popped up and yelled:

"YAAAAH!"

I literally scared the piss out of him mid-rain. He ran like he'd seen a ghost, pissing and zipping up as he ran. My first laugh in a while.

"I'm an alien Garbage Spelunker on Space Debris SD659-023 - a formerly inhabited planet several hundred thousand years ago - and I've just dug out part of a Homo sapiens arm bone in a layer of garbage about twenty feet below the Second Level. In some places the depressions where the liquid once was are now filled with decomposing landrollers, waterfloaters, flying mechanisms and other PLB's (Planetary Leave Behinds). Homo sapiens remains are rare and worth a lot of money to museums and collectors—"

Again awakened! This time by rapping on my back window! A white flashlight beam hits me straight in the eyes. I'm thinking, the friggin' drunk! Through the whiteout I hear: "Let's go Buddy! Move it! You can't sleep here!" The police officer informs me that to sleep in a domicile between the hours of midnight and 6 am in this area, the sleeping quarters of said wheeled domicile must also have a working lavatory - something that had never occurred to me or VW. According to The Law, in this area, I can be busted. I plead ignorance and ask for leniency and promise to never do this again. The officer lets me go with a warning, but I had to leave the area immediately. "'Immediately' means _Now_." I moved it.

*

Back in the day, what did Jesus mean when he said:

"It's easier for a camel to pass through the eye of a needle than it is for a rich man to get into Heaven."

Now, what did he mean by "Rich"? Rich compared to who? Rich compared to The Poor, of course: Jesus's poor. And who were His poor? The Destitute, The Lame, The Ill, The Lepers, The Forgotten, The Least Among Us: Rich compared to that. Among "us" - not among "them". Because that's who Jesus was talking about when he said the word, "Poor": The Least Among Us - Among Us. He was talking about Unemployable Lepers, People of Color. If you have a checking account and a safe, sheltered place to sleep tonight, you're probably going straight to Hell. According to The Son of God who told it to me personally in Bald Gary's dream and I was in it. That's what Doofo said Bald Gary remembers but it might be something else. Can I get a Heyman?

*

SMALL BUT COMFORTABLE

Kaye's out interviewing for a real estate gig this afternoon and I'm feeling and looking good but I'm still not perfect and I notice Kaye started talking about me maybe staying longer, I'm here now a lot and I'm thinking why not, pros and cons, what's in it for me, the usual crap, maybe me moving in with her for a month or two as a tryout and that'll make it easier for me to get back on my feet again and get a regular job instead of selling my pome books, washing windows, panhandling, and "Temping" or selling too much blood.

So, we, I, she, _we_ agreed to agree. I move in as a try-out for two months. It's kind-of weird but she also got a part time job with a real estate agency as a property hostess three afternoons a week, so I get some time in the place by myself.

Her apartment is small but comfortable. Everything here is hers. Just to put my toothbrush in her bathroom I had to shove aside multitudes of tiny palettes, packets, jars, tubes, and enough small brushes for an army of miniature Rembrandts.

Small kitchen. Homey, old-fashioned, kitchen table, a "Duke's" napkin dispenser, checkered tablecloth, two second-hand chairs; an old, gas stove. Lots of different spices. She paints: Makes these incredible paintings with wolves and clouds and mysterious, dark angels. It's nice. it's a safe place to sleep, but am I giving up too much? Of what?

*

This afternoon I was over the time limit for this side of the street and Babe wouldn't start. It's 2:15pm. I call Ron Rodriguez to drive over and give me a charge, sez he'll be over in 15 minutes. I'm waiting 15 minutes: No Ron. I fall asleep. Ron finally arrives at 3:45. C'est La vie. I get outta the bus, I see the Curb-Sweeper swept right around me; I didn't even hear it, nobody turned me in; no cops passed; no ticket; no pat-down; nada. Ron charges my battery, suggests I get a new one, and I drive off. Nothing happened. Made my day.

*

1 hour later: Babe wouldn't start again. Ron was right: The old battery was shot. I got a ride to my guy to get a reconstituted one, called Kaye and she put it on her credit card - I'll pay her later. I turned down a catalytic converter at an incredible price and took the bus back. Pomes, Slams, Parking, Public Facilities, Cops, Thieves, food, debts, time (and writing this bull-pucky, Theo!). I got a full plate.

I was watching NOVA on Kaye's TV: It showed a series of "glyphs" carved into the face of a 100-foot-high cliff in Northern France. The glyphs have been calculated to be over 100 million years old, are logical, mathematical, and have a definite meaning, but, until now, scientists have been unable to translate any of it until, with the recent help of A.I., scientists believe they've finally deciphered the message:

"We've left and couldn't take you with us."

I woke up.

*

Kaye and I were sitting at her kitchen table last night. She was reading 'Down and out in Paris and London', and I was writing my next rant on a yellow, legal pad when Kaye hits me with:

"I was just thinking, you have no religious affiliation of any kind, do you? Or do you?"

"Who wants to know?"

"I do. Don't answer a question with a question. Do you believe in God?"

"Hey. My partner is the Church."

"Your partner is God?"

"God has nothing to do with The Church. God and Mother Nature just Do It. All natural, all organic, no hard feelings. We have an infinite amount of matter plus, An infinite amount of nothing. We, on the other hand, can't do anying about that. Yet. We, on the *other*, other hand only have 2 choices: Keep on Keepin' on or Eventually Crash - into Something, or Something into Us. No church involved, that's it, and speed's not an issue in space. The Key word is "Eventually'.

"You haven't answered my question."

"I believe in the truth or the facts. Whichever comes last."

"You don't believe in God?"

"I don't believe Homo sapiens have quite got the handle on 'Consciousness' yet. Religion is small potatoes compared to that. Do you know how long it took an African ape to learn how to land a jet plane on an aircraft carrier in a rough sea? *At least* 300,000 years. Minimum.

"So?"

"*So*, we got a long ride ahead of us to discover the super equipment we got stored in our skulls right now, not anywhere near its Maximum Capability: It's the next Terra-Incognita."

"What about The Bible?

"A Self-Actualization Book whose Hero rose like a Greek Phoenix from the dead, Ultimate Proof Self-Actualization Works and God made females for bearing children, gathering, cooking, serving, babysitting, or posing angelically.

Way-Back-In-The-Day The Bible was The Internet, Newspaper, Bulletin Board, and Readers Digest all rolled into one. Along comes A Guy who just says, "Hey, guys, it's time to stop killing and just get along. Spread the word!" And what do they do? They kill him. And what does everybody else do about that? They don't stop killing each other: They start spreading the word about spreading the word about not killing each other. Now billions of Homo sapiens around the world spread the word. We haven't learned how to be a true Species yet. Now, wherever we live, our front yard is the rest of the planet. That never was before. Ever. Anywhere. And we're not used to it.

"You're not religious. Sorry I asked."

"There's some parts of religion make my job a lot easier."

"Like what?"

"Religion's Job is to Instill Guilt. My Job is to Leverage It."

"What about getting a real job and having some real compassion?"

"You can't depend on jobs or compassion - ever hear of Compassion Burn-Out" or getting bored or fired or both?   What I'm talking about. There's a reason why Adam and Eve got kicked out of the Garden of Eden.

*

The True Story of Adam & Eve

Once upon-a-time God had just about seen enough and was not pleased. He opened the Pearly Gates, stepped out and gazed down from Heaven to His Garden of Eden below. He'd been away for only a nanosecond or three, but what he saw on returning was shocking. He looked down and thundered: "Hey: you two! What the heck have you been doing?

Adam and Eve stepped forward out of the shadows - The only two Homo sapiens around.

"I leave for three nanoseconds and there's rotten apple cores all over the place, animals and trees are disappearing, mercury in the water, carbon monoxide in the air, I'm running out of trees, tigers, giraffes, elephants, bees, butterflies, arable land and potable water, the poles are melting because the oceans are heating up and Jellyfish are multiplying up the yin-yang. You know how long it took to get it the planetary temperature just right all over. Mostly. It's hard. You're uncool, you don't listen, you just use-up, throw away, get a new one, and fuck-all. The Garden is beginning to look like a garbage dump surrounding by neatly cared-for sports arenas, putting greens, and paved parking lots. Too many red flags: Get out. Now. And *put on some clothes!": Potso's Constant: Compassion Burnout.

*

THE BELLIGERENT DRUNK
&
THE DEMON WIFE

Kaye and I cornered a BBD - Belligerent Drunk - male, around 50- 55, last night at Duke's right before Last Call. I was waiting for Kaye to get off work and I was going to walk her home. This guy was pouring out his "poor me" divorce story with such sincerity I was able to sip his beer without him noticing. When he saw his glass empty, he just automatically ordered another and went back about his demon wife nagging him.

"She was needy. Neurotic. Nothing was good enough. She claimed I was a slob. An exaggeration. The wedding she was planning was -- I couldn't handle it. At first it was a small dinner in Queens with seven or eight close friends to celebrate the occasion - which grew into a banquet dinner in The Manhattan Embassy Hotel with over *145 invitations* and *"We" rented out their SkyView-Club for one night* just for 'Our Party: Invitation-Guests Only'."

Another beer was served. He took a sip, put it down, continued to Kaye.

I sipped his beer behind his eyeline.

"It took '*US*' three years and a heart attack just to pay off the 'Nightclub-Open-Bar' idea - *of hers*."

He was talking to Kaye. A quick slug - quiet replace.

"Did I bite off more than I can chew or was she holding me back? What I didn't have, she spent more of. So, I naturally back away. Her *wifely reaction?* She accuses me of messing around at the office sexually and files a police complaint on me *as fact and threatens divorce!* I figure if the law believes her, *I have the right to believe her, too!* At least let me see what I'm being accused of. Maybe it's okay. I cheat once. ONCE! She catches me! Spying! Before penetration! She sues for divorce: The car, the house – not "my kids"; No. Not: "Alimony"! "*MyKidsANDAlimony*"! The divorce was a horror. I lied, she caught me, so did the judge, I lost the house, the car, my personal nest egg, my stocks, my business, and my*kidsandalimony*. It was a mess, a nightmare I carried for years. I'm still going to therapy. You get it when you get it."

I finished his beer and placed the beer glass quietly on the bar slightly behind his eyeline. He looked at his empty beer glass, looked puzzled, and ordered another one. My dad never got it.

*

JOHNNY (WACKO) OBLONG

This afternoon Wacko and I were driving around near the Marina Del Rey pier, and we ran into a great parking space, so we threw Babe in, synched our cellphone timers and headed for the barren rock jetty dead ahead.

We walked out to the end, sat, and watched the ocean. The Ocean was weirdly calm, so we smoked a doobie to get us to the calmness of the ocean faster and mostly tried to figure out if we Homo sapiens are going to make it, near-term. I asked him if he thought the climate thing is getting worse. "Worser." I dared to ask again how he got his nickname 'Wacko'.

He took a puff, held it in a long time, blew it out, coughed like it was gonna kill him and stared at me:

"My older brother, Arnold, "Arnie", gave it to me. He was— You recording us now?"

"Yeah."

"Hey, Fuck you. Let's change the subject."

"No way. It's off. Look: See? It's off." I showed him the wrong button.

"It's off. Okay, lemme ask it to you this way: What would you _guess_ it would take to kill someone for money?"

"To Arnie, I was young and because I'd never 'Wacked' (killed) anyone for money, and because of my obvious naivete': So: 'Wacko.' Hey. Look, I never killed nobody, right? This is just a guess, right?

"Right. Of course."

"Okay, so, I'd guess it takes some kind of major invasion of your soul and a major refusal to believe it ever happened. And 'Feelings' would be proof it happened. Or prevent it from happenin'. It's a professional thing. The less emotional involvement, the easier it is. Less is more. That kind's thing. It works.

"Do you like the nickname, 'Wacko'?

"Why shouldn't I?"

"It's demeaning."

"To you. Don't mix me up with you. I was up for the job of a hitman, once. The guy who got the nod was a pro. I didn't get the job because I was "Cherry" – I never killed nobody (sic). I didn't get the job. This other 'Jalopy-Jim Jamook', he gets the job. *That's* demeaning.

Question: "Why does anyone take this job but not that job?"

The Job, The Specs, and-or The Money. You gotta keep it simple. It's just Business. You gotta tap into El Cajones Oculto - Deep strength, then: Who, why, where, when, how, and what's in it for me? I guess. I'm guessing, right?"

"It's off, it's off. Yeah, probably just a lot of Dark Angel type stuff.

Vengeance of God, Ultimate Power. Yeah. Could be. Or it's just a job: 'Exterminator': So there's one less asshole on the planet. No more, no less. 'Garbage Man'. Arnie chooses "Garbage Man". Serious psycho crap.

Hey, I'm a nice guy. Went to police officers training. I was a street beat cop. Two and a half years and then I flipped out. The general stress out there: A streetwalking target. I couldn't handle it. Did two-years in a mental institution; the insurance ran out, they released me too soon, nobody'd hire me, I started to regress, so I decided to commit suicide. But how? By cop, right? Die by Cop. Irony. I'll kill somebody and when the cops come, I'll shoot back and they gotta kill me, right? Irony. I am them; they are me. Get it?

"Yeah, but that's not *irony*; that's stupidity: Close, but no cigar."

"Exactly: 'Wacko'. Obviously, I was having a nervous breakdown. Thank God, In the middle of this, I get a call from Arnie. From Canada. My older brother. I got a younger, one, too: Mikey. Arnie lives in a huge mansion with his new girlfriend, Sylvie something, right up near the border with Alaska. Mulookumuk, Canada.

"Haven't seen each other in ten years. We're getting old, he wants to see me plus, he's doing well, he's got plans for both of us. He's got a great set-up: Right alongside a river made of ordinary, seasonal glacier melt. A rushing river of pure, fresh, ice water not from the ocean - from the glacier. He runs The Charon Ice Block Supply Company. Huge, 7'x4'x4'-foot blocks of ice for Reefer Trucks hauling perishables cross-country or for inside shipping containers on long-haul boats and trains. He lives in a big house on the edge of a frozen lake. No one around for miles except Sylvie; the Mill workers all live in a small town further down the road. Just what I needed, peace and quiet. Just me and my brother and Sylvie in the quiet, snow-covered woods up north. Perfect R & R.

"I fly up, he picks me up at the airport, takes me to his nice, big, comfortable house built on solid rock at the edge of a pinewood forest on the shore of a frozen lake. Perfect.   Plus, we both can add 2 + 2 and get whatever number you want, so he lays out the situation: Because of The Big Melt that's comin', men, women, and major corporations were sinking millions of dollars into land up there for mining Gold, Uranium, Jade, and Exotic Minerals. In the early '50's it was an old-fashioned American Wild West Land-Rush to California. Now-a-days it's North to Canada. Alaska. A couple of big Canadian and American syndicates used Arnie's company as… (pause)…Okay, you sure it's off? Or we gotta stop.

"It's off. I showed you. Jesus."

"No it's not."

"Look. (shows him) It's off."

"You promise?"

"Yeah."

"Don't turn it on again unless I say so."

"Okay."

"Okay. So, Where was I--!?

"Arnie was saying about the syndicates and companies."

"Okay, so Arnie was saying that it was a fact that 99% of murders are solved by something in, on or around the deceased victim's body. 99% of the time, in court: Habeas Corpus: No body, no crime. No crime: No Time: Punto final. Arnie was dumping several corporate hit jobs into white plastic bags, freezing them inside a 7'x4'x4'-block of ice and dumping the ice blocks into the conveniently-near glacial river which quickly flows out to the sea where very hungry carnivores live and thrive. The ice melts and bodies, trial dates, and jail times magically disappear. My brother's Ice Block Mill was the perfect solution for all the land- grabbers and hit men that went up there: Modern-Day carpetbaggers and lots of High Stakes Domino games were played while people were mysteriously disappearing in the north woods galore. Very High Stakes games. We never killed nobody. Swear on both my parents' graves. Me and Arnie'd receive a body or three or whatever, throw each into a white sack, freeze it in a 4x4x7-foot block of ice, dump it in the river, and out to sea she goes - or *he* goes, mostly. Don't knock it. It worked."

"Wow. So, what happened?"

"We got caught."

"How come you don't look caught?

"We-e-e-ll, it started with a shipping screw-up. Arnie's crew dumped a regular ice block in the river and put a frozen body in an ice block on a reefer truck delivering a load of salmon to some jerkwater supermarket on the east coast and the ice melted enough to see the bag. Me and Arnie didn't find out about it till The Mounties raided the house and caught my brother and Sylvie. Luckily, we had a slow month, so they only found one body."

"You still don't look caught."

"I was shopping in town for a pair of gloves. These." "Shows his hands wearing a pair of well-worn but expensive gloves."

"From the time sequence, I figure I was paying for the gloves just as the Mounties were busting him and Sylivia. busted in the door."

"Lucky you."

"Thanks. On sale. I like 'em. Wear 'em all the time now. Till Arnie gets out. It's something. I mean he was busted while I was paying for them. Right about the exact same time. I'm not emotional, so, least I could do.

figure, Venice Beach, California is the last place the Mounties'll look for me or, better still, hopefully they'll forget about me."

"I guess."

"This is my jail now. I figured hardship and anonymity beats three walls, iron bars and a roommate, right?"

"Welllllll,...-!

"Okay, discussion for another time, but Arnie was in business for ten years and nothing – not even a parking ticket - so he figured everything was honky-dory. I mean, people just disappear up north. Happens all the time. Perfectly natural for someone to go out for a walk and a bear drags 'em off or they disappear through a hole in a thin-ice-covered chasm. I tried Oregon first, but Portland's gone. 'Frisco is also starting to fill up. The northwest is Cloud Cukooland with needles. Arnie's in prison somewhere in Canada now, but I'm afraid to try to find out - those Mounties'll track me down - their smart them Canadians, least they used to be. I hear

Arnie gets out in three more years and is gonna marry one of his prison guards. A lady named Alice McBerny, which'll be his third wife. Him, her fifth.

It ain't a question of winning. Winners don't show me shit. I just wanna fuck with the point spread. Whatever happened to the Old Values?"

"They're in the attic with Eternal Verities and cast-iron baby shoes.'

"How're you and Kaye doing?"

"It is what it is for now. So, we'll see. I'll see." We spent the rest of the afternoon talking about where it all came from and when and how it all was and could be but c'est la vie, and, wow, so soon? We were both amazed but not surprised, which is happening more and more.

*

I HEARD KAYE LAUGH

"We need a Planetary Micromanager: A Planetary Superintendent."
I was sitting at the kitchen table talking to my hand-held recorder, exploring some ideas for a possible Venice Pier seminar. Kaye was in the bedroom, door open, reclining on the bed and reading something by Kierkergaard. I hear he's coming back.
I assured the microphone:
"Just to keep the planet running smooth, safe, on time, arable, and habitable." From the bedroom, Kaye shouts:
"Free Rent in any Major World City High rise goes with the job!" I quietly made a note of it and continue recording:

"Yes, I know about the graft and bureaucracy that go with the gig, but would we be doing anything worse any faster? Let's put greed, graft, and bald-faced stupidity to work on something that's worth the greed, graft, and stupidity." I heard Kaye laugh.

*

Duke's Bar is slow this afternoon. The afternoon Bartender, Brad, wipes and polishes the just-wiped-and-polished beer glasses and restacks them.

I'm sitting in our group's circular booth having a beer with Potso and Floe. Priest arrives with, "It's time to organize a Planetary Group Hum-in", explaining to us that the 60's "Spaceship Earth" has become a High-Rise, Ghetto-Apartment-House Earth that's just roundly and randomly ranting, hurtling, spinning, and babbling through the lonesome universe with a Holier-Than-Thou Absentee Landlord. That unspoken thought makes a lot of people nervous and paranoid and is the core reason for religion.

*

US

Kaye was talking about "us" and I was trying to follow her until I finally interrupted with:

"What are you really trying to say?!" And she just wiped the conversation away with--

"Never mind!"

Bam: Case closed – into the bedroom – DOOR SLAM! Which really frustrated the hell outta me. I went to the closed bedroom door and spoke to the room behind it.

"You mean to say you're trying to say you can't tell me…(silence…) Okay, correct me if I'm wrong: you're not getting what you need out of this relationship, but you can't tell me what because I wouldn't understand, and you can't tell me why.

(O.S.: thru door): "Right."

"Why?"

(O.S.) "Because I can't."

"Try."

(O.S.): "I don't want to."

"Why?"

Kaye OPENS DOOR:

"Because every time I try to explain how I feel to you, you interrupt, you never let me—!

"Bullshit!"

"YOU JUST DID IT! EVERY TIME I--!!!"

"THAT'S BECAUSE I DON'T-!?"

Kaye SLAMMED the door in my face!

*

TUESDAY

Today we got into an argument about how "sloppy" I am (her word, not mine). Kaye started picking up things and started ranting about my dirty socks on the couch and ranting about what I was or wasn't doing – what life wasn't doing – she wasn't doing - throwing things - not at me - around the room. I never felt in any danger, so I just backed off and watched, figuring she'll calm down, which she did, finally, but not before picking up anything handy as she ranted on about impermanence, men, my habits, politics, where this is going, money, the hair-dressing business, me, us, her clients, on and on, all around the room. I stood off to the side out of the way and my first thought was, she fell off the wagon - whatever wagon she was secretly on. Kaye was seriously angry. Then, I noticed she was picking up things that were *unbreakable* – like a cushion, or a book, an empty cardboard box, a coat, a shoe, a wire coat hanger – and throwing it where there was nothing to hit, or at something that would be okay to hit, like a wall's blank spot with the cushion, or her couch with the coat hanger – or my dirty socks out the open window! Her choices and aim were amazing. She was angry with an athlete's eye-hand coordination and a ladylike care for lamps, knick-knacks and framed art, which were never grabbed, snatched up, or disturbed. Nothing was being destroyed (it was her place). I saw it as a harbinger disguised as an athletic sissy fit performance show.

*

BABE

Not enough can be said about Babe and the debt I owe her, but right now, Babe's battery was stolen last night while I was at the 3rd Street Promenade listening to Bald Gary and Lori sing and pass the hat.

Where I parked was okay, but they were going to sweep the side of the street I was parked on at 10 am and I had to move Babe to the other side of the street before then or my Home Sweet Home's going to be impounded because somebody stole my battery. The Worst. The only pushers I could round up were Priest and Marley-the-Dog, Hair Gary, and M.E..

I pushed and steered from outside the open driver's side door while Marley sat in the driver's seat and patiently managed the move, tongue a-lop all the way. Everybody heaved where there was a place to heave, and we pushed her to a safe parking spot across the street and down the block where it'll be cool till noon. I called Kaye and she said she'd lend me the cash for a reconstituted battery for Babe before I have to move her again.

Finally, Kaye taught me the secret of most locals in finding a place to park overnight anywhere in the world: Chanting. Yes. Factually. It works. Nishron Shochu's Secret: "Sooner or Later". Its primal motivation is not Intent but Manifest Destiny: Sooner or Later.

So: I Chant. And sooner or later someone leaves a spot to go to somewhere after I've circled and chanted around the block for two hours.

'Nam-Yo-Ho-Ringey-Kyo, Nam-Yo-Ho-Ringey-Kyo, Nam-Yo-Ho- Ringey-Kyo, Nam-Yo-Ho-Ringey-Kyo, Nam-Yo-Ho-Ringey-Kyo, Nam- Yo-Ho-Ringey-Kyo on and-on-and on and - you get it. But it works. *In That*: it's a belief system based on *Sooner or Later*. Therefore: it works. Sooner or later, a priori. We call it Self-Actualization if the Sooner happens extremely soon. You literally talk yourself into believing or doing or connecting stuff that you really want to believe or do, or connect but are too lazy or afraid to, so you shop around for a God or App that will tell you you're not crazy, you're right on, it's okay, you're fine, go do it if it's pro-active. If not, you cannot have your money back. But we told you so. All religions are just different apps or doors to peace of mind and hope, and it's all just true or a lie or a crutch or a shoehorn. But it works. Sooner or Later. I chanted & chanted & chanted & chanted. It didn't work. So, I stopped. Nishron Shochu's Answer: "You stopped too soon."

At last, the modern-day, utilitarian application of thousands of years of meditation on lonely Tibetan Mountain peaks have rewarded us with a fail-safe method for finding an overnight parking space. I give Buddha props and a silent shout-out on that.

*

Got a check from Poetry Press this morning: 375 bucks! Paid Kaye back plus some rent and had enough left over for a celebration. We went to the Maxi's Burger & Fries on 9th and Lincoln with Priest. I know the owner. Marley was tied to a parking meter out front, red bandana, sitting on his old mattress.

(If it was 1844, Marley'd be a burro with a red bandana, tied to a hitching post. But it's not).

BG (Bald Gary), Lori, Emmy (Mother Earth), Fried Sal, Floe, Kaye, and me pushed 2 tables together and commandeered 8 chairs. I introduced everyone to Maxie, took him aside and told him it was Mother Earth's birthday and asked if he'd split the check with me for the occasion. He countered with the fact he was very proud that we had chosen his franchise to celebrate her birthday and, instead, would give us all extra sides-of-fries for free. We shook on it. His staff - two teen males working the kitchen and two female teens as servers - sang Happy Birthday to Mother Earth, and three other customers joined in. At the end there was a French Fries fight which made for a completely successful celebration and imitation birthday party. A good time was had by all, but our 2 tables were asked politely by one of the teen female servers that the owner asked that we don't come back until the owner 'Okays' it. A request not to be taken lightly in these parts without adequate financing and dependable shelter. I've got to keep reminding myself of what they think I am and how I act and react unconsciously because of it.

Places to hang out late at night are at a premium when unsheltered in the normal, Norman Rockwellian nonsense. So, though it was fun and funny in the late afternoon, I can't afford to be on the outs with the day or night shift at any place open after 11pm and all-night diners are few and far-between. The night crews know the score. You don't want the day crew bad-mouthing your presence to the night crew. If you serve coffee and a donut after 11 pm, you get respect. To me, All-night diners will always be coffee, a toasted bagel, respite and sanctuary.

*

IT'S GETTING WEIRDER.

11:45 p.m. Nuthin' on TV. I was minding my own business at the kitchen table casually skimming through an abandoned, business section of a two-week-old "N.Y.Times" I found on a bus, and I was post-checking-out their predictions and enjoying a cold beer. I notice Kaye comes into the kitchen and sits down opposite me like she's done a million times before. Sometimes we read the paper together or talk or she'll do one thing and I'll do another, less and less lately but whatever, so I just went back to The Futures section -- I'm suddenly aware Kaye is sitting silently, both elbows on the table, a lit cigarette stuck between her fingers, the smoke curling up past her face, leaning in: 2 Cold Blue Medusa's Eyes staring at me through cigarette smoke slowly curling up are definite "Tells".   I went back to the safety of comparative numbers. I hear: "You're blowing it, Barnum". She gets up, walks into the bedroom, and slams the door shut. I wait an hour - till

I figured she could pretend to be asleep. I quietly slip in, laid down on my side in my clothes and finally fell asleep…

> *It's winter, things are cold and slow, I'm driving southeast, through the Midwest. I'm hanging-out with the Home-On-Wheels groups on the open roads of the southwest till it gets way too hot. I drive back to the west coast, making full, proactive use of my ADHD, Dyslexia, and OCD proclivities which might explain my writing and driving or it may not at all or somewhat.*
>
> *It's summer hot and sweaty, I'm on the road driving Babe. I need a shower. It's too hot. I stick to the open tourist highway. A lot of motels along the tourist strip. I pull into one, park Babe in the lot, ask about prices, back to Babe, change, do a couple of laps and back on the road. 5 motel laps equal one shower.*

When I woke up, Kaye was gone already. I had some Fruit-Loops and left to make my usual rounds, repark Babe, and sell some books. No windows till this afternoon around 4. When I got back, Kaye was back but locked me out. I had my key, but she threw the bolt. She's still home! All my stuff was in there.

Through the door she accused me of cheating on her! Of having sex with another woman which is ridiculous. She wouldn't open the door. I'm innocent - obviously, there's a problem. I left.

Why would she say I did something like that? Premeditated plea for commitment? I got things to do important to my well-being. I don't know; something's wrong.

I must have walked a couple of miles. I called. She hung up. I went back. She wouldn't open the door. All my stuff is in there. I slept in Babe.

*

The Nightmare

Sometimes sex is hard, and love is soft
Sometimes love is hard, and sex is soft
Sometimes hard is soft and love is sex
Sometimes soft is hard and sex is love

It ain't her nose and she ain't too fat
So why accuse me of something like that
A fever dream that very night
Freaked me out, man; what a fright
A sinister angel put a hex on me
In a bad-ass nightmare in the first degree
I dreamt I woke to an acrid smell
Condemned forever to Don Juan's Hell

Smiling females tranced my mind,
And, late for dates, left me behind
Each left and cried, "it's me not you",
Which was a lie but also true

The first fair lady wore a satin dress
What the second one wore was anyone's guess
The third one never got mad unless
The fourth came over to play some chess

The fifth played more, the sixth played less

The seventh's sole purpose was to really impress
The eighth didn't talk, she'd just digress
The ninth I loved, I must confess

Whatever I damned, the tenth would bless
Eleventh ate nothing but watercress
Twelfth meant no when she said yes
Thirteenth left my place a mess
But I didn't care, and I didn't depress
We lived by our wits near the Scot's Loch Ness
She loved me a lot and her name was Bess
I'd write her for money, but I lost her address

Fourteenth said she couldn't grow
Fifteenth split for Mexico
Sixteenth ran with a rodeo
Seventeenth came late or just didn't show

Eighteenth followed wherever I'd go
Nineteenth was warm and sweet and slow
Twenty turned tricks at ten a throw
Came up to my waist on tippy toe

Twenty-third wouldn't wash, Twenty-fourth
couldn't sew
Twenty-fifth ran off with a guy named Joe
Twenty-sixth now lives in Kokomo
Twenty-seventh I guess I'll never know

She disappeared a while ago
I kinda' think she's pretty low
She stole my TV, all my dough
And the solid gold ring off my big toe

Twenty-eighth gave head in every state
Twenty-ninth got mad, broke every plate
Thirty got drunk and stayed out late
Thirty-first just blew with the winds of fate

Thirty-second, you know, was really great
Thirty-third could love, thirty-fourth could hate
Thirty-fifth jumped off a' the Golden Gate
Thirty-sixth did speed and never ate

Thirty-seventh smoked grass and just gained weight
Thirty-eighth moved in with my last date
Thirty-ninth turned out to be jailbait
Forty started with a nice clean slate

But it all just started to dissipate
When her mother moved in with her stuff in a crate
I couldn't make love or masturbate
I came too soon or came too late

And the motel rooms were second-rate
So, I put my money in Real Estate,
"Paint Your Wagon", and "Kiss Me Kate"
Made tons of money but I couldn't relate--

I woke up in a cold sweat. 5:30 a.m. I switched Babe to the other side for street-sweeping in the morning and finally fell back to sleep.

*

I just finished a seminar in the park - out of nowhere, Kaye arrives fairly stressed out and tells me her landlord's sales agent and some prospects were coming to inspect her building the next morning because the landlord was thinking of selling the property.

"...as soon as all the tenants are out."

"So? No problem. I'm not there anymore—"

"It's not you. it's me."

"...How do you mean that?"

"My cutting hair in the apartment for a fee without a business license is against the law. Between bartending three nights a week at Duke's, and real-estate hostessing and haircuts. - and when you were there whatever you chipped in. That's how I pay the rent and eat.

"What's illegal about cutting hair?"

"I don't have a Barber's License or a Business License, out of my apartment. Plus: To do business in this apartment, the law says I have to have a special drain, or the cut hair clogs the building's old waterpipes. And there's also Business Hygiene Laws."

"You've lived here for two years. Why, all of a sudden, now?"

"The Landlady is just looking for an excuse to evict me. The buyer only wants to buy the building without tenants so he can tear it down right away and build a better one . They'll be. here tomorrow morning at 10."

"Got it."

This was totally uncool news. Kaye and I were over. I've been working on it. This was unfair and Kaye knows it, because I wasn't over it totally yet and Yogi Berra's Law is an immutable Law Of all Universes Anywhere: "It's not over till it's over". This was a big weirdness for me.

She needed my help to dis-assemble her entire friendly barber- shop-themed living room and bathroom now. Visuals I helped create: down, gone, hidden, why'd she wait so long to tell me?   We could have started days ago. Or yesterday. She knew last week about this.

We had to remove the whole barbershop Mise-en-scene: hand mirrors, hair dyes, rollers, tin foil boxes, bobby pins, scissors, brushes, combs, towels, tensile hair-strength device, curlers--Bam! Gone. The director's chair, wall mirror, an old-fashioned stand-up-on-rollers hair dryer. Where? Anywhere they're not going to look: My van (her suggestion). We had to make it look like there's nothing to see here but a cheap, rental apartment. There're laws everywhere. This is not good. I'm becoming a Lone Wolf or an Accessory.

I didn't make any deal with Kaye before I agreed to this insane move for her – knowing full well I'd have to move the stuff back in - Back upstairs – even with an elevator. To it, load it in, unload it out, move it down a hallway and through a door plus now there's no place for me to sleep in the van. I didn't think of that until I saw Babe filling up. Too late. She offered her couch. Problem solved.

No sex. We were both exhausted. I had to be out by 9 a.m. because the building inspectors are arriving at 10.

*

Zeus and Hera

The Great-Couple Rulers of all the Other Gods. Zeus was A Heroic Hero. Hera was a Shrew. Zeus was a Leader God. A Leader Husband God. Perfect. He was always "sleeping over" with other goddesses, demi-goddesses, semi-hemi-demi goddesses, other god's wives, animals, clouds, birds – any vertebrate that moved was fair game.

"Hera – honey - it was a <u>swan</u>. A frickin' bird. Me and The Oracle at Delphi were sniffing some gas together and I ran into this woman who said she was a swan, and she looked like a real swan. Really. I believed her. I swear on my ancestor's graves. I swear to you and myself. I don't remember anything after that. I was out of my mind. It was nothing. I didn't enjoy it, I _had to_: It was a case of life or death: She was going to commit suicide if I didn't have sex with her - to save her life – so, <u>okay, _I became a swan_</u>! I didn't know what I was doing, I was high, she hypnotized me, it was _the gas,_ do you know where a swan's head is at?! Hera, she was Suicidal, Yes, I had Great sex with her! Lovely, Wonderful -- <u>to save her life!</u> I can't have sex with a suicidal voluptuous young thing and have bad sex with her. I couldn't do that to her.

Or - maybe I could: I'm the Head God; whose gonna stop me? No. Nonononononono. I don't think so. Here's a poor, forsaken human being going to take her lovely life and I should have bad sex with this poor lonely human being!? NO! I, Zeus, God of Gods made her come like Nobody's Business! If that's a crime, then call me Godless!"

But Hera never left him (a man's world-view).

Don't you think it's a little weird that Hera never told him to get the hell out and stay out - it's over?

Hera never stood up for herself, except for revenge. Hera spent most of her free time just thinking up ways to get even. All she did was to punish Zeus with dirty tricks. Never washed a dish, walked the dog, changed a sheet, ran a business, fought in Battle, raised money. No confrontations: No, "Zeus, we gotta talk." None of THOSE talks. Zeus: How about awarding her equal pay and let <u>her</u> pick you up in <u>her</u> chauffeured limo to the airport and fly you in her jet to The Bahamas for dinner - on <u>her</u>. Plus, Hera can go halfies on a bigger house and a bigger mortgage: All possible through equal pay. The 3rd way takes Time, timing, genius & awesome luck. However, never underestimate the genius of sheer stupidity: The broken watch that tells the exact right time twice a day. Through equal pay. The 3rd way takes Time, timing, & genius or awesome luck. However, never underestimate the genius of sheer stupidity.

The Hair Police never found any of Kaye's salon stuff. Yes, I carried most of everything out of my van and back where it all was. Kaye helped. We were a team for moving her Salon stuff - and our cleaning job worked: The landlady couldn't evict Kaye if she paid the rent every month on time, but Kaye and I: Not so much. She knew it, everyone at Duke's knew it. I refused to believe it, but I knew it too. A dead Shark.

*

THINGS HAPPEN

I miss Kaye. But she wants me to change. My friends think we were a cool couple. There is the word, the image, the thing itself, and her, and me, and us, and them. I understand the need, but I don't feel it. I don't grok it.

I went over to her apartment this afternoon. Took the stairs instead of the elevator. More time to relax. Burn off some energy, keep my mea culpa straight. I walked up two floors passed hers I was so lost figuring out what to say first - snapped out of it, went back down to her floor, down the hallway to her door. I knock. From inside, I hear Kaye's voice:

"Who is it?"

"Barnum."

"...What is it now?!"

"To apologize."

The lock clicks open. Kaye opens the door—THUUUNNG! A crack: The chain was still on. I didn't plead or get angry. I was just calm and honest: I told her where I'm at right now an' how I feel about where I think we are now. I told her about how my friends thought we were a really good couple. I told her I was willing to change. Ready to.

"Anything to be back with you." She undid the chain, grabbed me, led me into the bathroom, turned on the shower, undressed me, put me in the shower, undressed herself and got in with me. It only got better from there.

We towel dried each other for a while, she led me into the bedroom, and we managed to get along amazingly well. We smoked a joint, drank some wine, lit two candles, and when we tried some porno-movie improvs I nearly burned the place down by knocking over the one scented candle, relit it and burned her wrist with hot candlewax. We quickly put on salve - no time for a bandage – and back to business of pleasure.

She did me good, I did my best. Damn, all that horny, lonesome- anger-lust-energy letting go or coming through and she knew what I liked, and I assumed I knew what she liked, and we got along fine, even with all the instructions. I got some of my moves back. I gotta say, make-up sex is the best sex ever. Maybe that's what breaking up is for. Maybe I don't have to change. Maybe I shouldn't.

*

The Problems

Kaye and I have totally different senses of humor. I said something about her nose, and she took it the wrong way. She was really pissed. So, obviously, there's a problem. I swore to her I wasn't serious.

"That's the problem! You're <u>never</u> serious." She went for my satiric psyche, my imaginary brass balls. That's where she always went. A baseball bat to my psyche's nut sack. We were sitting at the kitchen table for some reason.

"What else is wrong with me?"

"You don't give me what I need." I was in way over my head.

"What do you need?"

Kaye walked to the kitchen sink behind me. I didn't turn to her. I waited. I figured she was picking up a steak knife from the sink. I refused to turn around. I waited. I didn't move a muscle. She came around and confronted me.

"Is there any future in this?"

She was grasping a large dish-sponge in one hand and nothing in the other.

"What do you mean?"

"What about <u>us</u>?"

It was way too soon for this conversation.

"What *about* us?"

--was all I could come up with, hoping what was coming wasn't going to come, but no such luck.

"Are you serious?"

"Of course, very serious."

"Will you marry me?"

"What?! --Now?! Why?"

She hurls the sponge at the sink—my eyes follow--off the tile and in! She scores. Three points.

My ADHD is doing somersaults. I'm thinking' okay, I was horny, maybe we both were, but this, "shelter from the storm" thing has gotten way out-of-hand. My feelings of guilt tell me I'm in too deep to pretend anymore. That's how deep my own personal feelings of guilt we're, right then: So deep I couldn't lie anymore. 'In Too Deep to Lie'. There's another pome for a hit song. I told Kaye I couldn't commit yet. I had too many plans and baggage and she was way too serious. We've got to lighten this whole relationship up.

I brought the whole subject up to Priest & Marley – Marley is fascinated by human speech and pays attention to it. He makes dog sounds back and sometimes is paying more attention than Priest – or possibly Priest isn't as polite as Marley. Priest fell asleep so I spoke to Marley and recorded it. He paid attention the whole time. Marley's cool. Once a week I talk exclusively to Marley and record it.

*

THURSDAYS WITH MARLEY

Today I had a good session with Marley. I let it all hang out:

"If guys want to fall in love, we gotta risk our lives. Oh, yeah. Sometimes I'll sleep in all-night movie theaters. Cheaper than a room and I learned how to sleep sitting up and not slouching for or 3 hours at a time. I like sleeping surrounded by a lotta people who aren't going to set me on fire. Color me cautious. However, if someone sets a dirty, smelly, sleeping, unhoused person on fire in a crowded movie theater, would it be okay to yell, 'Fire!'? What I'm talking about is this falling in love business and "The Three Rules of Chivalry for Heroes". King Arthur and this Mongolian Knight, Ivan Ho, made up these *Three Rules of Chivalry* so the poor heroes and knights back-in-the-day could fall in love and get around the fathers and arranged marriages and scary, shiny, tin-can, homo-pods they were forced to wear: Metal homo-pods for the men and metal chastity-belts for the maidens and wives. Back- in-the-day wedding nights must have been something else if you didn't have a can opener and the right key."

Marley got it. Marley's cool.

*

THE BANANA CREAM PIE

I thought about it all night. This morning, I was sitting at the kitchen table contemplating Kaye's table-napkin dispenser and assembling my good-bye speech to Kaye, who was out buying food, and I was about to rehearse what I was going to say to her before she got back. I hit 'record' and started - and heard her key in the door. I grabbed the recorder, left it on 'record', stuck it under the top, yellow, lined legal paper on a pad I was scribbling notes on and hoped for the best:

Transcription:

Sound: Door opens and...slowly closes.

"Hi."

"Hi."

She came straight to the kitchen table and just missed placing her loaded shopping bag on the notepaper hiding my recorder.

"Okay. Listen, Kaye, We – I mean I - think it's time we – I mean-um, I really thought---What? ...What's the matter?"

"Nothing. Why?"

"You look like something's the matter."

"...Nothing's the matter. What are you doing?"

"Thinking, writing. ...What'd you get?"

"Frozen Sarah Lee Banana Cream Pie, eggs, almond milk, olive—"

"Banana cream pie."

"It's got to thaw out first."

"Cool. Let's give it some air."

I started to unpack the frozen pie. She circled behind me. I could feel it. Something's coming. She came back to the table and defiantly sat down. I, now, carefully and slowly unpacked the frozen pie...

"We have to talk."

"About what?"

"Something's wrong."

"What d'yuh mean?"

"I'm not getting what I need out of this relationship."

"Oh. Wow. What do yuh need?

"Never mind."

"What do yuh mean, 'Never mind'?"

"It's not important."

"It's so, 'not important' you can't even talk about it."

"It's a joke. It's all a joke to you. Whatdyuhmean, What'ryuhtryin't'say, whatdyuhneed?"

"Is this still about your nose?"

"What about us, Barnum? Are you serious?"

"...Yeah. <u>Yes</u>. Very serious. Serious and a half."

"Marriage serious?"

"What? Wow. I-- No. Not yet."

"Why not?"

"Because I got too many demons and you're too serious. We gotta lighten this whole relationship up."

Kaye picked up the unpacked frozen banana cream pie and slammed it into my face!

"AAH!! What-the fuck!"

"...Oh my God! ...You're bleeding! ...Oh my God! I'm so sorry! Oh my God!"

The pie remained frozen, unmarred and unbloodied by the blow. However, my face hurt like hell and my upper lip tasted like blood. I hoped it was just my nose.

"*What-the-fuck...? What did you do that for??!!* What's bleeding? Where's a mirror?!"

She started to hand me a kitchen towel, stopped, pulled two napkins out of the restaurant napkin dispenser, and handed it to me.

"It's just your nose--I'm sorry—here, use this--don't touch your nose. Tilt your head back—No! You've got blood on your finger— Don't touch the pie you'll get blood on the--! No, no. Dammit. Okay. Leave it--Leave it! — tilt your head back! I'm sorry! I'm _so_ sorry! I didn't--!"

"What the hell was that all about?"

Kaye is attempting to stuff pieces of napkins up each bleeding nostril--

"I was just trying to lighten things up - keep your head back - it was a joke."

"Real blood kills the laugh."

I kept my head back and stared at the ceiling. She went looking for something. I was dizzy. Is she getting a knife? Kaye knocked me defenseless, gave me a bloody nose so I'd just tilt my head back so she could easily slit my throat: Clown, Cream Pie, Blood: Irony. But, in another hour-and-a-half at room temperature it would've be funnier. I chose to wait for a better time to announce my decision to leave.

*

THE NO-BRAINER

"Guys can't hit Girls. Bottom Line, Boiler Plate, A No-Brainer." I pointed to the portable white-board Erase-Board I held up on the table that I'd printed in erasable ink:

1. Guys <u>can't</u> hit Girls.
2. Guys <u>*can*</u> hit <u>Guys-who-hit-Girls</u>.
3. Girls fall in love with Guys who hit Guys-who-hit-Girls-or- save-them from Scary Dragons.

Classic Literature was written mostly by men about men for men and some were written for the 6 or 7 other people who could actually read. Strangely, none were female. You may say, "Bullshit", but I say that bullshit worked for centuries, at least until the latter part of the 20th Century. And then, out of nowhere, all these heroes had to deal with the Norman Rockwellian Theory of True Love: "You can't find your true love unless you're wearing clean, white underwear." How about simply: 'Nobody Kill Anybody', for starters. It's called Evolution. Onward, Upward, & Better. No Best. Only Better.

A couple of years later females were out burning their underwear in public. Fine. So don't wear bras. I thought they were useful like jock straps: support, but what do I know? The question then comes up: "Well, what if you're punched by a female weightlifter who knows karate, has just shot you but it's only a flesh wound?" The home office is dealing with that on a case-by-case basis. The next question is: "Why don't men burn their underwear and jockstraps in public?" But no question, it's much harder to be a hero nowadays. It certainly isn't what it used to be. She wants it down; I leave it up. It's a toilet seat: Who cares? She does. What I'm talking about."

*

DOOFO'S VAN

I had five storefront windows to wash on the same block today so, I decided to do three of them last night - the night before. I wanted to sleep late; I'm still healing. I found a place to park where I didn't have to move Babe 'til noon tomorrow and it was right near a bus stop – which could take me to my windows – which happen to be in Jimmy Doofo's neighborhood and I know for a fact Jimmy's currently out of town visiting his mom for her birthday and he always leaves the key in the place he always leaves the key for me because these night window-washing jobs happen a lot in Doofo's neighb' because of all the stores. It's planning. Simple: When the buses stop running and it's too far to walk back to where I parked Babe overnight, I get the key outta the exhaust pipe, and sleep in the back of Jimmy Doofo's '82 Dodge camping van.

So, I'm asleep in the back of Doofo's van - I wake up. It's pitch- black outside and I hear somebody outside jiggling the handle of the front passenger seat door – luckily, I locked all the doors, and I know Doofo's out of town, so--CRASH! A brick comes through the front sidewalk seat's window. I stayed as still and as low as I could. Nothing... no sound. Doofo doesn't have an alarm system because the statistics showed this model '82 Dodge Van is the least likely van to be broken into or stolen.

I'm frozen, down low behind the curtain. No sound. No movement. Finally, I come out from behind the curtain to look up front. A bright white flashlight beam hits my eyes! I hit the floor behind the curtain! I hear-- "Hey, I know you."   I kept my mouth shut and stayed low. "You're the seminar guy. You're a cool Dude, man. Barnum. Barnum Justice, right? I'm not gonna hurt yuh. I don't have a weapon." I peek out and immediately a flashlight shines right in my eyes and then back at a familiar kid's familiar, South American face.

"You know my dad, Carlos Siermos from the fires up north. I'm Ramone Siermos, his son 'Ramo'. We met. Sorry to disturb you like this,

Mr. Justice." I recognized his voice. I came out and recognized his still flash-lighted face.

"Oh, yeah. Right. Hi. I thought you were still in Juvie." Ramone is the oldest of 4 of Carlos's kids, maybe 15-16. He's one of two teen sons and two tweener daughters of one of the Newbies I been talking about. I met Carlos and family about three months ago, when they first got here from Redding, up North: They got burned out of their house because of the fires. Their house caught on fire and Ramo, his dad, mom, his grandmother - his mom's mom, his younger brother and two sisters came down here with nothing but what they could throw into their car in one trip - grab and run into the car and out of Dodge - or go up with the house.

Ramo's dad told me that on the way out his front-left tire blew and he didn't stop, just floored it, pedal-to-the-metal for two miles, and they drove across a bridge right before it collapsed behind them – the car just got across and Ramo looked back just as the bridge buckled and disappeared below the cliff. Bam! They got through and outta there and stayed with his mom's relatives for a month in East L.A. waiting for a government check that never came, into a motel room till their cash couldn't cover the bill, then the streets.

After that Carlos started to come to my Seminars with the kids. He chipped in. It helped. It's not a million bucks, but it's what I can do because it's getting crowded out here. But this one, the oldest, Ramone, he was having problems from the get-go.

The kid never learned how to learn. Could be the

ADHD thing. His subconscious brain is going faster than his conscious brain - too fast to imprint learning no matter how hard he tries to focus. We get a lot of 'em out here. Plus, Ramo's dad is borderline O.C.D. A lot of 'em end up out here or become CEO's of huge corporations or at least start their own businesses. Ramo seemed okay at the seminars, but I don't have to live with him. ADHD's and OCD's are great in emergencies like in the fires up north: They get real calm and sensible as fast moving emergencies finally catch up with their brains. I've seen it happen, but I'd recommend a different coach for the mostly normal times.

Ramo was going to therapy and some classes, hanging in, filling out the forms, going to the interviews, going to school, but he was obviously going through more than acne shaming. Weird parents and who knows what else. The kid's a mess. After a month down here, he got busted for breaking and entering. He's intelligent but for some reason I picked up he was going to do time for something stupid.

"I escaped from Juvie two nights ago and I'm working my way to Canada. One of the guards was a friend from high school. He helped me - I'm just looking for camping stuff for along the way. Sorry about the window. Is this where you live?"

"No, no: I'm guarding this for a friend. He's out of town and this is a very desirable model. These models get jacked a lot. So, but yeah, he's got insurance."

"Okay, so the window's covered: Attempted robbery, you fought me off - saved his van. You can probably get a few bucks reward. Say I was big, had a gun."

"Yeah. Wait".

I reached over to my plastic drugstore bag, took out a roll of toilet paper and handed it to him. He smiled, took it, and disappeared back out the window – and poked back in.

"Here."

Ramo held out a bill.

"Take it. I was looking for stuff for the trip. I got money. Take it - for waking you up. My dad learned a lot from your talks."

I took the money. Five bucks.

"Give my regards to your dad."

"Can't. Cops probably got the family staked out. If you see 'em, give 'em my love. Tell 'em I looked healthy and was heading for Mexico. If the cops ask, tell 'em I told you the same. Sorry about the window. Later."

And he was gone. I put the fiver in my left sock, and planned on getting some brownie points for defending Doofo's vehicle from a badass intruder who threatened my life. I put on another one of Doofo's extra blankets and went back to sleep. Another tricky day and I got another one tomorrow.

*

I feel guilty about Kaye. A new feeling. About not being honest with myself - so I can't be honest with anybody else till I get that straightened out.

For Kaye, I thought I'd try something normal yet scary, something Norman Rockwellian. I picked a bouquet of flowers in a nice, upscale neighborhood and added three long stemmed roses which I purloined from a local supermarket's exterior flower stand. Not an easy feat. Years of practice and self-denial. But I was willing to give ground, apologize, whatever was needed. My intent was shelter from the storm and do the right thing on Kaye's behalf. The elevator stopped at her floor. Crunch Time. Get it right.   Be serious. I got off, approached her door heart-in-hand and knocked. I heard her yell "Who is it?" "Me!" Silence. I gave it another shot: "Barnum!" The door opened four inches- THUNNNNG! The chain was on.

"Are you really going to keep the chain--!"

"Yes, I am. What do you want? You can't come in now."

"Why not?" "Because I'm taking a bath and I'm mad at you, that's why."

She saw the bouquet.

"What's that?"

"It's for you."

"Did you sleep with someone?"

"I don't believe this."

She claimed the bouquet was a cover-up for me sleeping with another woman: Because she claimed (concluded), I'm not the type to give her flowers *as I was giving her flowers.*

"No! See? I'm changing."

"You mean You're "Cheating."

She exchanged the word "Changing" for "Cheating" through several corrections. The truth was I was playing cards, but of course she didn't believe me, which I couldn't believe was happening. I risked getting busted for three roses.

"I'm innocent."

"No, you're not."

"You don't trust me."

"Why should I?"

"Why shouldn't you?"

"You're a male."

"You're a paranoid."

"Where were you last night?"

"Playing cards! Bald Gary, Potso, Fried Sal, Straight Sal, and Dante play Wednesdays plus a guest. I was invited so I went. It was tense, high stakes; once you leave you can't come back. *Call 'em.*"

"They'll tell me what you told them to tell me. You

could have called."

"Majority rules. I was busy."

"So am I."

She slammed the four-inch opening shut in my face. I spoke loudly to the door:

"I have never made a mistake in my life; I have never made a wrong decision or move, I've never said or done anything wrong, I've never been in the wrong place at the wrong time—!" THUNNNG! the door opened four inches on the chain.

"You are so full of shit!"

"Impossible!"

"Fact!"

"Like what?"

"You're _not_ going anywhere!"

"What's wrong with that?!"

She slammed the door shut and threw the lock. I heard it click. I left. I didn't realize I was still clutching my bouquet until I was out of the building and walking down the sidewalk. Up ahead, I saw an Open Trash Can. Further back was a Little Old Lady walking slowly towards me. Bouquet: OTC or LOL? I passed the trash can, slowed to her , and as she passed me, I smiled, and handed her my bouquet without a word. She graciously accepted the bouquet with a smile and eye-twinkle as we passed. After a few feet I turned back and saw the little old lady toss my bouquet into the trash can without looking, as she passed.

*

THE #1 THING TO REMEMBER

Jesus hung with US. Not with firemen, not with policemen, not with insurance agents, priests, politicians, real estate brokers, developers, movers & shakers, or CEO's. <u>"US"</u>: Me. *Jesus hung with thieves, prostitutes, lepers, <u>beggars, lawyers, and</u> <u>the rest of the least of us</u>.* Oh, yes, lawyers. Disciples had to know how to read and write. When you're going to Go Big, access to media and a lawyer is a must. Jesus figured it out. Jesus was no dummy. Of course, Jesus had a lawyer. He was put on trial. The whole "Up on The Cross" thing was a plea bargain. Think about the symbolism: the delicate, Gold Cross on a delicate gold chain hanging down between young pubescent female cleavage. Are you kidding? Definitely. Gold Cross. Resurrection from a lion's stomach? Too over-the-top. What's going to hang around that young girl's neck, a gold, gnawed skull?

If there ever was The One for Me, she might have passed away a couple years ago. I don't know if I've ever been in love. True Love. Love love. Where two become one at least occasionally, but over and over, easily. Naturally. Every time we both were convinced - one of us wasn't. Hell is other people except for the sex part. Females are closer to that stuff.

*

GREAT NEWS

This morning, I got some great news in my post office box. My publisher just sent me a $1,000 check for winning 3rd prize in the poetry contest he goaded me into entering plus, he's not taking a percentage. That's great because this entire check is going for the betterment of my brother and sister Free Range Urbanese. Only then did it hit me. It's a check. I have no bank account. Nobody but a bank will cash a stranger's check, and I don't know anybody with that kind of cash except 'D', one of Fried Sal's Suppliers. He remembered me because I accompanied Fried Sal twice, but strangely, the third time I was with Sal, 'D' wouldn't make the exchange until I left. He later told Sal that he didn't like me and didn't want me, 'Nosin' Around'. However, possibly 8% of $1,000 might move him towards a more positive reaction.

I went to D's apartment with enough sense to leave my recorder in my bus, and sure enough, D patted me down and still charged me 10% not 8, "Just because." I immediately hid my $900 (in various conditions and denominations) in Mylan's secret stash compartment under Babe's dashboard: Sacred money for The Team.

A few hours later Solly Greene told me that Fried Sal is missing and was last seen getting on a bus to The Valley, but that was all anybody knows. He took the bus out there two days ago to see marine buddies in Woodland Hills, but he never showed up. And nobody's heard from him. He's been missing two days now. He's not in any jail in L.A. County. So far.

My problem is I want to help find him, but I also don't want to waste money on all the gas to get to the valley and then drive around all day and night looking for the idiot. Solly volunteered to move my VW tonight to the other side of the street for me if he could sleep in it tonight. And I could look for Fried Sal in Sal's army bud's vehicles.   I called Potso but he's out of town so, Solly's idea was a good one except it was also an accident waiting to happen. I was leery, but Sal's situation had a seriousness to it an' I figured I got a Friendship-Obligation-Moment here, I gotta help find Sal.

Solly said I could park Babe on his street, and he'd change sides for me tomorrow morning before noon if he could sleep in it till I got back. That way, if I got hung up, Solly would move it for me - _not drive it_. _Just move it_. "Blah blah blah - …accident waiting to happen", but duty calls: Deal and done.

I explained to Kaye what's happened and what I felt obligated to do. She was pissed and thought I had more important things to do.

"Like what?"

"Like get a job."

"My job is selling stories and doggerels."

"Oh, right: There's big money in poetry; I forgot."

"And right this minute—I don't have to explain. Never mind."

I packed my backpack with my sleeping bag, Top Ramen, freeze-dried beef, and chicken soup packets, and Solly blocked off a space for Babe at the curb right in front of his tent - a major win. Taking a bus to the valley would save a ton of money on gas there and back especially if I had to look for him. That's why we have friends in The Valley. They pay for Search-Gas on their side of the Hollywood Hills. But just-in-case, I took $500 out of my Free-Range-Urban-Fund I'd hidden in my VW's secret compartment, caught the Bergamot Station train downtown, got on the bus, and departed. I was going to hook up with his buddies who're helping. There's also a couple of bookstores I want to check out.

Nobody knew how much money I was carrying but I was obviously carrying more pocket money than anyone in my karas except for D, one or two drug dealers, and probably one undercover cop - A whole different story.

I contacted my contacts in The Valley: Derik, Jay, an' Lena. They've been searching since yesterday and I could stay at their campsite tonight. Derik borrowed a van an' we cruised and queried in bars, parks, stores, policemen, cops, looking for Sal but no clues so, around 10 pm we packed it in. I went to a poetry slam and story reading, stayed late enough for the busses to stop running because I was prepared. I brought my sleeping bag and envelopes of freeze-dried soups: Chicken and Vegetable Beef. Slept at Eddie, Lena an' Jay's campsite, which was under a 405 overpass. They came up with a pot, some water and a fire, Lena cut in some fresh carrots and celery, and we had some hot soup all around. I slept in my sleeping bag outside as there was no tent. There was the usual talk of one, soon. It was a cold, hard night.

Three of Fried Sal's marine buddies and I spent the next day and evening looking, asking, cruising the streets in the area, ER's, Hospitals, police stations, morgues. 3rd day: I was honestly starting to worry. I called Kaye and told her we couldn't find Sal. She wasn't sure if she believed me or not. She was still pissed.

We made some more phone calls and finally: on the third day, The Police System came up with a Salvatore *Dentino* being held at a nearby Valley Police Station waiting on a $200 bail bond in jail, plus $200 dollars-worth of damage to a local bookstore's Poetry Section. According to Sal, he simply requested Tomes of Pomes, and the store told him they didn't carry it. He became paranoid, demanded to know why they were lying to him, pulled all the poetry books to the floor and kicked the bookcase that held them to pieces. the police were called. According to the police, when they arrived, one of the officers was Asian and Sal attacked him, a huge fight started, Sal was subdued, cuffed, busted, fined, and jailed. I paid for his bail, the bookcase, and books in cash. The Cost: $450. Fried Sal swore he'd pay me back. I didn't believe him my pocket. An unrecoverable 45% financial loss in just 3 days. Biorhythms? Dyslexia? Astrology? Get different friends?

> Dept. of Sanitation Street Sign:
> "All Debris, Detritus, Tents, Vehicles-as-Living-Quarters, and Etc., On This Street not removed by 10 am Monday, shall be removed/ towed by L.A.C.D.S. & C.R.D., at owners' expense."

At 9:40 am Monday, Solly Greene was first-in-line to get a free, 10 am breakfast at the Santa Monica Pier.

A Gut Punch. I proceeded to dutifully beat myself up: I knew it. Of course. I should have known. My trust mechanism needs an adjustment. He didn't tell me because he didn't know. *I* should have known. I hoped my last $50 in cash would be enough to bail my home and nest egg out of auto jail and this nightmare will be over in time for me to prepare for the next one.

At the Tow Yard my begging, pleading, and identifying the blankets in the back of the van on the floor plus my measly $50 dollars cash worked: They deigned to take me to Babe.

Babe's Secret Compartment under the dashboard was broken open and empty. None of the towing people knew what I was talking about.

"It was towed in the condition you see it now. Nobody touched anything, so you better get your ass in it and outta' here before we call the cops and it'll cost you twice as much to get your vehicle out plus a ticket and jail time."

All I'm guessing is, they figured since they got all the money out of Babe's secret stash, they could be big-hearted and give me my home back for (the worst curse of all) for my last $50.

I borrowed the bus fare back to Venice Beach from Lena. The trip to The Valley by bus to find Fried Sal and save the gas money I would have spent on Babe cost me my Slam book's cash prize money. But: What if I didn't win? Where would Fried Sal still be right now? Where would I be? So, maybe that's why I won. And Solly Greene is Solly Greene is Solly Greene and I'm me over and over and over and over and it's just another day in Peopleland and some days are just trickier than others.

I got back to Kaye's apartment around 3:30 in the afternoon. She wasn't home, probably doing her house-hostessing till 4. There was a note leaning up against Duke's Bar napkin holder:

> B,
>
> Please leave your key on the coffee table. When you leave, pull the door shut so it locks behind you. You won't be able to get back in. If you or any of your possessions are still in my apartment after 4:01 pm tomorrow, I will trash them and report you to the police as a dangerous stalker. I mean it.
>
> xox,
>
> Kaye

*

A BIT MUFFLED, BUT IT WAS ALL THERE

I finally fell asleep. It's now 9am tomorrow as of yesterday. We, It, I: lasted longer than 2 months, but it's over. I have till 4pm to get my stuff out for good. Plus, I have five storefront windows to finish before that: Three on Santa Monica's Main Street and two just off the boardwalk plus, the traffic on Lincoln was backed-up because of a stupid traffic accident. As I crawled passed, both drivers were just leaning against their dented and bent halted autos blocking 1½ lanes, sullen, silent, arms folded across their chests, avoiding eye contact waiting for the cops to arrive.

I silently cursed the Lookie-Lous to no avail and arrived at Kaye's apartment building at 3:15 pm and had to park in a supermarket parking lot two blocks away. I got there, got in, got my two backpacks stuffed with everything I cared about with six minutes to spare: 3:55pm. I was coming out of the bathroom with my large, plastic pharmacy bag full of my bathroom stuff when Kaye barges in pissed to see me still there. My recorder is in the pocket of the jacket I was wearing. I switched it on but left it in my pocket.

"It's not 4:01 yet. I was just leaving."

"Fine. Then just leave."

"If I'm so bad, what was I doing here in the first place? Why'd you invite me in here in the first place?"

She stopped and seriously considered my question.

"You're nice."

Threw me, totally.

"'Nice'? That's not a reason. What does that mean: 'Nice'?"

"You're the first man I've ever been with that didn't

beat me up." I stifled a mind-blowing: *"What?!",* held my breath, and wrestled it down to a sort of a cool-and-flat, "Oh. Wow. Yeah, but I don't think because I don't beat you up is a good enough reason to get married."

Kaye walked to the front door and opened it.

"Good luck, Barnum."

Fully backpacked, each hand carrying a stuffed bag full of clothes, underwear, and two rolls of toilet paper, I stepped out into the hallway and turned to her inside holding the door open. She honestly asked:

"Who do you think I am?"

"The one that got away."

"Nice knowing you."

"That's it? Nice knowing you?"

"It's either that or: "That's it, Chickenshit."

"I'm rubber, you're glue, whatever you say bounces off m-!" Kaye slammed the door in my face. It stopped inches from my nose. I heard the lock thrown and the chain put on. I checked: 4:00:34. Made it. Going down in the elevator, I listened to the tape. A bit muffled, but it was all there.

*

ENCORE

"I got busted again for Impersonating a Politician While Not in Possession of a Doorknob. "Vagrancy", my ass. The Judge gave me one-week whackin' weeds for The County. At the time I had forty- eight priors; I demanded a trial-by-jury. I got a hearing, which was exactly what I wanted: I use The Law to achieve personal goals impossible and crazy as that may seem.

In the Hearing Chamber, I was seated, my arresting officer was standing right next to me. I figured I already wacked enough weeds to start a dust bowl so, remaining seated, I slowly raised my hand in a fist _in a non- threatening manner_, bowed my head, and calmly announced:

"I will not whack weed one, no more forever." I grabbed my arresting officer's gun-hand and attempted to bite off his trigger finger. I felt a lot of hands grab me from behind. A knee went to my neck and pressed it into the floor. Several people held me down. I couldn't breathe. I blacked out.

I woke up on a cot-bed of a Solitary Cell. my arm was dislocated, and it hurt when I breathed too deep. I had a bloody-hair-knot on the back of my head. I grabbed one of my cell bars tight, threw my weight back hard – and popped the ball over the hump and back in the socket and I gave out a yell could have rose The Dead Sea. Nobody paid attention. Probably thought somebody was being raped. I found out her honor the judge said I fell in my cell and ordered no medical attention plus, ordered Solitary Confinement: Again, exactly what I was going' for: No roommates. Plus, I still had one phone call. Always be working The System in your favor.

I used my one call to Kaye and prayed she'd answer, and she did. I explained to her exactly what happened: "...Plus, I needed medical attention. I can't feel my fingers and I'm sure I got a broken rib and a concussion." She hung up on me.

My left, upper arm had teeth marks, and I was worried about rabies. Obviously, one of the cops bit me. But my arm was back in its socket, and I could use it. That night I dreamt I had a concussion and kept waking up because I didn't want to die in my sleep. I want to be awake when I die. It's not being alone; it's the walls. They make me sick and paranoid. The food's full of drugs and poison. They're trying to make me look like I'm well-fed by making me fat so I can't run fast. I started having nightmares about Kaye. In each nightmare she was kidnapped & taken hostage by Bloody Bloodo, the most blue-eyed Cyclops Viking Biker-Ogre, and taken back to Hell Froze Over on the back of Black Bess, The Amazing Flying Iron Firebird Hog of Speed and Power: The Devil's Own Machine. I had to chase and save her by catching a cross-town bus and transferring twice. I think of Kaye constantly.

Love Haiku

Love
The hard part's over
Now comes the hard part

The ACLU got a court order to get me to a UCLA Medical Facility in Santa Monica. I spent two days there while they checked my head for concussion and the nerves in my arm and hands healed enough for my fingers to come back so I can write semi-hemi-demi-legibly. I was released to my own recognizance and on the street just before the hospital served dinner.

*

Sundown

I can drive, thank whatever. I lucked out – got a parking spot on 6th Street where I could leave her for six hours because I had four shop windows all along the 3rd Street Promenade, so I could leave her and work the promenade.

Finished the last window just in time. Started to drizzle around 11pm. Walked back to Babe on a dark Main Street in Santa Monica. It started to rain so I stopped into Mickey's Place on Fourth.

With all the bullshit goin' on around me, I guess I was askin' for it. I was lookin' for sex <u>and</u> love. A no-no. My momma told me: "It's one or the other. Too much of a good thing is not a good thing." -- Long John

I headed back to Babe as soon as it eased-up to a drizzle. Plus, I'm carrying my bucket full of my gear: rags, towels, squeegees, solvents; all Eco-Friendly.

I pass a homeless couple huddled against the damp and cold under one blanket, sitting up against the library's dark, locked doors, back under its porticoed and dripping entranceway. Would I give them a job? A bath? A dollar? Shelter? A raincoat? I'm freezing. Is this it now forever? How long before I go insane and kill myself?   Got to get *me* a goddam a raincoat.

Some people won't change. Fried Sal just *won't*. Can Kaye? Can I? But somehow, for some reason, I still root for Sal. He's wrong but he's right. I care, but so what?

I'm walking in a cold drizzle on Santa Monica Boulevard. I cross at the light. An ambulance siren wails, red lights flashing by: Inside, a head-bowed priest in black. Death. I don't assume, I conclude. Fire engines roar passed. Down the street a fire in the rain. Fireman hose water into its charred black remains, white clouds of steam rise. The owner, standing in the street crying, still wearing his dirty white apron, his smoldering diner burnt to the ground. All I could think of was: The Hard part's over. Now comes the hard part.

Still raining, walking, carrying my bucket of gear and extension. I see a woman at the side of the road with an umbrella attempting to flag down passing cars in the rain, dressed inappropriately near a safe, pull-over zone of an exit ramp. Where's her disabled mode of transportion? Hooker. I don't assume, I conclude. Can I even get it up? If I'm paying, it's her problem not mine. I approach.

"'Scuse me, miss, if I can't get it up, do I get my money back? Or a cut rate? How does that--?!"

"Just a sec, just a sec."

She runs to the just pulled over new Porsche, shouts a few inaudible words into the opened passenger seat door, points to me, shouts again to the driver, smiles at me and waves goodbye, glides into the Porsche's front passenger seat, closes her umbrella, pulls it in, her arm pulls the door shut and the Porsche roars away in the rain.

2:30 am. I walk down to the beach, pass under the Venice Beach Pier. Tides out. The sky was black over a black ocean and boardwalk.

A piercing wind. Cold. Raw. I took my shoes and socks off and walked into to the cold wet sand of the water's edge. The ocean was freezing'! Black waves with white hair crash and spray, thin ocean foam rushes up to my freezing feet, tries to coax me in, retreats.

*

Kenny's Song

As I curse the dark & my fate assail,
Who should appear, from beyond the pale,
A ghost; not just any
But my long-dead friend Kenny,
His head half-gone,
shot, grey and wan
His song was one long wail:

Now this never happened to me
And I know it can't happen to you
But a lad met a maid on a mountain
Beneath a sky of blue

And she was twenty-seven
He was younger through and through
Her laugh was half of heaven
Her hands were ninety-two.

At seventeen she wondered
What other women knew
At eighteen she had mastered
What was known by but a few

Her hair fell in raven freshets
Her face retreated to
While waiting on the tables
At the local liquor zoo

And she was twenty-seven
He was younger through and through
Her laugh was half of heaven
Her hands were ninety-two

She went for days on pills and coke
And Miles on Bitches Brew
She lived two years with Billy Shears
And a French toboggan crew

And she was twenty-seven,
He was younger through and through
Her laugh was half of heaven
Her hands were ninety-two

Enraptured, he was captured
As all the men she drew
Becalmed in the straights of his manhood
Her blue eyes blew him through

And as he feared, she disappeared
Gone without a clue
There's few that know the wrack and woe
And nights he suffered through

He found her with a lover
He had a perfect view
He died beside binoculars
His nose inside her shoe

 And she was twenty-seven
He was younger through and through...

Kenny was 16. The wind and waves drowned out Kenny's words and his weird head wound faded into the black sky and I'm standing ankle deep in the ice-cold friggin' Atlantic Ocean next to the Venice Beach Pier freezing my ass off.

3:00 am: I went into Max's burgers & Fries on 9th and ordered a coffee and a toasted bagel. Jack Trent, A friend and the night manager comes over and tells me I have to leave. Max left specific orders that I'm 86'd from the place for the rest of the month. I protested, of course. He said Max told him the last time I was there I started a food fight, made a mess of the place, and insulted his menu after he gave my party free food.

It was no use. Jack, a friend from Duke's, was serious. He said Max would fire him if he found out he served me food or even let me in. I understood and left.

Places to hang out late at night are at a premium when unsheltered. So, though it was fun and funny in the late afternoon, I can't afford to be on the outs with the day or night shift at any place open after 11pm, and all-night diners are few and far-between. The night crews know the score. You don't want the day shift bad-mouthing your presence to the night shift. If you serve me coffee and a bagel after 11 pm, you get respect. Soaked and cold, I climb inside Babe, dried off, changed into dry socks and hiking boots and drove around chanting for an all-night coffee shop. Finally: A month's worth of gas for a hot cup of coffee (chanting works: Sooner or Later Someone Will Leave). The Perfect Reason for Failure: You quit too soon.

4:12 am. Coffee and a blueberry scone. The server doesn't care if I'm a spy. I talk low and into my recorder. Talking to the future. Giving 'em the low-down and a heads-up:

"I think the only people I can talk to anymore are

dead people. They're real good listeners; no judgments, no interruptions. A dead person'll never jump to a conclusion or finish my sentence. They don't assume, conclude, or over-react. Dead people are very deadpan. They have *Listening Down* (I know a real funny guy sez he could make a dead man grin a bit).

6:30 am. The boardwalk. Two people coming towards me about two blocks away. Everything else is asleep or dead. A cop is leading Priest by his upper left arm ala "In-Custody". Priest is clutching a Brand-New Doggie Mattress under his other arm and Marley trundling nonchalantly behind on a slack leash.

As soon as Priest recognized me approaching, he calmly waved me away: "Stay away, B. It's okay. Don't make trouble. I'm okay. I'll be okay", while obviously letting the non-committal police officer calmy lead him away, Marley dutifully just trundling nonchalantly behind, but with lots of leash-slack and keep-up.

I spent the next two weeks licking my wounds, mental and physical, washing windows, and doing my seminars, but my heart was broken and that wasn't part of my perfect plan.   Thankfully, I've got washing windows which is a blessing. My first bio's title is gonna be, "Invisible Panes": It's a song screaming to be written and backed by, "Hard to Come By, Worth the Price".

*

IT'S OVER

I was walking and talking with Fried Sal along the boardwalk, and Sal sees something dead ahead, grabs me and pulls me a sharp left turn into a convenient side street that deadends at the beach.

"Okay: What? Who'd you see?... Oh, c'mon.... Kaye?"

"In an outdoor restaurant with a gentleman in a suit."

"What's she wearing?"

"What do you mean?"

"What was Kaye wearing? What clothes-outfit-whatever."

"Stuff for lunch at a boardwalk outdoor restaurant in the neighborhood. Why?"

"Nothing. Just askin'."

It was a hot poker and a cold spike. It clenched my heart.

I wrote Duke's Happy Hour completely off my schedule. For a week I'd sit by myself on a park bench over by the Santa Monica Pier cliffs checking out the ocean and feeling sorry for myself until Priest comes up out of nowhere and concludes: "Sooner or later We all must face Happy Hour alone."

The last time I saw Kaye face to face was right before I saw her door slam shut two inches from my face two weeks ago. She broke my heart right then. Still on the mend but scarred forever, no doubt. But with Priest's short, weird homily, I knew what I had to do.

When I finally felt ready to go back to Happy Hour a week later, I went to Duke's reminding myself all the way: Be friendly, be nice. Nothing big happened. Two ships in the night; we're friends now. I'm over you. I am. Done. Definitely.

I walked in like nothing was wrong and was informed Kaye LaMarr had quit and moved to San Diego 5 days ago. She was gone. Officially Out of My Life. Just like that. It could happen. And did.

Wow. It hurt, but different. I felt lighter. Not much, but lighter: this time I knew I was better off and hoped she was too. "How do you get to Carnegie Hall?" "Practice." I think we both knew we each had to bring a little more to the kitchen table than each of us assumed (concluded) we had or were willing to modify. There's way more to it, hopes, fantasies, desires, needs, you name it. We just couldn't come up with enough for us to share. I'm obviously not ready. Will I ever be?

*

SALVATORE DENTELLO FUNERAL

To All Friends & Others: Salvatore Dentello (Fried Sal) died in his sleep on the beach near the Venice Pier, last night, November 9, 1999. He died of a heart attack complicated by Parkinson's Disease, which he'd been treating for years. The world lost a good man, the seagulls got his eyes, and two lifeguards, Straight Garry, and JJ Rodriguez found his body this morning. The Earth will take his body, yet his eyes will still sweep the shore like the birds in the sky.

THE FRIED SAL/SALVATORE DENTELLO MEMORIAL FUND

Please leave Donations with Bubble-Up cashier.

Funeral Services will be announced soon at:

The Bubble-Up Laundry bulletin board at Main & Ocean Park for time and place. *To Contact Barnum Justice: Leave messages there.*

March 18, 2000

Sal was re-buried and laid to rest one week ago, on a corner of a 2-acre, green pasture on Bob Halpern's farm outside of Costa Mesa, California. Babe and I left for Taos, New Mexico the next day.

I'm turning over what I've got so far to Kaye in San Diego. Kaye kept in touch with the new owner of Duke's, and I got her number from him. I invited her - among other friends of Sal - to the memorial. Some people've died (they've been doing that all my life, but lately I know them).

I left *in* what's supposed to be left *out*: stupidity, bad writing, nonsense, or things too scary, embarrassing, or boring for me to deal with in real life. Sal was family.

JUNE, 2004

We finally got enough donations to hold a memorial service for Fried Sal nee Salvatore Dentello and place a permanent plaque on one of the pier's upright supports, with legal, written permission from The City of Santa Monica, California to proceed.

Kay is married, opened her own salon, adopted her husband's son, and she and her new family took the train up from San Diego. I met her new husband, Tom Jefferson, a 67-year-old African American and his 37-year-old son Jeremy and Jeremy's wife Emily and their two- year-old son, Jamal. Tom is a middle-class businessman-furniture store franchise owner ("Jefferson's" - 126 franchises in 26 states, mostly in the southeast). He seemed comfortably successful, a bit overweight, dressed in a suit with a vest, salt & pepper hair. Nice. Safe. I bet he's a great guy to play golf with.

Tom and Kaye met at Deedee's Deli near the beach on Santa Monica Boulevard. He lives in San Diego, drove up on a business trip, dropped into Duke's, she gave him her card, a haircut, He got her a nice cheap apartment near his place in San Diego, she moved in, he invested in her hair salon, they dated, he helped her with the salon, they got engaged, married, she adopted his son, Jeremy. Salon's doing fine: Five chairs. Kaye rents out four and she works the fifth three days a week. She showed me a picture of the wedding cake. It was pink and blue, real high, and covered with white roses made of frozen yogurt. She was very proud of it. Tom had it made special.

Somewhere there's got to be a Norman Rockwell Post Magazine cover painting of Kaye's new family: five healthy, smiling Jeffersons posed with Homeless Clown-Saint: *Emmett Kelly*, the sad, Barnum & Bailey Hobo holding the long stem of a drooping flower. If there's not one, there should be.

At the end of the Salvatore's memorial, Kaye, Tom, Jeremy, Emily, Jamal, me, Potso, Wacko, B.G., Lori, M.E., and Priest (pretty much Fried Sal's family), went to the spot near where Straight Gary and JJ found him, and Priest intoned a Memorial Goodbye Chant-Prayer to Fried Sal's Spirit which was amazing and managed to close with, "Can I get a Heyman", to great applause and "Heymans!" from the group. Priest's ever mesmerizing.

Then all Sal's Family plus a gaggle of Sal's other mixed bag of friends and strangers affixed the plaque to the nearest support to where his body was found so his local, old, and young beach buddies had a place to leave notes and flowers, come together, grieve together, and pledge to rock on because he'd want us to. Rock on, Salvatore. We all rock on with you.

*

First There Was Hercules

First there was Hercules, Jason and the rest
Of those heroic and semi-unknowns
Then came Quixote & Wild Bill Cody
And then came Roadrash Jones
Now, Dulcinea she walked the streets
Of La Mancha's thoroughfare
Until that Knight in Rusty Mail
Offered her a chair

And Lady Roxanne's chambers
Was a circus of pumped-up young nerds
But she stopped the show for Cyrano
That brave-nosed fool of words
And Katrina Van Tassel's tiaras
Caused her nothing but heartache and pain
So, on Saturday night while her suitors would fight
She went dancing with Ichabod Crane

And Rapunzel, Rapunzel lived locked in a tower
Alone with no one to care
'Til a faint-hearted Prince Quite bravely convinced her
To let down her long, golden hair
But then there was Catherine, the best of them all
She had 'em all beat by a mile
With a hand on her hip and a smirk on her lip
She could turn on a room or a smile
She sure could be funny, she sure could be sad
She sure had 'em doing her will

*But they sucked out her heart and that tore her
apart
'Til one day she became deathly ill.
So, they sent for the doctors, the best in the land
And they came with their powders and pills
Some said sore throat, and some said a cough
And some just said fever and chills
Near death and quite pallid, her skin was like
glass
Her body grew withered and cold
But her mind was still keen and her eyes were still
clear
So, she looked like a girl-child grown old
Oh, Rusty Knight Errant, Oh, Ichabod Crane
Cyrano, and Prince with your tricks
Where are you now that the best of them all
Is nearing that black River Styx*

*She just stared out the window and looked for a
sign,
A signal, a sound, or a touch
And she swore to her doctors that miracles come
But the odds a' that happenin' ain't much
Then, lo & behold, the air it was filled
With a terrible, ear-splitting sound
And a chugging and smoking, two-wheeled
machine
Circled her house twice around*

*And on a lean cycle, all battered and bent
Rode a tall clown so thinly surreal
He looked like he hadn't slept for a month
Or taken a bath or a meal*

But he rode with a spirit of je-ne-seis-pas
That hunger and rain couldn't quash
And his gauntleted gloves and white tattered scarf
He wore with certain panache

Then he shut off his racket and parked that steel steed
And faked out her parents and staff
And bounded upstairs and bent to her ear
and said something that sure made her laugh
Then he balanced a wheel on the end of his toes,
Bowed and pulled Daddy's beard,
Stepped out the window, and off the porch roof
And in a blue, smoky roar, disappeared

Well, needless to say, she got better of course,
And conquered the whole U.S.A
On stage and on screen, and T.V. to boot
And she's doing quite well to this day
And Ichabod, Cyrano, Quixote, and the Prince
Are just semi-hemi-demi-unknowns
When compared to a two-wheeled and down-trodden clown
Who calls himself Roadrash Jones

*

THE ONE THING I COULD NEVER FIGURE OUT

You ever notice how youth is always right? Yeah. You notice how young people are right? And the younger you are, the righter you are. And the older you are, the wronger you get. And you keep gettin' older and wronger and older and wronger 'til, finally, when you're extremely wrong and old, suddenly you're wise and then you die. I could never figure that out. Somehow it doesn't make sense - perfectly. That's the whole point of irony.

-- Barnum Justice

*